RAISING THE STAKES

C.L. LEDFORD

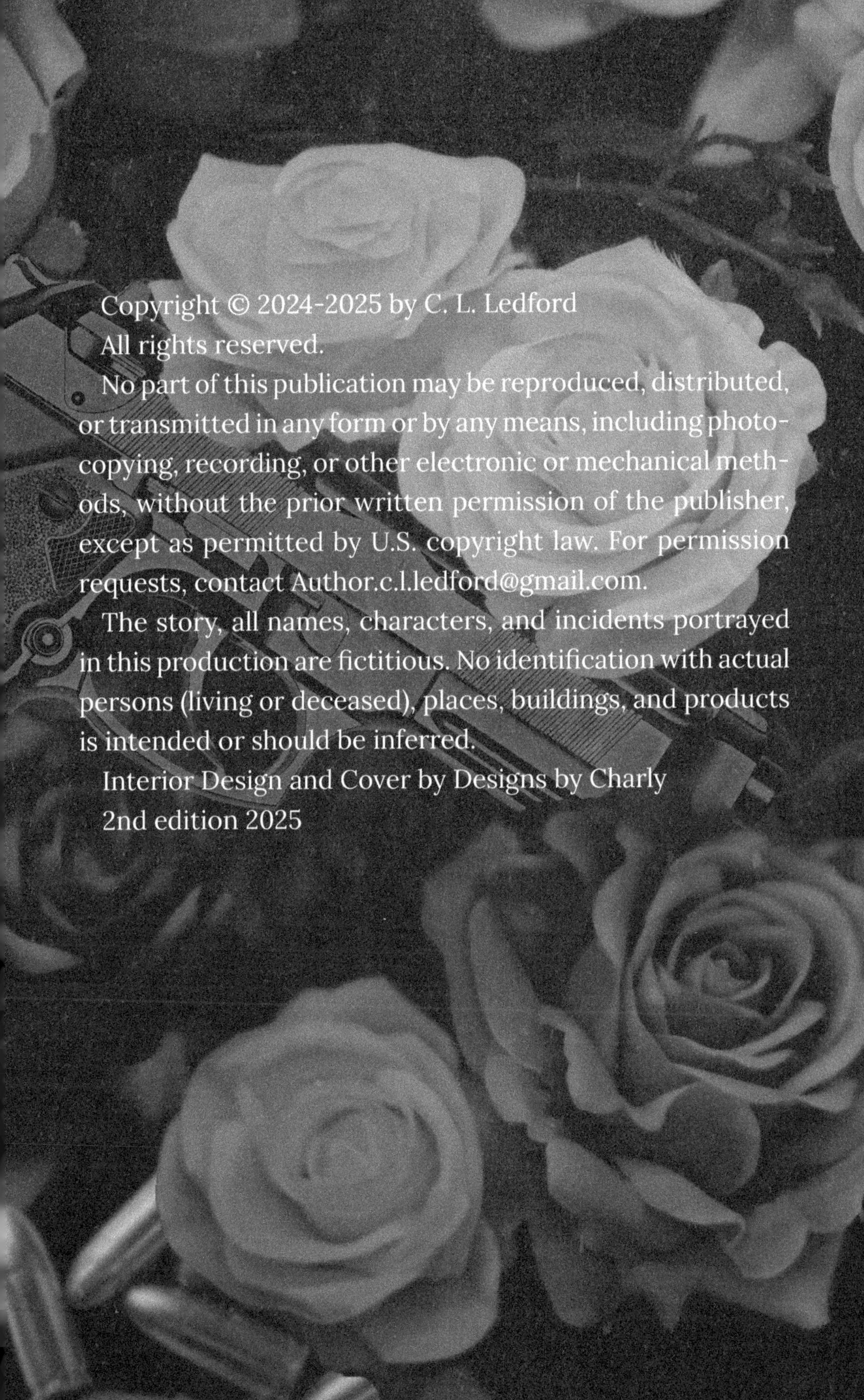

For those readers that want a man who is kinky and isn't
afraid of a little blood and torture.
This book is for you.

Content/trigger warnings

This book is part of my Dark Era series. It contains the below warnings and kinks:
Gangs, Death,
Killing/murder,
Drugs,
Mention of poverty,
Addiction,
Dead bodies,
Mutilation,
Scars,
Kidnapping,
Period play,
Fisting,
Arranged Marriage,
Piercings,
Anal,
breath play,
Pregnancy (end of book)

My story isn't all sunshine and rainbows. No, my story is dark and twisted. Well, before I met the Churchhills, that is. My adoptive family changed my life for the better. Because of the wealth and connections that the Churchhills had, I was able to escape the gang life that I had been leading. I was able to start making something of myself. To have the public see me for what I could do. Not for what I had done in the past.

But it didn't last. For an entire year, I was able to be a normal teenager. I went to school, and I met a girl. A girl with chocolate brown hair and grey eyes. A mouth that was plump and inviting; she was everything that any teenage boy would be obsessed with. Aurora's my father's best friend's daughter, and I formally met her at my introductory party. After embarrassing her in front of everyone, she never spoke to me again.

She hung out with her group of friends, and at school, I stayed with mine. After graduation, we went our separate ways. She went to a college across the country with her two best friends, and I went to the prestigious private college with Drake, the man who would become my Chief Operations Officer.

Six years of college for my undergrad courses in business and DBA were tough. The courses were intense, and keeping up with the work was demanding. But I played as hard as I worked. I always turned in my work on time, but there wasn't a party I didn't crash. On the weekends, I could always be found with a drink in my hand and a woman on my arm. Sometimes more than one woman. In the end, I graduated at the top of my class.

After graduation, my adopted father handed Churchhill's Logistics over to me. Drake's father retired and handed his COO position over to Drake. But not without stipulations.

Chapter One

TC

The moon was high in the sky as I sat at my desk; my father and Mr. Emerson, my father's friend, awaiting my reply. Jake, my bodyguard, stood by the door waiting for this unscheduled meeting to end. I glanced up at him and motioned for him to leave. He nodded, before exiting the room.

Apparently, this arrangement had been in the works since I was adopted at seventeen. The only reason I was in this situation was that my father was getting older and wanted to retire. That day at the orphanage would always be the day that a family had actually wanted to give me a chance. I lay there on my cot thinking about where my gang was. But it was Emi, my younger sister, who decided that my life would become what it is today. They had approached me while I was still asleep with the director. A man who hated me just as much as I hated him. Little fingers prodded me awake, and as I came to, a set of green eyes were staring at me with a grin.

As I focused, I realized that a little girl stood beside me by the bed and squealed as she jumped up and wrapped her arms around her mother. I had sat up and surveyed the people around me; the little girl was a mixture of her mother and father, with dirty blond hair. The little girl seemed to be the type to always smile, her eyes were bright with innocence. My gaze landed on the director, his stern face glaring at me the whole time. He had then turned to the husband and told him that I was basically no good, and that they should pick someone else. For the life of me, I didn't know why they even wanted me. Until Emi had run up to her father, and I assumed had given him her puppy dog eyes and pleaded with him that I was the brother that she had always wanted. The man would do anything for my sister, and when I actually started to let myself become part of this family, he did the same for me.

I knew there were stipulations for me to take over. But it had been three years. Why had they waited until I took over the company to spring this on me? I had brought this company further than my father had, but he was still holding that Snapchat post against me.

Which was Aurora's fault. If she hadn't sent it to my mother, my father would have been none the wiser. I glanced down at the glass I had been twisting on the desk. Being an adult should serve as being able to make my own decisions about my life. But if there was one thing that I learned about coming from money, it was that you never truly were your own person, and things like this happened all the time.

"Tom, this needs to be announced soon. Your mom has already been planning this for years." My father's voice brought my attention back to the men in front of me.

"And my wife has picked out Aurora's dress for the betrothal announcement and found the perfect venue for the wedding and reception. You won't have to worry about anything," Mr. Emerson chimed in with a grin that I didn't return. I didn't know why they wanted me to answer them when it was already in place. It's like they wanted me to agree.

"How would my answer make a difference? You both have had this planned for years. I couldn't care less about any of this. But if this is the way I can keep the company, then fine," I answered, picking up my glass of whiskey and tossing back the rest of it. "But don't expect this relationship to be a loving marriage."

Mr. Emerson glanced over at my father with a concerned look. My father knew the reason for my words. Aurora had done me dirty, and if this was the way I could get revenge, then that was what I would do. My father nodded and pulled Mr. Emerson to his feet. They both made their way out of my office and closed the door. My father knew when it was time to push and when not to.

I glanced down at my phone, at the text that had come through from my flavor of the week. It was a picture, and I knew what kind it was. She had been sending them since she woke up this morning. Standing, I grabbed my phone and unlocked it. The woman's picture flashed onto the screen. She was naked on the bed with her legs spread wide. Perky, fake tits standing to attention as her hand played with her cunt. Brunette hair stretched above her head; her mouth opened in a moan. She was one hell of a gorgeous specimen. One that had been different from the other women I had as my flavors of the week. Who had all been blond.

Snatching up my keys, I proceeded to the door. Loosening my tie as I went. It was already after hours, and very few lights were on as I made my way to the elevator. Boarding the metal container, I pressed the button for the garage. I glanced down at the phone now ringing in my hand. The screen flashing with my father's name.

"Yes, Father." In his rush to get Mr. Emerson out of my office, he must have forgotten to tell me something else that was going to alter my life.

"Don't make plans for tomorrow. We are going to have a dinner party, and we will be announcing your betrothal." I rolled my eyes as my dad made his demands. Yes, it was childish, but I didn't fucking care.

"Why do I need to be there?"

"Tom, I know you don't like Aurora, but you need to be a little more flexible about this. This is the company's future as well as yours. Go home. Rest. Get your head right for tomorrow." I could hear the sigh in my father's voice. I didn't know why they would want Aurora and me together. Just because I was marrying her, it didn't mean that we would have a genuine marriage. There would be no love between us, and I had needs that I doubted she would be able to fulfill.

"Well, I'm not going home. I have a date tonight and I'm already running late. I'll see you tomorrow." I hung up the phone as the elevator door opened. My black Bugatti sat in its assigned spot closest to the doors. Being CEO had its perks.

As I reached for the door, a chill ran down my spine, and I glanced over my shoulder. Taking hold of the Glock concealed by my suit jacket, I turned and found myself face to face with a man covered from head to toe. The only characteristic I could identify was their green-colored eyes. This wasn't the first time I had seen this fucker. The last time was at a club. But now he had followed me to work, somehow getting into the secure garage.

"What the fuck do you want?" I kept my voice even as I shouted my question. Gripping the butt of the gun, I pulled it out and let it hang by my side. My stalker came toward me until they were a car's length away from me. Their hands were out, and I didn't see anything bulging at their sides. He was just a messenger.

"He's been looking for you. You can never escape him." The voice behind the mask was muffled, but I could tell he was just a kid.

"I wasn't hiding. What does he want?"

"You didn't come back. Now you must answer his call. It's time to go." The kid went round to the other side of my car and waited for me to unlock it. This kid was ballsy that was for sure. What he didn't know was that this life was going to get him in jail or, worse, killed.

"Why don't you go back and tell him that I'm too busy for the likes of him and that he will have to make an appointment." I stood there locked in a staring contest with some random kid.

"You know you can't tell him no. If you do, your loved ones will go first. He will make you watch as he tortures your adoptive sister. And let's not talk about the woman you now call Mother." The threat in the kid's voice reminded me of him. I knew he would send someone to handle those tasks if I didn't comply.

Unlocking the doors, I opened my door and got in, and the kid entered the passenger side. Snapping the door shut, the kid stayed quiet as I backed out of the parking spot and exited the underground garage. I stopped at the red light when the kid turned to me in his seat. "You remember how to get home, right?"

I nodded, and he turned back into the seat and stared out of the passenger window. I grabbed my phone and texted Jake to let him know that he needed to track my phone. Just in case something went down, and I couldn't make it back to the penthouse.

At the last turn, I spotted the house that had been my home for most of my teenage years. It had been years since I had been here, and nothing had changed. The windows were smashed, and the paint had peeled on the siding. As much as Marcus made off the drugs that he sold and the shit that he stole, he still couldn't fix this shithole up. Shutting off the car, I pulled my Glock from the middle console and placed it back under my suit jacket.

Stepping through the door, my eyes scanned across the room, only to find the inside wasn't much better as my gaze went around the place. There were a couple of guys off to the side cutting and bagging what looked like heroin. As we moved to the second floor of the house, there were grunts and moans from inside each of the rooms. The kid brought me to the last room down the hall and opened the door.

Smoke filled the room as my eyes leveled with his. He was behind the table that he used as a desk. He had aged since I last saw him almost ten years ago. Marcus had been with me the day I was caught by the cops after the robbery. I was his first lieutenant then, so it wasn't like I was a nobody in this world. The way he glared at me didn't make me as uneasy as it used to. His black eyes were two unending holes that sucked you in. "Well, TC, long time no see."

"Marcus."

"So, it looks like you made it rich. You weren't going to spread the wealth?" Marcus stood and marched over to me. I was finally his height and a little bulkier. It helped when you had three square meals a day.

"You left me to rot. You didn't even think to see if I was doing time for keeping them off you. I'd say we were square." I came back at him. I was no longer the teenager under his wing.

"You know the rules. We don't go back for people who get caught, but we expected you to come back to us when you got out. So? What were you doing?" Marcus was face-to-face with me. His breath almost made me gag. It was just like I remembered. The pungent smell of smoke and infection might have even been worse because I wasn't used to it anymore.

"Yeah? Well, I guess I forgot about you while I was living a life of luxury. You know, it's hard to remember the little guy when you make it big."

His fist connected to my face with a crack, swinging my head to the side before I could block it, and I staggered backward into his desk. As I regained my footing, he lunged at me, fists flying. He had always been quick to anger.

I pushed him back, and my left fist landed on his nose. The crunch of the cartilage and small bones shattered under my punch. Blood rushed out of the orifices as he shook his head, trying to regain his footing. Marcus had never been much of a fighter. He always used me or one of the others to do his dirty work.

I pressed him up against the wall, pounding into his face. The splatter of his blood on my fists and the cracking of my knuckles, as they landed on my target, sent a thrill through me. It had been years since I last used my fists to silence someone. But the greatest thing about this was that I was able to show him just what he sent out on those he couldn't deal with himself.

Marcus slid down the wall with blood streaming down his face. "Stay out of my way, Marcus. If you come at me again, I won't go so easy on you. I'm done with this life, done with you."

Turning, I headed out of the room and closed the door. The kid that brought me here was no longer around as I made my way down the rickety stairs. Blood dripped from my knuckles, and I passed the men who stared at me from the table. I was out of the door and making my way to my car as quickly as I could.

I hopped in my car, the tires squealing as I fishtailed out of the drive. Gunshots rang out as Marcus' goons spilled out of the house. I hunched down as my back windshield was busted, glass raining all over my backseat. I took the corners dangerously fast as I tried to outrun their bullets. My heart raced in my chest, but I kept an eye on the rearview mirror. After a few miles, it was clear they hadn't followed, so I slowed, not wanting to get pulled over by a cop. I guess telling Jake to go ahead of me wasn't the best thing that I could've done tonight.

Back at my place, I pulled out my phone, surprised to see that I had missed so many texts. The one from my father would have to wait, I didn't have time for him now.

Drake, the man I had spent six years of my life with at college, had sent a picture of my flavor of the week, with her kneeling in front of him, her lips around his cock. It was apparent that she didn't like that I had bailed on her. I shrugged. It was just pussy. Now that she had gone out on me, she wouldn't be part of my rotation anymore. I sent him a thumbs up emoji before checking the text from Jake.

I was just about to open the text, when the elevator doors opened. Jake stood in the doorway, gun out, doing a visual sweep of the parking garage. When he saw me, he lowered his gun and moved forward.

"What the fuck happened, TC? You said you were going to a woman's house."

"That didn't happen. Apparently, my message didn't send to let you know where I was going. I need you to get in contact with your team. I want more bodyguards watching my family." I stepped out of the black car and spotted the fucking bullet holes in the rear. My insurance company was going to have a field day with this. "Get this fucking fixed."

"TC, are you okay? You're bleeding." Jake's voice became more gruff as I glanced down at my hands and then back at him.

"It's not mine." I was starting to come down from the adrenaline from showing Marcus just what I was, and the bullets raining around me as I sped away from the assault.

"No, I mean at your shoulder. You've been shot!" After he mentioned it, I felt a sharp sting in my right shoulder. Glancing down at the wound, I could see the spreading stain of blood on my now ruined suit.

"Let's get up to the penthouse and call Sam. We will deal with this in a minute." I pressed my left hand over the wound to get it to stop bleeding. It hurt like a bitch.

Jake stood at the door to my office, his arms crossed over his chest. Sam was one of my rookie bodyguards who had come on board after I became CEO. He had been a combat medic before being honorably discharged and coming to work under Jake.

I sat at my desk as Sam dealt with my gunshot. Luckily for me, the wound was a through and through, meaning I didn't have to worry about him having to dig out a bullet. Sam was an excellent field medic, so I knew I wouldn't have to take a trip to the ER. Which was fortunate since it would have been reported to the police, and I didn't want to deal with that hassle. Not to mention having to explain it to my parents. They were too wrapped up in the upcoming marriage, they didn't need to worry about this.

I glanced over at the clock on my desk and sighed. It was already almost midnight, and I wasn't looking forward to what was going to happen tomorrow when my father announced the betrothal to all his friends and family. I still couldn't believe that they were doing this to me.

There was no telling what Aurora would do once I got to her home, and the thought that her parents hadn't even told her about the marriage ran through my mind. She might have even known this whole time and wanted to make my life a living hell. After Sam got me patched up, he stood and headed for the doorway.

"TC, tell me who did this." Jake was getting frustrated with me as I sat there at my desk. I could barely keep my eyes open, the only thing I could think about was crashing somewhere. Because at this rate, I wouldn't be making it into the office tomorrow.

"It was the leader of my old gang. I beat the shit out of him and then left. Then he sent his goons out to try to stop me." He raised his eyebrows and came over to me, helping me up.

It had been a long time since I had felt like this. Being shot wasn't how I had planned on spending the rest of my night.

"Well, let's get you to bed so you can sleep off some of those pain meds and the numbing agent in your shoulder." I nodded and leaned into Jake as he took me to my room. He placed me on the edge of the bed, and then dialed a number as he headed out of the room.

I didn't even pull the quilt back before landing on my back on the soft mattress. It didn't take me long to fade to black. I didn't know if it was the fatigue of the day or the loss of blood from the gunfight.

Chapter Two

Aurora

When my mother told me I was going to marry Tom Churchhill, I thought she was joking. This was the cruelest thing she could have done to me. He and I had nothing in common. He wanted to be in the limelight, whereas I wanted to be left alone and stay away from everyone's view. Besides, calling him a man-whore would be an understatement even on his best days.

He hadn't changed since high school. How could those women be with him knowing that he was just using them? He was still a player, and they were eating out of his hands. The only reason I knew that he had been with so many women was Chloe searching every media and finding him with a new one almost every week.

They were all the same. Blond hair and blue eyes, fake tits, and caked-on makeup with skimpy clothes. Tom had a type, and it wasn't me. I wore very little makeup unless there was an occasion I needed to wear more. But it still wasn't caked on. My clothes covered more than what theirs did, but I wasn't a prude. And the biggest difference was I had long, chocolate brown hair and grey eyes.

I think one of the main reasons I didn't like him was because I found him fucking that girl in the band room. I say one of the main as there was one that surpassed all the others. Sitting down right after lunch with my flute and piccolo in my first chair spot., I was about to get ready to practice my solo piece for the showcase when I heard something coming from the storage rooms.

Part of me told myself not to go find out what was going on, but the curious part of me wanted to know. So, I headed to the back of the room to check. As I had gotten closer the sounds were more recognizable. Someone was fucking in the band room. My heart was pounding. Normally, no one tried to do this in this room. Because there was always someone there practicing.

Continuing forward, I spotted them. He had the girl up on the counter, her moans loud and obnoxious as he pounded into her. My hand had come up to my mouth to stifle the gasp when I realized who he was. The way my stomach turned and twisted as I tried to pull my gaze from them made me want to throw up. If I hadn't backed into those stupid cymbals, I wouldn't have been spotted. But that wasn't my luck. The cruel ice-blue gaze he graced me with back then was something I couldn't pull my eyes from. It sent chills down my spine.

I remember how horrible school with Tom was, and I was so excited to leave to go across the country with my friends, Chloe and Elizabeth, to get away from him for college. Only to get back and be told he was going to be the one I was going to spend the rest of my life with. What had I done to have such luck?

I stood in my childhood room waiting to head down for the dinner party. My family and the Churchhills had invited everyone to this. The driveway was full of cars as valet personnel parked the cars down the long, paved avenue. It was crazy the amount of people who wanted to see this drama that was now my life. I wanted to throw up at the thought of having to be near him the entire night.

There were bodyguards galore here tonight. But I hadn't spotted the man of the hour. Would he come with another woman? Or would he come alone with Drake? I was hoping he would come with another woman so I could throw it back in his face and refuse this arrangement. There was no way my parents would continue this if he brought another woman. Right?

But when he got out of his hunter-green Mercedes G-class SUV, he was alone with Jake, his bodyguard since high school. I hadn't seen him since graduation, but I couldn't mistake his dirty blond hair. When he glanced up at my window, those hard ice-blue eyes locked on my grey ones.

Tom's expression didn't change as he moved his gaze from mine. He was too handsome for his own good. I couldn't help but wonder whether he was doing this because of what had happened all those years ago.

A knock on my door brought my attention away from the window. The curtain fluttered out of my hand. My mother came into the room, her nude dress swishing with each step. She was a beautiful woman, and a few of our friends told me I looked just like her. I could only hope that was true when I was her age. She smiled as she let her gaze look over the dress she had bought me for this party.

The dark green strapless number hugged all my curves. It came down below my knees with a split in the front. I wasn't too sure about wearing this around Tom. It didn't leave much to the imagination, and like I said, I wasn't into things like this much. But my mother had thought it was appropriate, even though I was old enough to pick out my own clothes.

"Everyone is waiting for you. You look beautiful!" my mother cooed. She stopped a few steps away from me.

I took one final look in the full-length mirror to make sure that everything was in place. My makeup had been professionally done, along with my hair. I wore it down with loose curls falling over my shoulders. The only thing I had requested from the stylists was that they didn't cake on my makeup.

Diamond earrings hung off my ears to draw people's attention to my face. I wasn't opposed to getting married, but why did it have to be with Tom? My mother motioned for me to follow her out of the room, so I squared my shoulders and did as I was told.

My heels clicked on the tiled steps as we headed down to the party. This was going to be a long night. As we reached the doors to the large ballroom, so many people were in there, and most of them were around Tom. He always had a way that attracted people to him. Which was probably why my dad loved him so much. That and he now owned the wealthiest logistics company in California.

The room had been lavishly decorated with gold and silver strands, and flowers were in pots near the columns. My mother had gone all out for this party and she and Mrs. Churchhill were already planning the wedding. I just hoped that they didn't make us go on a honeymoon.

I followed my mother into the room to my dad, who was standing beside Mr. and Mrs. Churchhill. The Delucas were beside them since they, the Churchhills and my parents had all grown up together. Drake was the Delucas only son. I didn't ever hang out with him because he was two years older than me. But that didn't stop Drake's eyes from roaming my body, and the heat in those dark brown orbs told me he wanted more. He was another playboy who had been in the Snapchat pictures with Tom during college.

This had to all be a nightmare. The guys from school were all grouped together near the bar. Drinking their body weight in alcohol. They didn't even try to hide the lust in their eyes as they roamed my body. Chloe and Elizabeth were near the food table standing there in beautiful black dresses. I had texted them both about what was happening tonight. They were here for moral support, and if I could get out of here, we would go to the club.

Mr. Churchhill motioned for Tom to come to join us, and I kept my eyes averted from him as he strutted over to us. I stood there in the middle of my parents and his. Tom settled in beside me, and I glanced over at him from the corner of my eye. He had gotten bulkier and had acquired a few more tattoos that played peek-a-boo out from under the sleeves of his suit jacket.

Being this close to him after all these years was a little intimidating and also brought back the emotions of the day that he embarrassed me in front of everyone. I took a deep breath and then raised my head. If I had to be here beside him, then I wasn't going to let him shame me again.

Mr. Churchhill moved forward and hushed the crowd's mumbling. His smile was genuine as he gazed over the group of people. "I never thought I'd see this night ever happening. But now it has. We are here to celebrate the betrothal of my son, Tom, and Mr. and Mrs. Emerson's daughter, Aurora."

He turned to face us as the crowd clapped and cheered. The way they acted; it was like this was something they had been expecting. Did they really think that we should be together? Were they crazy? I continued to smile at the people surrounding us. My mother's hand landed on my forearm and her mouth came up near my ear. "It's time for your dance. Don't do anything crazy, okay?"

Sighing, I glanced over to Tom, his blue eyes cold as he stared down at me. His hand was held out, and I slipped my small one into his. The grip was crushing, but I didn't make a sound to indicate that it hurt. Tom led me to the middle of the room and turned me to face him. The cruel smile on his face sent a chill down my spine, and when he pulled me close, it was like I was ten years younger again.

Everyone stared at us as the music began. He swung me around the dance floor. His vice-like grip on my hand and waist held me at just the right length from him. Tom's right shoulder trembled every time he spun me around. He crashed my body to his hard chest, his mouth close to my ear. People close to us sighed as we danced past them. "This marriage is just so I can keep the company. So don't be a fool about what this really is."

"I wouldn't have thought of this as anything but an inconvenience for you. But I guess when we have time alone, we need to flesh this whole thing out." I whispered back to him as the song ended, and I broke the grip that he had on me. If he thought that he was going to hurt me with that comment, he was sadly mistaken. I was no longer going to put up with his bullshit.

If he only wanted this for his company, so be it. I wasn't going to stop him. Curtsying, I turned and left him in the middle of the floor to head over to Chloe and Elizabeth. He wasn't going to be the one to leave this time.

Chapter Three

TC

I watched her leave me in the middle of the dance floor. It wasn't lost on me that she was trying to put me in the same situation that I had put her in. The dark green dress hugged all the new curves that she had grown into, and she held her head up high. She had grown into her backbone as well. Aurora was gorgeous tonight, but that didn't really shock me. Those grey eyes penetrated mine each time they locked with mine as we danced.

She didn't want this as much as I did either. But we were stuck with each other because I wasn't going to give up my company. I had put a lot of hard work into showing the board members that I was worthy of being my father's successor. In the three years that I had been running the company, I had transformed it, and it was now booming with shipments.

We didn't have to love each other or even like each other to make this work. Hell, we definitely weren't going to be husband and wife in the sense that these people thought. All this meant was that my dating life was going to get a lot harder. Because the media loved it when they saw me out in public with my flavors. So, my flavors wouldn't be getting dined out anymore once I was married.

A hand landed on my left shoulder, and Alex came into my peripherals. I hadn't seen my redheaded best friend in years. He hadn't changed much. Still tall and lean, with his freckles on his face, but he now had a thick beard. I turned and reached out with my hand to shake his. "Alex, how's it been, man?"

"Going well. Not as well as you, though! Big-time CEO and bachelor? Well, not a bachelor anymore." Alex brought his glass up to take a sip with his other hand. His eyes went to Aurora and her friends before winking at me. Something inside of me wasn't too sure about him staring at her, but I shook it off. "So, how's this going to work? I didn't know you two had a thing for each other."

I shook my head no and headed over to the bar to grab a drink. This was going to be a long night, and I was in desperate need of some whiskey with this feeling messing with me. Alex followed me and ordered another round for himself as we leaned against the bar, drinks in hand. "We don't. This has been arranged for years."

"Yeah? Well, I think it would do you some good to get away from the office for a while." Drake's deep voice brought my attention beside me to face him as he flirted with the brunette bartender. He turned with his drink in his hand, a wide grin on his lips. "Guess that means no more women for you. I finally have a chance."

"No, I'll still have my women. I just can't bring them out in the open anymore. I'm not going to touch Aurora." I glared over at Drake, and he raised his hands with that stupid smile still on his face. Sometimes, I didn't know how we even became friends.

"She's hot, I don't understand why you wouldn't want to fuck her?" I glanced over at her as she stood beside another man and her friends. She was laughing and cutting up with him. I threw back the contents of the glass and slammed the glass on the counter. When another appeared beside it.

Alex leaned up and chuckled, motioning with his drink to Aurora. "Because she's the reason he almost didn't get the company."

"Ah! So that's why Daddy Dearest stayed on for as long as he did. Didn't think he would ever let us be." Drake laughed and finished off his drink. He thought it was funny. I didn't. I had worked too hard in that fucking school to be denied what I was meant to be given.

"Keep laughing. I'll make sure you stay overtime every night," I threatened as I glared at him over the rim of my glass. Turning, I waved down the bartender to get another drink. She came over and poured my third glass of my favorite drink before heading to the other side to get someone else's drink.

I glanced over the thinning crowd and couldn't see Aurora or her friends anymore. Thank God she had the decency to make herself scarce. It was one thing being here in her home, and another with her being here as well. My gut also didn't like that she could be with that man. I finished the rest of my third glass and stepped away from Alex and Drake.

"Where are you going, man?" Alex's voice questioned behind me. I didn't answer him and continued my search for the right person. Just because I was engaged now, didn't mean I couldn't find one last fling in public.

I found a blond near one of the columns and started chatting with her. Her dress left nothing to the imagination, and my eyes continued to roam her body as we stood in front of each other. She flirted back before I asked her to follow me. She nodded, and we made our way through the crowd. No one would think anything about two people walking through them.

We headed down the hall I had walked so many times as a teen, and I found the door that I needed. The Emersons had redecorated since the last time I had been here. This room was hardly ever used, and it wasn't being used tonight. At least not yet. I smirked as I opened the door and grabbed the blond's hand.

Pulling her in, I took hold of her wrists bringing them up above her head and crashed her against the now-closed door. She moaned, and the lust in her green eyes had my zipper uncomfortably tight. She knew who I was, and that I was going to be married, but she didn't care and neither did I. I bit her above her left breast, and she gasped with a moan.

"Will you be bringing women home after we are married?"

I froze at her voice and let go of the woman in front of me to turn to face my fiancée. She stood there staring at me. Just like she had when she caught me with the girl in the band room in high school. Only this time, she decided to make herself known instead of trying to leave. Her grey eyes seemed to darken as she glared at me.

The woman I brought in here slipped quietly out the door. She was smart. She didn't need to hear anything else of our conversation. I locked the door for good measure and stalked forward. Aurora didn't budge but continued to keep her eyes trained on my face. "No, because once we are married. If I want a fling, I'll go to her house."

"Good, and as we are alone, we need to handle this situation now. I want to know what I should expect and what not to." Aurora crossed her arms under her breasts making them pillow even more in her green dress. I never noticed how big her bust was, or maybe I had.

"Fine." I went over to the leather couch and sat down, motioning for Aurora to do the same. She strolled over to the other couch, sat down, and crossed her lightly tanned legs. Her green dress slid up, showing off a little more leg, like when she backed into the cymbals and landed on her ass in the band room. Fuck, that day was still probably one of my better memories of her.

I remembered thinking that if I wasn't already hard that day, the sight of her skirt almost showing me her pussy would've got me there in seconds. Aurora had always had beautiful legs, and the guys in the school didn't miss it. She had them because she was the top keeper in the county and had almost become the top in the state.

The girl I had been fucking rearranged herself and scoffed before Aurora covered her eyes and got up, leaving me and Alexius in the storage room. Aurora's grey eyes had been eclipsed by her pupils, and I had to admit it was a turn-on knowing that she had watched me fucking someone else. When I had gotten older, I thought having another woman in the room with me and the one I was fucking would have the same effect, but it didn't.

"We've established that there will be no other women where we share a home. Other than the staff, that is." Aurora's grey eyes simmered as she stared at me. Since I had become the CEO, no one really held my gaze, but here she was barely even blinking. She was ballsy. But what was I to expect when she was the daughter of a CEO. If she had been a guy, she would have taken over her father's company.

"When we go to the courthouse, you will sign prenuptials. Oh, and since no women are to be in the shared home that goes for men as well, other than the staff, of course." I smirked at her. Aurora didn't even shift at my comment. I wondered if she had been with anyone. The thought of her being a virgin intrigued me. I mean, it wasn't that often you found a woman that hadn't been with someone. But if she was a virgin, it would be bad news for me.

"That won't be a problem either. Besides, I don't need your money. I have my own," Aurora answered me, her plump lips pressed together so it was difficult to tell the top and bottom. Her manicured hands lay neatly in her lap as her silver-heeled foot slowly twitched as if she was dancing to a song in her head.

"Not as much as I do. We won't be sharing a bed." I scowled at her, and she glared at me.

"That's fine with me. There's no telling what you have. I'd hate to tell my lover that he wouldn't be able to touch me without the worry of getting something," she snapped at me, and I repositioned myself, which brought her eyes to my lap. "When the minister tells you to kiss me, don't do it. I don't want your lips on me."

The mention of my lips on hers in front of hundreds didn't sit well with me. I didn't want to kiss her anyway, so her bringing it up kept me from having to.

"You don't have to worry about that." I glared at her as she stood, throwing her curled hair over her shoulder, and her dress slid down, hiding the part of her leg that it had been showing me just seconds before.

Aurora opened the door and strolled out into the hall. I sat there thinking about everything she had just told me.

According to her, she had someone else, but I doubted that she was still with him because of the way she mentioned him.

I stood from my seat and glanced down. Fuck, I was hard and had to get through the house without someone seeing me. Rearranging myself, I left the room through the open door to find Drake.

Chapter Four

TC

Drake followed me out of the Emersons' house and down their stairs with Jake a few feet behind him. My shoes echoed off the stone drive as I walked to my vehicle parked next to my parents. All the noise was inside the house, and the outside was as silent as one of the many jobs I had done before this life. As many times as I had been here, you would think I would be fine staying here. However, the reason I was here this time made me start to dislike the place.

Reaching my green SUV, I slid into the back. Drake got on the other side as Jake closed the driver's door and started the vehicle. Jake looked in the rearview mirror silently asking me where I wanted to go. It took me just a moment to figure out where.

"Take us to Hyde Sunset." This club had the best VIP areas—that way I could people watch and wouldn't have to be in the middle of the room.

"Damn, dude. I thought you were going to get your cock wet with that blond pussy." Drake chuckled as he glanced at me. It was a good thing that he didn't talk like this around my mother. She would have freaked out a little bit.

"Yeah? Well, you thought wrong. I need some good whiskey; that shit that Mr. Emerson had wasn't hitting the spot. Besides, Aurora fucked up my chance of getting anything at that house." I ran my hand down my face as I winced.

The pain meds that Sam had given before were wearing off, and my right shoulder hurt like a bitch. But I couldn't let Drake know. What was I going to tell him? *Oh, I was in a gun fight last night, and I was shot.* Even though I had known him for almost ten years, it didn't mean that he knew my past. And I was gonna keep him from knowing if I could.

I needed to get piss drunk and then go home and sleep. The wait to marry Aurora was going to be the worst part of this. It was a good thing that there were new clients coming to meet with us in the next few weeks. That would keep my mind off having to marry that bitch.

"Damn, are you really going to talk about your future father-in-law that way? His ass likes you for some fucking reason." Drake sat back in the leather seat getting comfortable, texting on his phone as we rode through the city to the club.

"I know he likes me, but that doesn't mean that he didn't buy some shit whiskey," I snapped back, and Drake threw up his arms in surrender. "Drake, I don't know why they want us to marry each other. My mother knows that Aurora intentionally showed her that picture. So, I just don't get why they want to make my life miserable."

"Maybe they think that she will keep you in check. I mean that's what they thought when they left Jakey-Poo with you in college." Jake glared back at my friend before he flipped him off. I couldn't help but chuckle at that.

Jake had done a great job when I was in college. He made sure I didn't get too fucking drunk, but then there was that one time when Drake and I left without him. Which is when the picture was taken and then shared to the whole campus.

I was surprised that we didn't get expelled, it was either our fathers' reputation and money, or because we both had really good grades. One or maybe both.

Jake stopped in front of the club, and one of the valet people opened my door. Drake and I exited the SUV. Walking up to the bouncers, they let us through, and I headed straight to my VIP spot. It was good to have enough money to have a VIP saved every night, even if you didn't come. I didn't have to wait to get anything in this place.

I dropped down into the brown leather, seat and one of the waitresses came up with a tray. They were all dressed in cosplay tonight, and mine was dressed as some anime character I knew of when I was younger. "What can I get you Mr. Churchhill?"

"Bottle of your best whiskey and two glasses."

The waitress nodded and headed down to the bar to get my order. The place was packed tonight. If it wasn't for getting married in a few weeks, I would probably have had a couple of women sitting beside me as I drank through the bottle of whiskey with Drake.

Drake was already tapping his foot to the beat of the music. I would have to make sure his ass didn't get too drunk, otherwise, I would have to head home sooner than I wanted. When the waitress came back with my bottle and two glasses, there wasn't a part of me that was excited about it.

She sat the bottle down along with the crystal glasses before she asked, "Is there anything else I can get you? I can get you an appetizer."

"No thanks."

The waitress nodded and left us as I tore the golden wrapper around the top off and uncorked it. I poured both of us a glass and downed mine. Tonight was going to be all about me, and I was going to have as much of this as I wanted.

"So, I think I'm going to have a running bet with Alex."

"About what?" I asked him while I glanced over the rim of my glass at him.

"To see which one of you falls first." He laughed, his dark eyes staring at me over the rim of his glass as he downed its contents.

"That will not happen. We both hate each other," I told him as I settled into leather.

Drake reached forward to the bottle and filled his glass again, sitting back and placing an ankle over his other knee. "That's what you say now. But I think one of you will fall. There's no way that someone who lives with someone else can avoid having some attraction to the other."

I shook my head. He was an idiot. When I first met him in college, I had been asleep in my bed. He came into my room and started messing with some of my boxes that I hadn't gotten to the night before with Jake.

"Damn, dude you have a lot of shit."

Opening my eyes, I spotted the dark-haired guy standing in the middle of my room. The dorm was a three-bedroom to allow Jake to stay with me. I sat up on the back of one of my arms as I shielded my eyes from the assault of the bright LED light. Before I could completely sit up, he had found an open box and was going through it.

I jumped out of bed, grabbed him and pushed him into the only part of the wall that was empty. "Keep your hands off my shit. Who the fuck are you, and why are you in my room?"

"Ah I forgot, we haven't met yet. I'm Drake, Drake DeLuca." He held out his hands with a mischievous grin.

This guy had something up his sleeve, but I took his out-stretched hand and shook his hand until he pulled me into a headlock. I grabbed hold of his hand, pulling it away from my neck and pushed him out of my room as he chuckled. "We are going to be best buds!"

"Dude, I just met you. I don't know if I like you," I told him as I folded my arms over my chest in my door. He was sure confident that I would like him.

Drake plopped down onto the couch and kicked his shoes off as he placed his feet on the table. For him to be brought up in a wealthy family, he sure acted like a pig. Jake emerged from his room and grinned.

"Mr. DeLuca."

Drake's head snapped from me to Jake, and he jumped up and went over to Jake. Shaking his hand as Jake continued to grin.

"Jake, buddy ol' pal. How have you been? Looks like you are having to protect the Churchhill protege, huh?" Drake turned his gaze to me and winked.

Rolling my eyes, I didn't know if I would be able to deal with this shit for the entire six years that I was going to be here. I just hoped that he would calm down once he was settled in the dorm.

That had been ten years ago. He was still fucking crazy, but I could handle it to some extent. The good thing was that he didn't act like that at work. Drake took whatever silliness he had and buried it deep inside of him when it was time to be in business mode. So, dealing with it outside of work was fine.

Taking a sip of my whiskey, I glanced around the dance floor and spat out my drink as I proceeded to choke on what was already going down my throat. Drake sat forward and slapped my back a couple of times before I regained my composure.

"Dude, are you okay? You wasted a good bit of that drink."

"Yeah, just saw someone I was trying to get away from." I leaned forward in my seat and realized that she was not only here, but so were her two friends, Chloe and Elizabeth.

Fuck, I wanted to get away from her and not have to see her again until the day I had to marry her. She seemed to be having fun dancing with her friends and some guy who was grinding on her from behind.

"TC, man. Chill your face. You look like you're about to kill someone." Drake downed another glass of the whiskey.

I continued to watch as my betrothed danced away from the guy while I poured more of the whiskey into the glass. For the life of me, I didn't understand why I continued watching her as she made her way over to the bar. Another guy at the bar started to make small talk with her and even ordered her another drink.

Rolling my eyes, I glanced back at Drake, the corners of his lips were raised as he took another drink. My gaze went back to Aurora as she continued to laugh and talk to the man beside her. That poor man, he didn't know what he was getting into with her. He didn't know that she was already betrothed. Hell, he might not care—I didn't care if she wanted him.

"Are you going to come back to earth, or are you going to continue to stare at your gorgeous fiancée all night?" Drake's voice broke through my empty thoughts and brought my gaze back to him.

"I'm not staring at her." I scoffed as I looked back at the empty bottle on the table. I decided in that moment I was going to fuck with Aurora.

I motioned for the waitress to come to me. "Yes, Mr. Churchhill."

"Can you grab me another bottle and make sure you ask the bartender who's serving next to the woman in the green dress. Be sure to mention my name."

"Yes, sir." She scampered off and made her way to Aurora. Catching the attention of the bartender for the new bottle, I could tell right when she mentioned my name because Aurora turned and locked eyes with me. Grinning, I saluted her with my glass. Drake burst out laughing beside me.

Chapter Five

Aurora

As soon as the name left the woman's mouth, I froze. It had to be someone else. There was no way that he would be here. My heart began to race as I turned my gaze from the man who was happily talking about his dog to glance around the room and then up to the VIP tables.

And there he was with a shit-eating grin on his lips like he had caught me doing something wrong. Drake was beside him laughing as I watched the waitress get his bottle and turn to take it to him. I grabbed her arm, and she squeaked before she realized who I was. "I need to borrow that bottle for a moment."

The waitress glanced at Tom up in his VIP booth, sitting all cocky, before she shook her head.

"Don't worry, he's my fiancée." I grabbed the bottle and tore the foil off the top and tugged the cork out before tipping it and downing some of the liquor. I had never been too much of a whiskey drinker, but this was to piss him off.

I glanced over to Tom, his lips a straight line as he stared back at me. Smiling, I flipped him off and left the man at the bar to find Chloe and Elizabeth. Fucker wanted to make his presence known, then I would make sure he didn't get any more evidence from me. Finally, finding my friends at a table further away from the VIP balcony, I sat down as Chloe hung on every word from the blond who was sitting between her and Elizabeth.

"Where did you run off to?" Elizabeth asked as she turned her gaze to me.

"Oh, you know, getting free drinks. Mr. I'm Too Good For Others is here," I answered her as I glanced over my shoulder and noticed that he and Drake were walking down the steps.

"Really? I didn't think that he would wander off from your dad and his. He's so stuck up their asses."

I shrugged as I watched them both walk out of the door. I was here first, so it was a good thing that he left because I wasn't ready to. He always had to ruin things. The whiskey that I had chugged had made me warm, and I was starting to feel good.

"Yeah, well, Tom Churchhill can suck it. He's nothing more than a brown-noser."

"You know TC Churchhill? You know he's the most eligible bachelor in LA?" the guy who was talking with Chloe inter- jected as he looked at each of us.

I cocked an eyebrow at the man before turning my back on them all. If the way I was feeling right now was going to mean anything. Things were going to be bad in the morning, and my mother was going to be pissed with how drunk I was going to be. I didn't even know what the percentage was on that whiskey.

"He's not so eligible now. He's engaged now," Chloe in- formed him, bringing the guy's attention back to her.

"No! For real?"

I could hear the sorrow in his voice without even looking at him. What did it matter if he was engaged? It wasn't like he would be faithful. Maybe with the right woman, but even then, it was doubtful. I stood and the entire table stared back at me.

"I think I'm going to leave. Do either of you need a ride?" Elizabeth stood and nodded, and then glanced back at Chloe.

I worried about Chloe because one day, she was going to meet the wrong man, and we would never see her again.

"I'm going to spend some more time with Spence here." Chloe winked at me, and Elizabeth and the guy chuckled.

I nodded, "Okay. Well, call us when you get home."

She knew that it meant for her to text us. Because we didn't want any guy that we were talking to know that all they had to do was text and that we had a code. So, even if they did text us, it wouldn't mean what it looked like.

Chloe nodded and then waved us both off. She was getting laid again tonight. I swear her body count was up in the double digits. Not like I was judging her, hell, she was a gorgeous woman, why shouldn't she have whatever man she wanted.

Aurora

> Orson, can you come pick me and Elizabeth up?

> On my way, ma'am.

We both went outside and stood in the valet area. Waiting for Orson to get to us in the long line of cars the valet was bringing to the other patrons who were leaving. Luckily, I didn't have to wait long as the valet allowed people with drivers to park their vehicles.

Orson got out and opened the back door to the DiMora Natalia car. This was probably the most expensive car that my father had ever gotten me, and the only one who ever drove the car was Orson. I didn't trust anyone else.

I slid into the leather backseat with Elizabeth, and Orson returned to the driver seat. He pulled away from the curb and into traffic and back to my house. I wanted this night to end already. I didn't want to see Tom again until the wedding day. Which was all too soon.

After the whole talk with him in the drawing room, I had come here to avoid seeing him again. The decision to chug his whiskey was a stupid move on my part. But I wanted to show him he wouldn't be able to intimidate me. Now, I don't know if that's what I showed him, or whether I showed him how much of a child I was.

"Are you okay? You look pale." Elizabeth's hand rested on my forearm.

"Yeah, I think I just had too much to drink. It's been a crazy couple of months since we've been back." I glanced over to the window and noticed that I was pale.

"It has. I'm sorry you are having to go through this arranged marriage. It's horrible that they would do this to you," Elizabeth commented as she stared at me through the dark window. "But did you tell your parents what he had done to you while you were at school?"

"No, I dealt with it myself. What were my parents going to do to him? He was the heir to their company. We were small compared to them. I think that my father thought with me and him together it would pull our family in the same status as the Churchhills." I sighed as I leaned further into the back seat. I really needed to get home.

If I didn't, I was sure that I was going to vomit in my favorite car. Orson finally pulled into our driveway and put in the code to the gate, and I was sure the party was over. Since Tom and I were no longer there.

"I'm sure they have a reason other than companies merging for this arrangement. Didn't your mother tell you that this had been planned since our senior year?" Elizabeth asked me.

I shook my head. My head was pounding as I tried to open the door. The whiskey was going further in my system. Whatever he had must have been high proof because I had never felt this way before. The handle to the car became two as I tried to open the door.

"Ms. Aurora, Ms. Elizabeth, we are at the house now." Orson had my door open, and there were two of him as well. He grabbed my reaching hand and helped me out of the vehicle. Elizabeth was behind me and wrapped her arm around me as I stumbled.

"I have her, Orson. Thank you for driving us." Elizabeth led me to the front doors where the butler had opened them and stood aside to allow us in.

I stumbled up the stairs, while Elizabeth helped me up to my room. In all my life, I had never been this drunk before. At this moment, I wished I hadn't chugged that drink.

I woke up with the worst headache I had ever had before. Turning over to my side a bottle of water and a couple of aspirin were on my bedside table. The last thing that I remembered from last night was walking up the stairs with Elizabeth. Trinie must have brought in the meds and bottle of water.

There was nothing in this world that would make me drink like that again. I was done with liquor. I didn't ever want to feel like that again. Ever.

Sitting up, I grabbed the aspirin and bottle of water. I downed the medication and some water to make sure it went down. My head continued to spin as I stood to go to the bathroom. Everything was still reeling.

I knelt down next to the toilet and threw up the water, aspirin, and whatever else that hadn't digested over night. Luckily for me, I had my hair up in a bun, so I didn't have to worry about it getting in my hair. My throat burned from the acid that came up, and my sides hurt as I heaved one more time into the porcelain bowl.

He was the one who made me do that. All so that I could pretend that I was one-up on him. I hated this feeling that was going through my head. Why did he have to stir up these feelings in me? The ones that brought me back to school, and the mean things that he did to me.

I stood and went to the sink. Taking my toothbrush, I put a heavy dollop of toothpaste on the bristles and wet it with the water. I brushed away all the nasty tastes in my mouth. This wasn't how I wanted to spend my morning, nursing a hangover because of Tom.

A knock sounded on my door as I finished with my teeth and placed the brush back in its holder. I dried my mouth and walked out of the bathroom just as Elizabeth came into my room. She looked a whole lot better than I did.

"Well at least one of us isn't hungover."

Elizabeth laughed as I went to the vanity in my room. The brightness from the lights hurt my eyes while I really looked at myself. Bags were under my eyes, and I looked a little pale. Makeup would be helpful today as my mother had something planned for us. I just hoped that I didn't have to deal with Tom. Because that would just be torture.

"I can't believe you were drunk last night. I didn't think the drinks that you had were anything that you hadn't had before." Elizabeth sat on the end of my bed as I started putting on the foundation.

My stomach rolled like I was about to vomit again.

"Yeah, well, you know when I told you both that Tom was there. Well, I'm sure he told the waitress on purpose to come down and get his bottle of whiskey from the bartender. Because I know for a fact that they normally get the new bottles from the back."

"Yeah, so you did what?" Elizabeth stood and came to sit beside me on the bench.

"Well, I looked up at him and he had that shit-eating grin on his face. So, I stopped the waitress, told her I was his fiancé and opened the bottle and chugged some of it. I didn't check the proof, so I don't know what the percentage of the alcohol was. I hate when people try to intimidate me," I continued while finishing up with the foundation and moving on to the eyeshadow.

"Oh, girl. You should have looked at the proof before doing that." Elizabeth grabbed a brush and began to untangle her hair as I continued with my makeup.

"Yeah, I should have. But I know one thing: I will never drink anything that he is having ever again."

Elizabeth chuckled as she stood and pulled her hair up into a ponytail. I finished my makeup just as another knock came upon my door. My mother came in, already dressed in a flowy dress as she came up behind me. "You look beautiful. Make sure you put a nice dress on. We are meeting Laura to taste cakes and figure out the food for the reception."

Great, I just hoped that it was just Laura going and not Tom as well.

Chapter Six

Aurora

My mother allowed Elizabeth to come with us because we were going to look at wedding dresses. I swear they were making this seem like me and Tom were in love. The owners of the shop had pulled out every dress imaginable. Jewelry, corsets and shoes lined the walls of the large room we were in. Laura and my mother sipped on champagne as Elizabeth sat with them.

We spent hours in the shop while they pulled me out of one dress and then into another. I declined each one of the white dresses. My mother was getting pissed, and when I picked out a dress that was plain, it took everything in her to smile. I knew that she hated the dress, but I wasn't going to pick any of the others.

"Aurora, you look gorgeous in this and all the other dresses you were in." Laura came up behind me, her hands on my bare shoulders as she stared at me in the mirror. She had always been very sweet to me. Probably because she had a daughter herself. "Whichever dress you decide to wear, you will turn heads. Now, why don't we get you out of this dress and find out which cake we are going to get, and which one we will pick for Tom."

I rolled my eyes, and the two ladies helped me out of the dress. It felt nice to be back in my normal clothes as we headed out to the car. With Elizabeth beside me, we both slid into the car.

Laura and my mother continued to talk about the wedding, about how our families would now be linked. I had to turn away and stare out the window. This shit pissed me off, but there was no way I'd be able to tell them no.

We arrived at the bakery I had always wanted to make my cake. But it was bittersweet, especially as I was getting married to Tom. Laura patted me on the knee and then exited the car with my mother.

Sighing, I followed them with Elizabeth right behind me.

"Well, isn't this awkward?" she whispered to me as we all headed inside.

"You're not telling me anything I don't already know," I answered her as the attendant held the door open for us.

I was going to hold Laura to the cake thing, I was going to make sure that I got a cake that he hated. If he was going to make my life miserable, I'd do the same, and I wasn't going to back down.

Walking further in the wonderful smell of the bakery flooded my nose. This was my favorite place to get my birthday cakes. When I was a little girl, I always dreamed that they would be the ones to make my cake for my wedding. They were so delicious and soft.

The owner came around the counter and hugged my mom and Laura. With a smile, she glanced over and came to me.

"Oh, Aurora! How I always dreamed of making your cake on your big day! Come let's pick this out!" Gretchen took me by the hand and brought me over to the sample table. "Where's the groom? Is he picking out his cake?"

"No, he is trusting us to do that for him." Laura smiled and put her hand on my shoulder.

"Very well! I know TC has always been one to put things off." The pixie-haired lady answered before bringing her attention back to me. "So, Aurora what do you think? Go through these and see which one you want, and then we will go through TC's cake."

I nodded to her and looked over the options. All of them looked so good, but I knew the red velvet wouldn't be an option. I didn't care for it.

The little signs in front of the plates indicated the flavor along with the icing and topping. Picking up the small fork, I cut into the white chocolate with cream cheese icing and strawberries and placed a small piece in my mouth. The explosion of the sweet berry and the tartness of the cream cheese brought out a moan. Damn, Gretchen was good!

I didn't know if I wanted to try any of the others because this one was amazing! Turning the sign around so I could come back to it, I went on further. I didn't like lemon, so I didn't even try it, and coconut was out too. A chocolate cake stopped me in my tracks.

The dark chocolate with its chocolate icing made the raspberries stand out, and they pulled me to it. Taking the small fork beside it, I cut into the small square. I couldn't help the small moan that exited my mouth as the flavors hit my tongue. Fuck, I needed both this one and the white chocolate together.

I sliced another piece of the dark chocolate and went to the white chocolate. Cutting a small bite from it, I placed both in my mouth and that was it. Both of these needed to be my wedding cake. I didn't care what Gretchen needed to do to make this work, but it needed to happen.

Turning from the samples, my gaze went to Gretchen, and she smiled with her eyebrows raised as she held my eyes. "I want both of these. I don't know how you can do it, but I need these both as my wedding cake."

"Of course, I will do whatever you want. Now, which cake do we want for the groom's cake?"

I had been so interested in what I wanted that I had forgotten about choosing Tom's. Part of me wanted Laura to pick it, but I wanted to find something that he would know that I picked. Nodding to Gretchen, I went back over to the samples and spotted what looked like a nice vanilla cake.

Grabbing the fork in front of it, I didn't even look at the sign. I cut into the sample and took a bite to attempt to show them that I had tried it. There was no way I was going to make a scene with Laura here. Even though I was choosing this for Tom, the flavors were amazing, and I felt a little warm after I swallowed the bite.

It had the right amount of banana, caramel, and cinnamon. This one would be his. I didn't know if he would like it, but if he wanted something that he liked, he should have been here to pick it. Turning back to the ladies, I pointed to the sample.

"I think this one will be good." She nodded and took the three that I had picked to the counter. Laura and my mother followed her leaving me with the rest of the samples.

"Well, you are now that much closer to getting married to the man you hate." Elizabeth slipped her arm in mine as she stood beside me.

"Yeah, it will be more like roommates that hate each other. I'm sure I won't see him much, if any." My gaze went to the three women at the counter as they laughed and talked while Gretchen made note of my order. I wondered whether Laura would tell Tom what I had picked for him.

"Hey, just think it will be an easy life. You won't have to put out when you're not in the mood." Elizabeth laughed, and I smiled.

"This is true. but then I would need to find a guy that didn't care that I was married."

"Honey, there are plenty of them. And when we go on our girls' trip here in a few months, we will meet plenty of foreign hotties." She nudged me and pointed out the window.

I spotted the bike before he took his helmet off. He was gorgeous and the Ducati that he was riding was bright red. If he didn't want the attention, then he was losing that battle. Slinging his leg over the bike, he placed the helmet on the tank and turned to the building.

"Yeah, but you can't be posting pictures. Tom cannot know about the girls' trip." I answered her as I pulled my gaze from the biker.

"You know that I won't, but you never know what Chloe will do."

I spent the rest of the day at home going through things in my room to go pack up what I didn't need. Elizabeth had gone to her apartment when we got back to the estate. Staring at the walls of this room made my stomach bunch in knots.

This would be the last few weeks that I would be here. After the wedding, I would be living with Tom. Thankfully, I had been told by Orson that I did have a room to myself at his place. At least he wasn't going to make me sleep in the same bed with him. Hell, he probably wasn't going to be there at night, so it didn't really matter where I slept.

I would miss Sandra and her cooking, along with Jeff's breakfast. Hopefully he had a decent cook because then I would have to go out to eat. Which he probably didn't from what Laura had talked about on our way back that he worked a lot.

When they started talking about babies, it took all I could not to scoff and roll my eyes. Tom wouldn't come near me with an eight-foot pole. That dream wouldn't happen, besides, I was on the shot, and I wouldn't be stopping that anytime soon. It wasn't that I didn't want kids, I did want them. But not with Tom.

Fuck, with all my inner thoughts, I had stopped packing things and was sitting on my bed. This was bullshit with a capital B. I now knew what the girls in the past felt like when they were arranged to marry someone. How the hell did they survive like this?

I shook my head and stood, pulling a box to me to place more of my stuff in it. My mother had wanted to have Tinzi to help me pack everything. But I needed some time to myself. I was tired of putting on a smile when I wanted to throw a tantrum and tell them all to go to hell for making me do this.

A knock came on my door. The only one who ever knocked was my dad, and maybe a maid who cleaned, but she never came around unless I was gone.

"Come in!" I yelled to my dad on the other side of the door.

The door swung slowly forward as my father stepped in. He had gained some weight while I had been gone for college. He used to be my knight and shining armor but now he has become the villain in my story. My heart broke as I stared at the man that was my whole world.

"It's been a while since this place has looked like a disaster like this." He moved further in my room fingering the things that had been pulled down from the shelves on my walls.

"Well, things happen when you grow up, don't they, Father?" I didn't miss his flinch when I called him father instead of dad. I wanted him to know that I was angry with him. Because he was just as much at fault as my mother.

"That they do, Aurora. Tom isn't as bad as you think he is. He has grown up from the person that you saw in that photo." My father turned to me, and there were tears in his eyes that hadn't fallen. "I hope that one day you will see why this arrangement was made, and on that day, I hope that you don't hate me as much as you do right now."

You see, that was the thing about me and my father. He knew me. So, he knew that I hated the world right now because *he* was my world. I doubted I would ever see why I needed to marry Tom, but I was sure that one day I would stop hating him. But not right now.

Chapter Seven

TC

I sat in my office signing off on papers for new ship-ments while the sun rose behind me. Drake had left to talk with another company to get more trucks. We had been expanding more recently, and the need for truck drivers was growing with it.

"Mr. Churchhill?"

Glancing up, I spotted Lindsey at the cracked door. I motioned for her to come in. Her heels clicked on the tile floor, and she stood in front of my desk until I looked up at her.

"Yes?"

"Sir, Ms. Petticort has been calling and wants to sched-ule a meeting. She has been calling multiple times to get this scheduled." Lindsey's Southern California accent caught me off-guard with the nervousness in her tone.

"Okay, schedule her in." I turned back to the papers that still needed to be signed.

"That's the problem, Mr. Churchhill. She wants to meet with you when you are already booked."

I dropped my pen and massaged my temples. Fuck, this was the part I hated. All of this bullshit with other company CEOs thinking that they could dictate when I could meet with them just because they were who they were. "Well tell her we are booked, and she will have to wait. I've put off some of these people a few times."

"I've tried, but she is refusing anything after four months."

"Fine, do what you need to do. Lindsey, can you pull the records up from four years ago? I need those before the board meeting."

"Sir, I was told by your father that you would be taking a two-week vacation for your honeymoon. I've started to clear meetings with the board."

I slammed my fist on my desk and groaned. Lindsey jumped, bringing my attention back to her. Fuck, why didn't I think he would try something like this? "Sorry Lindsey. Reschedule those meetings. I will not be off for two weeks. Thank you."

"Yes, sir." Lindsey left me sitting in my office. She had started only a couple of years before I became CEO and had remained with me.

My mother had called me earlier about cakes and food for the reception. I never understood why she continued to ask me questions about shit with the wedding. It didn't interest me in the slightest.

I finally broke down and told her to get me whatever cake she wanted because I really didn't care. Besides, she knew what I liked and would be able to pick food for the reception.

My mother and Aurora's had been doing everything in their power to get us together to do wedding shit. But I refused. They were not going to paint us as a happy couple when this was just an arrangement.

Now, my dad had done this to me with the honeymoon. We were not going, he would just have to take Mother. I didn't understand them trying to make us spend time alone together.

Picking up my cell, I called my dad. I really did not want to argue with him this morning, but I was not going on this trip with Aurora.

"Tom! How good to hear from you! Are you with your mother and Aurora picking out cakes?" The soft hum of the golf cart could be heard in the background.

He was already on the golf course. I swear he spent more time there since he retired than at home. But my mother sometimes went with him.

"No, I'm at the office and was told some news I had not been made aware of." I sat back in my chair and turned around to stare out over the city.

"What news would that be, son?" He chuckled at someone on the other side of the phone.

"That you had told my secretary that I would be gone for two weeks for a honeymoon? Dad, I'm not going. You and Mom will have to take the tickets," I answered him. My father had never really pushed me to do anything I didn't want to, other than this marriage. But I wasn't about to go on a honeymoon with this woman when she was nothing more than a compromise to allow me to keep my company.

"Yes, I think that being with her for a honeymoon would quell the disagreement that you two have from your younger years. Besides it's a good way to get to know someone." The voices around him became quieter like he was walking away from anyone that was around him.

"Like I told you and her father that night you met me in my office. I'm not going to treat her like a wife. The only thing that I'm marrying her for is to be able to keep this company.

Father, I don't understand why you want her and me to be married. We have nothing in common, and you and her family are just going to make us hate each other more." I was getting annoyed with this situation even more, and I had let it come out when I didn't need it to. Again.

"Look, Tom. If your mother and hers didn't think this match would work, we wouldn't have arranged it. But if you don't want to go on the honeymoon, I won't make you. However, I do want you to try to leave the things that both of you have done to each other in the past. I will let your mother know that you do not want the honeymoon. If this is all I have to go, eighteen holes will not putt themselves."

"Thanks, Dad. Yeah, that is all. Good luck on the range today." My father chuckled again, and we both said our good-byes.

I was glad that he didn't fight about the honeymoon. If I had to spend that amount of time with my future wife, I would lose my mind.

For the last few weeks before the wedding, my phone had been blowing up. My flavors of the week were upset that they wouldn't be the ones with my last name. Not that I wanted

Aurora tied to me for life. But keeping my company was my priority, and I didn't want to screw that up. My mother had been upset that I had refused to go on the honeymoon, but my father had talked with her, and she finally relented.

The last time I saw Aurora was the night in the club. My mother had tried to get me to do cake tasting and to be in on the food for the reception. I had told her that I had a very important meeting that day, and I couldn't miss it. And that she should just go without me. Hell, she knew what foods I liked, and it wasn't like I was really interested in what happened after the wedding anyway.

Today, Aurora and I were getting married, and I was sitting in a mahogany-walled room with Drake and Alex along with my father and hers. I just wanted this day to be over. Everyone around me laughed and drank, I just drank. When I woke up today, I had hoped that I still had a few more days.

Glancing at the watch on my right wrist, it was nearing time for the ceremony. I wasn't exactly ready for this. The door to the room opened and my mother stood scanning the room before she came in wearing her knee-length burgundy dress and shawl. Her blue eyes landed on me, and she marched up to me. She took my third glass of whiskey from my hand and pulled me to a standing position. "What are you doing? Are you trying to get drunk and embarrass us?"

"Mother, I'd never do that to you again. I'm just trying to relax," I answered her without a slur. This woman didn't know how much I could drink and still walk a straight line. I smiled at her and then kissed her cheek.

"Tom. You need a mint, your breath reeks of alcohol. How do you expect to kiss your bride like that?"

"I don't plan on kissing her at all, Mother." My mother slapped my cheek before she got in my face. The room had gone quiet, all the men turning to watch our interaction. I hadn't ever been afraid of a woman in my life, and the one before me had never slapped me before. "You will find a mint, and you will kiss your bride. I do mean a kiss, Thomas."

"Yes, Mother." Taking orders from people wasn't my forte, but my mother and father were different. I grabbed a mint from the candy tray that sat on the circular table on our way into the church and popped it into my mouth. If I knew my mother, a peck on the cheek would not suffice. Aurora wasn't going to be happy about this stitch in our agreement. But there was no way I would be able to tell her.

Drake and Alex stayed at the doors as my father and I went into the chapel. People who were friends of the family and family members were already seated in the pews staring at us as we headed down the aisle to the front of the church. Their murmurings were not lost on me as I continued past them, some of them didn't care that I could hear them.

Red cloth hung off the pews with white Gladiolus bouquets in stands beside them. If this were something I wanted this place would be beautiful, but it wasn't. I stood in my black tuxedo with a red pocket square peeking out from the left breast pocket. The minister gave me a quick nod and smile before resuming his gaze down the aisle.

My mom had stayed behind to shepherd the ring-bearer and flower girl down the aisle. I didn't even know who they were, some cousins from someone I had never met. It was stifling in here, and I pulled at the collar around my neck. I was never one to be claustrophobic, but this was definitely doing the job. I was ready for this to be over.

The music started and they opened the doors. Drake came out with Chloe first. She looked pissed, and I could imagine why. Drake would have already berated her with inappropriate pick-up lines, and her quick pace told me that she wanted to get away from him as soon as she could. They split, and Drake came up behind me, nudging me in the ribs with a smile. "I think she likes me."

I grinned at him and watched Alex and Elizabeth come down. They had gotten engaged once she got back from college. He had finally been able to get her to say yes after all these years. He was the only one in our group who was happy today.

All of this seemed to slow down. The kids, who my mother had acquired from family members, walked up to us: the young boy brought the rings to Drake, and the girl went and stood by Chloe. Emi sat in the pew up front with her date. I didn't know whether I liked the man or not, I was still deciding.

All that was left was Aurora, and the music changed again signaling that she was at the door. Turning my gaze to the door, I froze. Aurora stood there in her white dress. The thing hugged her body like it was a second skin and then flared out to trail behind her. The shoulders laid lightly on her arms, and if she weren't carrying the bouquet, I'd be able to see the front of the dress. Mr. Emerson stood beside her with a wide grin on his lips that looked forced, Aurora's arm looped in his as they waited for the song to change so that they could make their way to the front.

Chapter Eight

Aurora

I stood behind the massive oak doors with my father. My heart was racing while I waited for the music to change and tell us it was our turn. The heels that I had to wear with this dress hurt my feet, but I wasn't going to complain. There was no use at this point, all I could do was go down that aisle and be bound to a man who I hated.

"Are you okay?" My father's voice was close to my ear. It wasn't like the two men in tuxedos who stood at the door to open it would say anything. One had eyed me at one point, but the other one was a statue.

"No, but what choice do I have? You and my mother had this planned as soon as the Churchhills adopted him," I remarked out loud as I shuffled from foot to foot again.

I didn't know if I hated the man at the end of the aisle or the damn shoes more. My mother must have wanted to punish me even more by making me wear these damn things. It wasn't like we couldn't have gotten this dress altered.

"Aurora..."

"Don't. I don't want to hear it again." I sighed and held up my other hand as I shifted my feet again. The waiting was making me feel claustrophobic in this tight dress. "When are they going to change the music?"

The sound in the chapel went silent and then the change of the music gave us our cue. I took a deep breath and stood straight. My arm wrapped around my father's, and the two men manning the door opened it. Mother had made sure that the bouquet that I carried included my favorite flowers. Even though I had told her I didn't want them. The music became louder once the doors started opening, and we waited for a couple of extra seconds before moving forward into the room.

My father led me to the man who I would spend the rest of my life with. If I didn't hate him as much as I did, I would have thought he was quite handsome in his black tux and the red handkerchief in his breast pocket. He seemed to be standing there frozen as I made my way up to him. I wanted this to be over with. The people sitting in the pews were just there to see whether there would be any drama.

Chloe and Elizabeth looked gorgeous in their dark red bridesmaid dresses, and the little flower girl was sweet as can be with her red bow in her hair. She was a third cousin of Tom's mother. My father brought me up the small set of stairs, and I stood in front of Tom before handing the bouquet over to Chloe. If I hadn't been paying attention, I'm sure I would've missed the quick flick of Tom's gaze over my dress.

I kept my hands folded in front of me, and when they came back to my face, I held his ice-blue gaze . The stares from everyone in the pews made me uncomfortable. My mother had picked this thing out when I had refused to make a decision. I wasn't even fazed by what she had gotten me. It was just something to walk down this aisle in to marry a man who didn't even want me.. But I should have picked the fucking heels, with my feet already hurting I didn't know if I would be able to concentrate on the preacher.

Even though the dress was gorgeous, the way it allowed my breasts to almost spill out over the top and the low-cut back pushed my self-confidence to the max. It showed a little more skin than I thought my mother would ever allow me to show. Especially in front of friends and family, but then again, I figured she would want something to entice this cold man in front of me.

"Family and friends, we are gathered here to bring these two young people into holy matrimony. Is there anyone here that would object to this marriage?" The old minister gazed out over the full church. His worn book was open in his withered hands as he waited for someone to stand.

I wanted to tell him that I objected to this marriage, that I didn't want to be bound to this man. But I stood there waiting for the objection that would never come from someone else in the sea of spectators. The minister cleared his throat and went on with the ceremony. Flashes went off somewhere in the room as I tried to not fidget. The dress' tightness made me feel like I needed to rip the thing off.

"Tom, repeat after me. I, Thomas Christian Churchhill, take you to be my wife, and these things I promise you: I will be faithful to you and honest with you; I will respect, trust, help, and care for you; I will share my life with you; I will forgive you as we have been forgiven; and I will try with you better to understand ourselves, the world and God; through the best and worst of what is to come and as long as we live."

Tom repeated him, but I knew these words had no meaning to them as we had already agreed that I wouldn't be holding him back from the women he actually wanted. Which also meant that I was able to do the same.

"Aurora, please repeat after me. I, Aurora Evangeline Emerson, take you to be my husband, and these things I promise you: I will be faithful to you and honest with you; I will respect, trust, help, and care for you; I will share my life with you; I will forgive you as we have been forgiven; and I will try with you to better understand ourselves, the world and God; through the best and worst of what is to come and as long as we live."

I repeated them, but in my heart, I didn't mean any of the words that I uttered. I didn't understand why we couldn't have just had a courthouse wedding to keep away from all this bullshit. Spending money that didn't need to be spent. The minister nodded with a smile and motioned for Tom's best man to bring over the rings. He handed Tom mine and then gave me Tom's with a wink. I fought hard not to roll my eyes.

"Now again, repeat after me, Tom. I give you this ring as a sign of my love and faithfulness. Receive this ring as a token of wedded love and faith."

Tom repeated him and slid the ring on my left ring finger and then dropped my hand like it had burned him. I took his hand, noticing something dark peeking out from his cuff, and glanced over to the minister.

"Aurora, repeat after me. I give you this ring as a sign of my love and faithfulness. Receive this ring as a token of wedded love and faith."

I repeated him as I returned the gesture and dropped his hand. The next part made me nervous as I didn't know if he was actually going to kiss me on the lips or not even kiss me at all. I hoped that he didn't kiss me because mixed with the mint in his mouth, I could detect the subtle hint of whiskey. But I didn't know whether he was buzzed or drunk in front of me.

"I now pronounce you man and wife. You may now kiss the bride." The old minister snapped the Bible shut and proceeded to stand there. Waiting.

Tom took a step toward me and wrapped his left huge hand around the back of my head, holding it steady as I stared back at him. My heart was racing again as thoughts whirled around my head.

He wouldn't dare have our first and only kiss in front of all these people. We talked about this. The scent of the whiskey floated from his breath to my nose. His full lips brushed mine before he pressed his harder against them. Between the smell of the liquor and the way he kissed me, I couldn't help but reciprocate the kiss.

My heart raced harder in my chest as his tongue swept with mine. I had never been kissed like this, and if this was going to be the only one I ever had with Tom; I was going to make sure I remembered it for the rest of my life. Even if it was with a man I detested.

He broke the kiss, and the minister's voice sounded muffled as I tried to regroup from what had just happened. Tom was a good actor and an even better kisser. He took my hand, and we led the wedding party out of the decorated chapel.

I dropped Tom's hand and continued beside him. My heart was beginning to slow down as we headed over to the reception area. My heels clicked on the ceramic floor before we stopped at the doors. My thoughts no longer on the pain coming from the heels.

My mother came up to us and ushered us into another large room away from the reception. There were photographers waiting to take our pictures who had set up their camera equipment . It looked like a whole studio had come in and had taken up residence.

I glanced over to Chloe and Elizabeth, and they shrugged before I went up to my mother's side and whispered, "Mother, what is this? Why are we having pictures? Do you think we need to have these?"

"Of course, Aurora. You will thank me later in life for these. You'll look back and see how much you both have grown." She smiled and then patted my arm before heading over to one of the photographers to talk with them. I groaned. This was an arrangement. Why did she want to have all this? What was the point?

I turned to face Chloe and Elizabeth and the glare that they sent my mother was how I was feeling. Tom was standing against the wall at the back of the room with Drake and Alex. His arms crossed over his chest, his ice-blue eyes trailing my body. I didn't understand why he suddenly had an interest in me right now. When our eyes connected, he turned his gaze to Drake when he jabbed him with his fist.

The red-headed male photographer and my mother came up to me and my wedding party, pairing us off to take pictures of each of us together. Drake said something to Chloe, making her elbow him in the stomach. He was never going to find someone to put up with the shit that came out of his mouth.

Alex and Elizabeth were probably the only couple here who loved each other. They were so gorgeous together, and I was surprised that Elizabeth had finally caved and accepted his proposal. Their pictures were gonna be gorgeous!

One of the female photographers had me pose against Tom with my head and my hand against his chest while looking down. She dropped the camera and sighed. Her comment about us being so in love was a little far-fetched. There was no love in this relationship. There wasn't even mutual likings.

For the next couple of hours, we posed in different ways for more memories of this day. Pictures with the whole wedding party were easier as I was able to relax beside my best friends. If they hadn't been here, this day would have been the worst day of my life.

Chapter Nine

Aurora

My stuff had been moved over to Tom's penthouse, and I had made sure it had been put in one of the other bedrooms. It was on the opposite side of the penthouse, and it was better than what I expected it would be.

To be honest, I didn't know what it would be like once I started living here.

I had been living here for a few weeks, and my life had been very comfortable since Tom and his bodyguards were pretty much always gone. I had the house to myself most days, besides the staff.

I sat on the main balcony by the kitchen reading most days. Other days, I went out to eat with Elizabeth and Chloe. Today was one of those days, we were having lunch and had gone shopping. We had started early today so that we could get to all the shops that we needed before having lunch. I hadn't gotten much, only what I needed for our girls' trip that started tomorrow and lasted for the next couple of weeks.

Being able to get away from Tom and that penthouse for a few days had me in a high that I hadn't felt since I married him. Not that the staff were bad to be with, they left me to do what I wanted. But I was running out of books. So today, I bought an e-reader so that I could get more.

We sat outside as it was so pretty. The weather was just right, it wasn't too hot, nor was it too cold. Being in my favorite teal strapless dress was heaven. Today's lunch was from one of our favorite restaurants on Rodeo Drive. The table sat on the sidewalk behind the iron railing.

"Aurora, have you talked to TC about our trip?" Chloe's voice brought my attention to her as she stirred the hot tea in her mug. Her hazel eyes held my attention. I hated it when people used that name. It made me think things I shouldn't be thinking of.

"What does it matter what he thinks? Just because I'm married to him doesn't mean he can dictate what I do," I told them. They both stared at me like I had two heads. "What? Our marriage isn't normal."

"That's true. Okay then. So, we will meet at the airport as usual. You want us to pick you up?" Elizabeth asked me. I sighed as I played with the dessert that I had ordered. It looked good in the picture, but I was no longer interested in it and pushed it aside.

"Yeah, that's fine."

"Anything I can get for you, ladies?" The server came up with her tray, and she took the empty dishes and glasses.

"No ma'am. Can I have the check?" She pulled out a tablet and sat it down on the glass table in front of me. I pulled out my phone and tapped to pay my check. "Oh, can I get a box too?"

"Of course, Mrs. Churchhill." My eyes snapped over to the pixie-cut, red-haired server. No one had ever called me by my married name. She took the tablet and left to go get my box.

"Damn, girl, you gave her the bitch face when she called you that." Chloe laughed as she looked over at Elizabeth.

"Yeah, that was a little out there. I'm just not used to people calling me that yet, and I forgot my card had my married name." I shrugged as the server gave me a box to put my dessert in. Glancing up I gave her a smile, "Thank you."

She smiled back at me and left. I stood and grabbed my purse, the box, my bags full of clothes and other things I was excited about trying. My hand went to my purse and rummaged around until I found it and pulled out my phone so that I could text Orson to come and get me. Bringing my gaze back to my friends, they both stood and we exchanged hugs. "Thanks again for the invite. I'll call you guys when I get home."

My driver pulled up to the curb, and the valet opened the door to the car as he grabbed my bags and placed them in the trunk. I slid into the leather seat, and the door snapped shut, letting my driver know that we could go. Orson had been with my family for years, and when I married Tom, I had asked if he could be my driver. That way I would have some normalcy. My parents didn't care, and neither did Tom.

He didn't care what I did as long as I wasn't in his way. He went to work and then came home and headed straight to bed. Jake and Sam followed him like little puppies when he left. I had noticed that they had started meeting him in the mornings and then would leave once they searched the penthouse. I couldn't even figure out the reason. I mean, other than me, there were only the two maids and then the cook.

Maggie and Diana had come after I started living here because I didn't think that Gwen, the cook, should be doing everything. Especially as there was another person in the house. Jake had made sure to do a background check along with random drug tests. I didn't care, if they wanted to go the extra mile to check people, then more power to them. Gwen appreciated the extra help, and I had gotten close to her. She was easy to talk to when I was home alone and didn't want to read or sit on the balcony watching the people down on the street below.

"Ms. Aurora, how was your day today with Chloe and Elizabeth?" Orson looked in the rearview mirror at me. I sighed and stared out the window. Going back to that penthouse was not what I wanted to do, but in two days I would be away from this place for a couple of weeks with my girls.

"It was fine. I love getting to be with them, and I'm excited about the girls' trip coming up."

"Have you talked with Mr. Churchhill about the trip?" My head snapped back to him. I stared at him in the rearview mirror, and he shrugged before returning his brown eyes to the road. "I'm just asking because you are married to him."

"Why is it that I have to ask permission to do things when he can freely move about his life without asking me?" I didn't like that I had to ask whether I could go or not when he left me on the weekends and did whatever he wanted with whoever he wanted. This was what we had agreed before. But that was before he kissed me.

That kiss has been on my mind since that day. Hell, it had even helped me pleasure myself each time I was frustrated. I had even gotten some toys. My others were getting a workout now that I had so much time to myself. It had gotten so bad because I didn't know if or when he was home, and I didn't want him to hear me. Or the name that was on my lips.

So, I waited until the weekend. When he was almost always gone.

The first time his name crossed my lips shocked me. Since I didn't realize I was thinking of him, but fuck, the orgasm that followed. It was mind-blowing, and he wasn't the one making me come.

When we were home together, I stayed on the balcony while he was in his office with Jake and Sam. We didn't act like a normal couple, which was fine by me. But when he came out of his room in his black sweatpants and no shirt, I couldn't help but allow my eyes to roam.

The tattoos on his arms were not the only ones that he had. They ran down his back and across his chest. I was never close enough to see what each one was. It reminded me of some of the Mafia books I had read.

There was one day I could have sworn the light glinted off something on his chest. Those cold blue eyes very rarely locked with mine, but when they did, they held so much ice I looked away from them. I didn't blame him. I had been the reason he almost didn't get his company.

He had been out partying, and I had seen on Snapchat that had been sent to me by Chloe. He was doing drugs off some bimbo's stomach. I had forwarded that to his mother. Yeah, it was a bitch move, but that was my revenge for him embarrassing me in front of every one of those kids at school. But I got played by my mother and his with this damn arranged marriage. So, I guess karma got me back.

Orson pulled up to my building, and a doorman came and opened my door before going to the popped trunk to grab my bags. I entered the lobby of our building, even though I could have entered from the garage and come up the private elevator. The white marble floor and tan walls held paintings and tables full of flowers. The valet carried my bags in behind me and then placed them in the elevator with me before I pressed the penthouse button. My reflection stared back at me, and the woman in front of me didn't look like me.

She had the same chocolate hair and grey eyes, but she wasn't happy anymore. I hated not being happy. I hated being in this house all alone. Which was why I was going on this girls' trip whether he liked it or not. The elevator dinged, and I picked up my bags and headed into the foyer before I saw him sitting on the couch, nursing a glass of his favorite whiskey.

His jacket was thrown over the arm, and his ankle rested on his other knee. Tom's arm laid comfortably on the back as he stared back at me over the glass. It was as if he was a statue sitting there waiting for me to make a move. I glanced around to see if Jake and Sam were here, but I didn't see them anywhere in the living room. But that didn't mean that they weren't around somewhere.

Tom was home early. He never came home at lunch, much less drank while he knew he was going back to the office. If that was one good quality that he had, it was that he never put his company in jeopardy by being drunk. But those eyes made me think that everyone in that building knew that his word was law and that they better hope that he was in a good mood.

I watched as his eyes roamed my body, and part of me wanted to snap at him for it. But then the other part; I part that loved it when he was in my head as I made myself come. I wanted him to come over and show me just what he could do to me. My panties were getting soaked at the mere thought of him, and if he didn't leave, I was going to have to wait until he went to bed.

If he ever found me pleasuring myself, I'd be humiliated. I turned my head and headed over to my room. This wasn't good that I was starting to think about him in that way. So, leaving him in the living room was the best thing to do.

Chapter Ten

TC

Aurora came in with bags in tow. She had been out shopping with Chloe and Elizabeth again. I watched her almost walk past me before she stopped and noticed me sitting on the couch. She had been on my mind for the last several weeks. Ever since I kissed her on our wedding day, if I had just given her a peck on the cheek like I had wanted to, this wouldn't have happened. I wouldn't be here at lunch, waiting for her to get back from wherever she had been. Because that wasn't what I did. I didn't get infatuated with a woman.

After a moment, she turned down the hall to the left and headed to her room. As much as I wanted to get up and follow her, I made myself sit there and take another drink. Being with other women wasn't as exciting as it had been before I had married her. As she walked, her curls bounced with her strides. She was wearing a teal strapless sundress and the silver heels from our engagement party.

I placed my glass down and quickly went over to her. The scent of her perfume assaulted me. Goosebumps rose on her arms, and I knew that she subconsciously knew I was behind her. Aurora dropped her bags when my exhale caressed her ear. She turned to face me, which was a mistake on her part.

Using my body, I pressed her up against her door and ran my nose up her neck, making her shiver. I grabbed just under her chin, leaning her head back into the door. Hell, I was getting hard just being this close to her.

"Tom, what are you doing?" Her voice came out breathless, and her chest heaved into my body as her hands went to my chest. I didn't know if it was the liquor in my system or if I wanted her to break this obsession that the flavors couldn't anymore.

"Can I not touch my wife?" My other hand went to the small of her back, bringing her lower body closer to me. I knew she could feel my cock through our clothes.

"That's not what we agreed on. You wanted the other women." Her voice became a pant as I slid my hand down her ass and then to the hem of her dress. Yeah, that was what we agreed on, but there wasn't anything that said I couldn't change the agreement.

"Then we need to go into negotiations," I told her as I nipped her neck. She shuddered as I pulled my mouth away.

"Tom, the only way that agreement would change is if it was just us. And I know that wouldn't satisfy you. So, stop this and let me go. I need to pack." I didn't hear anything but the word pack. Letting go of her jaw, I took a step back and my brows furrowed.

"Where are you going?" Aurora hadn't said anything about leaving. Was she moving? I mean, I hadn't actually been around. The company took a lot of my time, and then I had tried being with my flavors of the week. But that hadn't been fruitful.

"If you must know, I'm going with Chloe and Elizabeth on our girls' trip. It's something we do every year around this time," Aurora snapped at me. Her arousal disappeared as fast as it had come. She crossed her arms under her breasts and cocked her hip to the side. Fuck, she was gorgeous today.

There was a faint tint of red on her cheeks as she noticed my gaze go to her cleavage. Aurora rolled her eyes when I made my way back to her face. "So, were you going to tell me you were going? Or was I just going to come home and find the place empty?"

"Tom, don't play me like that. You hardly ever come home, and when you do, it's always late." Aurora's door had opened, and she stepped back into her room while she grabbed her bags. "Besides, when was I going to tell you?"

While I was thinking of a response, she slammed the door in my face. I tried the doorknob, but she had locked it. She just shut me out, and it pissed me off. I had banged on the door for a good five minutes when someone behind me cleared their throat.

Jake stood behind me, his brows raised as he stared at me, a grin starting on his lips. I straightened up my hair, walked past him, and went back to my glass of whiskey. Picking it up, I drank the rest and took the glass to the kitchen. Aurora was the only one, other than my parents, to call me Tom. "What do you want, Jake?"

"Nothing, sir. Just thinking, if you are actually wanting to make an effort with Aurora; banging your fist on her door isn't going to help."

"Yeah, yeah. What does it matter? Huh?" I asked him as I left him in the kitchen to go to my room. I didn't know why I had tried to start anything with her. Being at work hadn't taken my mind off her. Then someone had gotten into the parking garage and shot up another one of my cars. I was getting tired of the bullshit that Marcus was playing.

Ever since I had noticed the masked boy at the club multiple times, I had started to carry my sidearm again on my person, instead of just in the car. It was like an old friend had come back to me. Jake didn't like that I was carrying again, but Sam was all for it. If something had happened to them, I would have been able to take care of myself. He didn't know that I didn't need a gun to be able to deal with anyone. Especially anyone from my old crew.

Taking a deep breath, I turned and headed back out to go back to the office. I still had a number of papers to sign. One was giving a raise that the employees were desperate to have. With the rising cost of living, I didn't want them to have to worry that they couldn't make ends meet. I had been in that situation when I was younger, and it wasn't pretty.

I grabbed my suit jacket and glanced down the hall to Aurora's room. She was just going to leave me for this girls' trip, and I wouldn't have been any the wiser if I hadn't come home. Which didn't help since she cock-blocked me again. I didn't understand why she wouldn't get out of my head, and the only thing I could think would help was to fuck her and get her out of my system.

"Sir, I thought we were staying for the rest of the day." Jake took his place a few feet behind me as I pressed the door to the elevator.

"No, I need to get back to the office. I need to sign a few more things and then we can come back," I answered him as the doors opened to allow us in.

"Whatever you say, sir." Jake pressed the garage button and then pulled out his phone. He was going to let Sam know that we were on our way back to the vehicle.

Damn, what was I thinking when I came home early from work. I didn't need to blur these lines, but there had to be a way to get my sex life back. Because my balls were going to rupture if I didn't get to come soon.

When we reached the garage Sam already had the SUV at the elevator, and Jake opened the back door so that I could get in. Jake hopped into the passenger side, and we were on our way back to Churchhill Logistics.

Reaching the building, Jake opened my door, and I headed into the lobby. Most of the employees knew what I looked like but hadn't met me. The ladies at the reception desk nodded and then continued their work.

The elevator to the top floor opened, and I bumped into someone. Glancing down I realized that it was Emi. I crossed my arms over my shoulders and stood there as she backed up a bit to let her make eye contact with me.

"Emi, what are you doing here?" I cocked my head as I stared at her.

"I was looking for you. They said you weren't here, so I figured I'd leave and come to the house to see you and my new sister-in-law." She glanced around me as if she was also looking for someone else.

"Where is your bodyguard?" If that fucker wasn't around her again. He was going to be demoted to washing vehicles here at the office. The reason I attached someone to everyone in my family was not only because Marcus was out to get me, but he would want to try to get someone that I loved to hold over my head.

"Well, you can't actually be mad at him. But I gave him the slip. TC, I don't understand why I need him anyway." Emi gave me a smile and then her puppy dog eyes. She had found out when we first met that I would do anything for her if she just gave me those eyes.

"Emi, that guard is supposed to be with you at all times when you are out in public." I ran my hand down my face as she wrapped me in a hug. "You need to come with me until Sam gets up to the top floor. He will take you home."

"TC, I think I can make it back home without Sam's help." Emi made to walk around me, and I took her by the elbow leading her back into the elevator. "Why are you doing this?"

"Because, I have a bodyguard for a reason with you. Stop trying to keep away from him. Jake, message Sam and tell him to meet us up on my floor. He has my little sister to take back home." I smirked, and Emi rolled her eyes.

"You know, when you are being like this, I sometimes wish I didn't choose you." Emi grinned. I knew she didn't mean it.

We stood in the elevator until the last floor, and Lindsey was there to meet me.

"Sir, I thought you were taking the rest of the day off." Her eyes went to Emi at my side, and she raised her eyebrows..

"I was, but I have other things I need to do here. Just make sure no one disturbs me and let Sam in when he gets up here. He has to take my darling sister home." I walked past her, and Jake and Emi followed.

"Of course, sir."

As soon as I entered my office, Drake came in and then froze for a moment before continuing forward. I didn't miss the look that he gave my sister as he went by. Emi sat on the couch as Jake took one of the high-backed chairs near the door.

"Well, looks like someone couldn't stay gone today." Drake strolled up to my desk rolling up papers in his hands. He plopped down in one of the chairs in front of my desk and propped up his leg on his knee.

"What do you need Drake?" He had a habit of coming to my office to sit while I was working.

"Well, I was thinking about talking to you about that old warehouse by the coast..."

"I told you, I'm not selling it. It will rot there until I figure out what I need it for."

I sat in the Mercedes SUV in front of the Churchhill Logistics building, waiting for Drake to get his ass out here so that we could meet up with one of our new clients. Aurora has been gone for the past two weeks, and if I was being honest, it wasn't quite the same. I had been stalking her on her Instagram with Chloe and Elizabeth. With little luck on hers, but on Chloe and Elizabeth's she was everywhere on the platform.

The little two-piece yellow bikini barely covered her most intimate parts, which was annoying the hell out of me. But what really got me was the man that had her in his arms. Aurora was smiling, and she wasn't wearing her ring. I might have been fucking other women, but my ring stayed on, and they knew they wouldn't be anything more than a fuck toy.

But she was out there in another country, letting some man touch her. He didn't know who she belonged to. That was okay. As soon as she got back, I'd show her whose she was.

The door finally opened, and Drake entered the back of the SUV. I glared over at my COO as he grinned back at me. Jake cleared his throat bringing my attention from my partner to him.

"Head on out, Jake, now that Mr. DeLuca has decided to grace us with his presence." Between him making me wait to meet this new client and Aurora in some other man's arms, life was really starting to upset me.

"Look, when an employee has a question. You have to answer it." Drake laughed as he straightened his suit jacket and then sat back.

"If it wasn't more important than this new client, you should have had her email you," I snapped.

"Touchy touchy. I didn't think those types of emails were permitted through work email. But I'll let her know in the future." Drake winked at me, not figuring out that I wasn't in the mood for his stupid comments.

We sat in silence with Drake texting someone on his phone. Sam and Jake spoke quietly up front as I tried to keep from going to my phone to check on Aurora. If I didn't have to be at this meeting today then I would meet her at the airport and really show her and her friends who they were messing with.

Jake stopped the vehicle at the front of our client's building, and we exited the SUV. Drake stretched like he had been cooped up far longer than the thirty-minute drive. Normally I would have Lindsey here with us, but she had requested the day off and wasn't able to come in. So, Drake carried everything we needed in the suitcase.

Entering into the lobby, I realized it was being renovated. Walls were being painted and new trim and flooring were being laid. At the reception desk, a redhead glanced up as we approached. She smiled before standing. "Hello, I'm Cassandra. Assistant to Ms. Petticort. She requested that I wait down here to bring you up to her office. She is expecting you both."

I nodded, and Cassandra led us to the elevator. Not many women took over their family's company, but I had heard of this one. She was brutal in some ways, but only to the men who thought she was ignorant. Which was a lot of them, and they then found themselves losing more than their ego.

The doors opened and Drake and I entered the elevator with Cassandra taking her place in front of us. I didn't miss his eyes lustfully roaming her backside before he nudged me. I cocked an eyebrow up at him, still not in the mood for his shit.

Cassandra entered the code to get us to her boss' floor and continued to stand in front of us with a confident air. She was very relaxed being with us in the elevator. When the elevator dinged, Cassandra stood to the side, and a scrawny man stood in the opening.

"Here we are. Jay will show you the rest of the way." Cassandra held the door open for us to exit. I stepped out first, Drake was behind me.

Jay quickly made his way away from the elevator, making Drake and I follow him at a quick pace. His hair was gelled back, and I didn't miss the glare on his face when he turned to lead us to Ms. Petticort. I didn't like this guy already, and I would make sure that I had Drake deal with him if we ever had issues.

He stopped and knocked on Ms. Petticort's office door and then entered without waiting for her to invite us in. Jay stepped to the side and let us in the room. I could tell that it had been recently renovated because the desk and floor gleamed in the sun's rays.

Ms. Petticort sat behind her desk like the queen she was. Softly curled blond hair and natural makeup. This woman knew she had power and wasn't about to take a step down from that. Her eyes came up and locked with mine, and she smiled.

The woman stood from her desk just as we made it to her desk. She rounded the furniture and held out her hand to me. Her tight-fitting dress hugged her body like a second skin. The red brought out her skin color. "Mr. Churchhill, thank you for meeting with me here. I know that it takes you away from your business, but I figured it would be good to get you out of your big building."

"You're welcome Ms. Petticort. This is my COO, Drake DeLuca." I released her hand, and she crossed her arms as she allowed her eyes to roam my partner.

"Yes. Now why don't we get down to business, shall we?" She motioned to the chairs in front of her desk and then rounded it to sit in her seat.

Drake and I sat in the chairs offered to us and waited for her to go on. Ms. Petticort leaned forward and threaded her fingers under her chin. She looked between both of us and then grabbed a folder that was sitting to her right.

"So, I was thinking about getting into international shipping, but to be honest, this is something new to me, and I wanted the best to ship out my products." She handed me the folder.

I opened the file and read through what she was proposing and what she wanted in return. It wasn't what I normally gave clients, but I could negotiate.

After a grueling three hours, we finally decided on a figure for both international and national shipping. Ms. Petticort was everything that I thought she would be. She had to be in this male-dominated world.

After being in this world for the past three years, I could see why my father didn't want Emi in this world. Not that I didn't think she would be able to take care of herself— because she could, that was a fact—but in his eyes, she was something to protect, and protect her I did.

"She was gorgeous. But fuck she was intense. I don't think I've seen a woman like her before," Drake rambled on beside me in the car.

I had half a mind to get some tape to shut him up. My brain hurt from the three hours of going back and forth with that woman. I was ready to go back to my office and get some of my work done since my other appointments had been pushed back.

"Can you not just shut up?" I massaged the back of my neck. I really needed to go to the chiropractor.

"You need to get laid. You're too uptight," Drake countered me as he pulled out his phone and started scrolling his social media.

He was right. I did need to get laid but laid… by the right person. This past week, I had been through most of my flavors, but none of them had satisfied me. Which was a problem, and I knew the reason why. It was my wife, even though I had yet to touch her skin to skin. She was all up in my head and senses.

Whenever I walked into my home, her perfume greeted me first. There were times when I would find a book on the coffee table. I had never gone over to see what it was since it always had a cutesy cover on it. It had 'Hallmark' written all over it. So, I could only assume she was vanilla in bed. That was something I couldn't get into.

"Sir? We are here."

I glanced up and noticed that Sam had my door open, and Jake was staring at me from the rearview mirror. Damn, I had allowed my thoughts to take me out of my surroundings. Sighing, I nodded and then stepped out of the SUV and onto the sidewalk. I still had a few more hours to go before I headed home.

It was late when I got home, and I shrugged my jacket off at the door. Aurora had been back for a few hours, according to Gwen, who had messaged me as soon as she had arrived. Gwen had been gone for quite some time. The lights were off in the house, and the kitchen was as clean as before I had left this morning. I grabbed a glass and poured a glass of whiskey when I heard a moan. Stilling my hand with the glass near my mouth, I sat the glass back down on the counter carefully and turned.

Kicking off my black leather wingtips, I padded down the dark hall to Aurora's bedroom in my socks. The drink on the counter was the last thing on my mind. Did she bring someone home? I didn't even do that, which was part of our agreement. As I approached her door, it was cracked open. The vibration and her soft pants brought me closer to her door.

Aurora was laid on her bed. Her legs opened wide with a blue toy on her clit as two of her fingers slipped inside of her cunt. Her tan skin prickled with goosebumps. I tore my eyes away from her shaved pussy and up her stomach to her ample breasts and peaked nipples. She was barely heaving as she pleasured herself. Her mouth was slightly open, and her eyes closed as she arched her back with a moan, I heard what I never thought would come out of her mouth. "TC"

I had never pegged her for someone who used toys, but what would I know. It was like she was very intimate with her toy and her fingers. I felt like a peeping Tom watching her, but I didn't want to stop because it was turning me on as I had never been before.

My cock pressed against the zipper of my Hugo Boss slacks. Loosening my tie and the top button of my shirt, I pushed the door open with my shoulder. Aurora's head snapped up as the door swung on its hinges. The pupils of her eyes were huge as they followed me into the room. I slipped the tie from my collar and then unbuttoned the rest of my shirt before I discarded it to the floor. Aurora's beautiful bronze legs were still wide, and her toy continued to buzz while her hand stilled at her center. Her eyes never left me as I knelt between her beautiful knees and said, "Don't stop. You're doing such a good job."

Chapter Twelve

Aurora

Shocked wasn't even the beginning of my emotions when TC strolled into my room. After I had moaned his name, I couldn't move as he stripped off his white shirt and red tie. TC's muscular tattoo covered chest and arms were on full display as he came near the queen bed. The light from my room glinted off the silver barbells in his nipples. He hadn't been on this side of the penthouse since I moved in. Well, since before I left to go on the girls' trip. He must have heard my toy . My heart was pounding as we continued to stare at each other. I didn't know what he wanted me to do.

His husky voice sent a shiver down my body. My brain was having a meltdown, and his eyes traveled up and down my naked body. I should have been ashamed of myself when he caught me with his name on my lips. But as much as I should have been, I wasn't. TC's pupils had dilated so much that the blue of his irises were tiny rings, and his tongue ran out over his lips.

I didn't have the courage to speak before I closed my eyes and tried to pretend he wasn't between my legs. My clit was swollen under the vibrator that I was using, and I could feel more wetness near my entrance as I pumped my fingers into my pussy. Every time I got close to the edge of my orgasm, I couldn't get over to the other side. It was like my body was holding me back now that he was no longer just a name on my tongue.

I hadn't ever played with myself with someone watching me. One—because every man I had been with was too eager to fuck me and then be on their way. Two—I just couldn't get over my insecurities to allow someone to watch me bring myself to orgasm. If they watched me, I didn't know if what I was doing was exciting them or making them cringe.

TC's hands ran down the inside of my thighs, kneading them as he went. His semi-calloused fingers were dangerously close to my center before he pulled them away and back to my knees. The way his hands felt against my skin as I doubled down on my effort to bring myself to climax was nothing more than amazing. I had never felt this way with a man watching me, and I didn't think I would ever feel this way again. Heat and desire ran through me, so I stuck a third finger inside my pussy; using my middle finger to rub up against the ribbed roof inside me.

The groan from in front of me made me open my eyes and glance down. TC was still bare-chested and panting, and he couldn't take his eyes off me. But his pants were still buttoned and zipped with his cock rigged in his pants. He licked his lips, and when his eyes locked with mine; I came undone. My body went tight and began to spasm around my fingers with the toy pressed against my clit. "Such a good girl, Aurora."

TC slid down to his stomach and took my hand in his as he wrapped his lips around my cum-soaked fingers. The nerves in my body fired constantly as he sucked my cum off my fingers and with a pop, he smirked at me. His head ducked down to my pussy and licked up the juices that surrounded my entrance. My hand itched to thread into his hair and bring him closer.

He thrust his tongue inside me, and his moan vibrated against my core before he took the toy and laid it to the side. I had never had a man go down on me before. The sensation of his tongue in my pussy, and when he sucked on my clit, my thighs tightened around his head. My hand gripped his hair and pressed him closer to me. I couldn't get enough.

TC wrapped his arms around my legs, pulling them apart as he brought me to another orgasm. *Damn, this man and his experience!* My body shuddered, and my high faded. Glancing between my legs, I caught him staring at me with his lips and chin glistening with my cum.

I would probably hate myself for allowing him to do this to me. But at this moment, I realized I needed this release. As much as I hated him, TC had my body responding to his touch like I had never responded to any other man.

My pussy was begging for something more. TC crawled over me, his hips resting between mine. I glanced up as he pulled my hands above my head and wrapped his tie around my wrists. He moved up my body and tied the red strip of cloth around the wooden prongs on the headboard.

"What are you doing?" I had found my voice as I brought my gaze to his. This was something new. I'd been with a few men, but they had never tied me up before. It sort of scared me, but it also turned me on.

"I'm going to give you the best orgasm of your life." TC stood from the bed and unbuttoned and unzipped his slacks. He then pulled down his boxer briefs, and what I saw made my heart skip.

Not only was he massive, but he also had a double piercing on his head. Removing my eyes from his cock, I brought my gaze up to his face, where the not-so-subtle smirk rested on his lips. *What have I gotten myself into?* I could tell him to stop. But part of me wanted to feel what those felt like inside of me.

TC kneeled back on the bed, spreading my legs wider as he lined himself up to my entrance. When he entered me, it wasn't as painful as I thought it would be, but damn, those piercings slid across my G-spot, making me arch my back. His groan brought out the moan that was stuck in my throat. I pulled on the tie that held my hands above my head.

His huge hands tightened on my hips as he stilled inside me. I tried to pivot my hips to make him move. I *needed* him to move. His taunting chuckle brought my eyes open again. Veins in his arms and neck strained as he sat there, holding my hips still. "Mmm, such a temptress. You want me to make you come?"

TC slid slowly inside me from his seated position, making me arch again and close my eyes. He slammed into me crashing into my cervix as he brought my gaze back to him. "Keep those beautiful grey eyes on me, Aurora. I want to see your eyes as I make you come all over my cock."

Why did his voice have to command my attention, and the way he held on to my hips as he rammed into me, making my tits bounce with each contact of our bodies. I pulled on the tie again, not used to not being able to use my hands.

I couldn't help but to close my eyes. TC's cock felt too good inside me as I met him thrust for thrust. A sharp pain on my left nipple snapped my eyes open to meet his icy blue eyes.

TC's teeth clamped on my nipple, and his eyes narrowed on mine. "I told you, temptress. Keep those eyes on me."

TC bit me!

He draped over me, his hips low and deep inside me as he kept hold of my nipple. Changing from suckling on it to biting it. The moan from the stimulation of my breast and G-spot brought me ever closer to my second climax with him.

"Yes! Right there!" I moaned, but I never took my eyes away from him.

"Fuck!" TC groaned as he went rigid and crashed one last time into my cervix. All those sculpted bands of muscles holding me tightly. My body quaked as the orgasm hit me. His cock was twitching inside me.

No man had ever been able to bring me to orgasm like this. I had always felt unsatisfied after and needed to finish myself off. If this continued, there would be no way I would be able to turn back.

TC had always been one to use a woman and go on his merry way. So, he shouldn't be opposed to me doing the same to him, right? I could use him to be able to have this same orgasm again and again. Right?

He untied my hands and then pulled out. I kept the whimper from the loss of him to myself. Rolling from the bed, I grabbed the still buzzing toy and turned it off. I stood and headed to my bathroom With both of our cum running down the inside of my legs. His eyes bore into my back, sending a shiver down my spine.

When I turned to close the door, TC still sat on the bed. I couldn't help but look and notice he hadn't ever gone fully soft. His hand went to his cock and stroked it, making himself hard once more.

"If you want to wash up, you better do so now. Otherwise, I'll take you against that wall." He nodded to the empty wall to my right. The lust in his eyes warned me that it was a promise. I snapped the door shut, locking it. My heart raced as I leaned against the door. The bed groaned, and I heard TC's confident steps coming to the door.

What was I thinking when I let this happen? The knob twisted as I stepped away but didn't allow him access. A smirk graced my lips as I pulled my bottom lip between my teeth, and I backed up just as the door burst open. "What the fuck, TC!"

"You're teasing me, temptress." The deepness of his voice held me still as he came to me and pulled me into his arms. His hands went under my ass, and my legs wrapped around his hips. TC's massive cock rubbed against my entrance and our cum, and he took me back out of the bathroom.

We crashed onto the wall beside the bathroom door. His lips on my neck, and my hands in his hair. When he entered me again, I couldn't hold back the moan that escaped. What this man was doing to me was nothing short of ecstasy.

TC's hands held tightly on my hips while he rammed into me while using the wall for leverage. My orgasm was building as those piercings slid inside of me. His chest against mine and those cold steel barbells rubbing my sensitive nipples.

It was amazing what he could do to my body. The fire down below continued to build along with my moans.

"Talk to me. Tell me how good my cock makes you feel. The way it fills your cunt." TC's husky voice caressed my ear. My brain was mush as he continued to thrust inside me. How could he expect me to speak as he talked to me in that tone?

"I... Right there! I'm so close!" Finding my voice in the throws, my head leaned into his shoulder as my orgasm came closer. I could feel him slowing but still making each thrust count. It burst from me, and my nails dug into his arms.

TC stilled and pulled me so hard into him that it was like he was going to connect us inside me. I lifted my head, and our eyes locked just before he removed himself from my cunt.

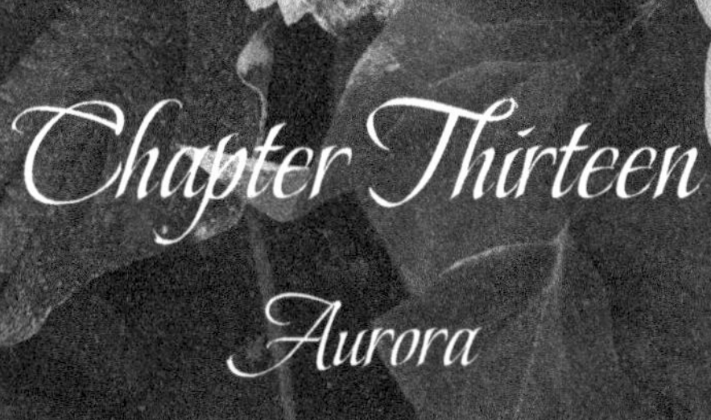

Chapter Thirteen

Aurora

The sun peeked through the blinds as I opened my eyes. I glanced at my wrists; the angry red abrasions stood out against my skin. TC had been rough last night, but as much as he had been, I didn't mind. I could still feel him inside me.

Sitting up my entire body screamed at me. I was sore all over, but my pussy was worse off. Every time I moved, my muscles in my core wailed. I made my way to my bathroom realizing the door was no longer usable from TC busting in.

Well, he had the money to do what he wanted, I thought as I ran the water for a bath. Grabbing the bath salts, I dropped them in before submerging myself in the warm water with a sigh.

As I soaked, I couldn't help but look back to last night. What I had done and allowed him to do still stunned me. I should probably have him use a condom next time. There's no telling what he had contracted from all those other women.

A doctor's appointment was in my near future. I was covered by my birth control shot. So, children were not my concern. But I wanted to make sure that I hadn't caught anything else. Finally relaxing in the bath, I was jolted by my phone ringing in the bedroom.

With a grumble, I got out of the tub and padded over to my nightstand, leaving puddles in my wake. My mother was calling me after dozens of texts she had sent while I was asleep.

"Yes, Mother." I turned to look in the mirror as I answered. The image staring back at me stunned me as my eyes surveyed my body. Bite marks and hickeys were everywhere. The deepest one on my left nipple, where he had got my attention. I shook my head, thinking that it was a little too late to deal with the marks now.

"Aurora, did you forget about the dress fitting? You were supposed to be here thirty minutes ago."

"Dress fitting? For what.... Oh shit, the Gala!" My forehead. "Can they still fit me in?"

"You better be glad that you are now a Chruchhill. Otherwise, they wouldn't dream of not waiting for you." Her tone made me fully aware that she was upset with me.

"Give me fifteen minutes, and I'll be in the car," I told her, hanging up and messaging Orson to bring the car around.

I headed back into the bathroom and let the water out before searching for clothes that wouldn't show my mother the bite marks. The marks on my wrists would be harder to hide.

I sat in the back of the car while Orson took us to the dress shop downtown. How the hell I had forgotten about the dress fitting blew my mind. I was tired from the lack of sleep and the way TC had used my body. My only wish was that my mother wouldn't notice the bags under my eyes. So, I had made sure to wear makeup today, but even with all of that, I could still see the puffiness and darkness underneath.

As Orson pulled to the curb, my mother was by the door tapping her heeled foot. The frown on her face told me that she wasn't happy that I was late. Orson opened the door and helped me out of the luxury sedan. His eyes went to my wrists. I had found silver bracelets to hide most of the angry red marks on my wrists. But Orson knew better than to say anything.

"Hurry up! You are an hour and a half late" She motioned to me as she opened the door. She opened the door and motioned for me to follow her. As soon as I went through, I spotted the dress she had picked out. The groan that left my mouth at the design made trying to hide these marks a moot point.

I headed into the dressing room, and two of the staff came in with me, hauling the dress behind them. My heart hammered. Why did she have to pick the most floozy dress in the shop? What was the point? Did she know that me and TC weren't fucking? Well besides last night.

"Mrs. Churchhill, can you take off everything but your underwear?" the red-headed woman asked me as she stared at me in the floor-length mirror.

I took a deep breath and shimmied out of my leggings and then pulled the oversized sweater off along with the bra. My breasts bounced just a bit while I stood there in nothing but my underwear and bite marks.

Red didn't make a sound and didn't even change her expression. The blond, however, gasped, and her wide eyes told me she had noticed the bite marks and handprints on my ass.

"Can you stop staring and help me into this dress?" I snapped at her. She shook her head and went over to the dress, helping Red to bring it over. The glare from Red to the blond told me she was newer.

They made short work of getting me in the skin-tight black dress. The neckline was cut low, at least three inches below my bust. It showed off two of the bite marks underneath my breasts. Two slits ran up to my hip bones, showing off the sides of my panties.

Red brought me a set of silver glitter heels and helped me into them. Other than the marks, I felt sexy in this dress. With one more look at myself, I turned to show my mother. I just hoped that she didn't say anything to me about the marks.

I stepped away from the curtain and spotted her talking with the store's owner. My mother glanced over to me; her expression didn't change, but I could tell she was pissed by the look in her eyes. The owner nodded and walked up to me with my mom.

They both circled me before they stopped in front of me. The owner studied me before turning her attention back to my mother. "It looks good on her. It needs to be altered a little, but I know it will be done by the Gala."

TC

Last night had been on my mind the entire day at the office. Aurora had me so hard with my name on her lips while she was playing with her pussy. It was euphoric. And it wasn't 'Tom' it was TC. None of the women I had been with had me jonesing this bad for a second round with them.

Sitting at the front of the table with Drake sitting to my right, and the board members rested in their chairs. I wanted this meeting to be over with, I had other things that needed to be done. And if I was being honest, I was hoping that Aurora would let me fuck her again.

"Mr. Churchhill?"

I glanced up from the sheet of graphs I wasn't really looking at. Mr. Dunn's expression seemed to be of concern. Drake's brow was arched with a smirk on his lips. "Mr. Dunn was just saying that you made a good call on the expansion to ship internationally. Profits have been higher in these past three years than the past decade."

"Good, and the projections?" I sat back in my chair as I surveyed the men who had bucked my father for years about this same expansion. They were now reaping the rewards of the venture I had pushed so hard.

"Sir, we expect them to keep rising," Lindsey said from behind me.

I nodded in acknowledgment and stood. "Perfect, this meeting is adjourned."

Everyone nodded and stood before they left through the boardroom doors. Lindsey went with them. Drake, however, stayed behind the smirk still on his face.

"What has you all smiles today?" I asked him while heading over to the windows looking out over the City of Angels.

"Seems you need to get laid. You were spaced out badly during that meeting. And that's not you. Let's go to the club. Find some girls and get you laid." Drake clapped my shoulder with a chuckle.

"No, I need to make arrangements for the Gala."

Aurora was at the dress shop trying on her dress for the Gala. Ollie had texted me, informing me that she had made it a little late to her appointment.

She had slept in. Which I couldn't blame her for. It had taken me a lot longer to get up this morning. I had never been that tired in all my life.

"I thought you already had your tux?"

I turned to my best friend and coworker. Telling him about last night wasn't an option. Even though I had spoken with him about my other conquests, I wanted to keep that to myself since he had said this would happen that night at the club.

"I don't think you need to know everything going on in my life," I hurled back at him with a glare.

Drake raised his hands in surrender, that cocky smirk still on his lips as he backed up and walked out of the boardroom.

"Good afternoon, Mr. Churchhill." Gwen's voice came from the kitchen. But my eyes were trained on a chocolate-haired woman on the balcony.

She had a book in her lap, her head laying in her hand while her elbow rested on the chair's arm. Aurora's tan legs stretched out and rested on the cushions. The memory of those beautiful legs wrapped around my head as I ate her out had me hard yet again. Her moans and sighs resonated in my mind.

"TC, I think you need to see this." I turned to Jake, taking the phone from him. One of the flavors I had been with right after the wedding was hanging all over another dude. I was about to hand the phone back to him when I noticed the gang tattoo on his right forearm.

This wasn't good. My old gang was getting closer to the life I had built. If they had gotten the slut drunk, she would've told him everything. She never knew when to keep her mouth shut. I glanced up at Jake, he knew what I was thinking.

Aurora did as she pleased most days, but it looked like I would have to send a bodyguard with her from now on. She wouldn't even have to know, and I knew the perfect one to have watch her.

"Call Sam. Tell him to get here now." Jake nodded as he took his phone back.

Glancing back to the balcony, Aurora had gotten up and gone into the kitchen with Gwen. I followed behind her and leaned against the door frame. She had become close to Gwen and the other staff.

The way her lips wrapped around the wooden spoon to taste the food that Gwen held up made my cock harden more. I wanted those plump lips around my cock, making her gag on it until I slipped it down further in her throat.

Damn, those legs of hers. They made my cock twitch with each movement. My tongue darted out wetting my lips just as Gwen turned her attention to me. She cocked an eyebrow before she threw a smirk my way.

"Mr. Churchhill! How nice of you to join us. Would you like a plate of the manicotti?"

At the mention of my name, Aurora spun around. Causing the long T-shirt of mine that she was wearing to twirl up, showing me the bottom of her ass cheeks. God damn, I needed that ass in my face.

"Sure, Gwen." I smiled and sat at the island. Gwen nodded and plated some of her famous manicotti. She placed it in front of me before turning and making Aurora one.

"Thank you, Gwen." Aurora took the plate from Gwen, kissed her cheek, and walked past me with her hips swaying.

Aurora went out of the kitchen, leaving me in the barely-used room. Gwen leaned against the cabinets wiping her hands on her apron. "Sir, if I may?"

I nodded.

"That woman. She is one sweet lady. You'd know that if you got to know your wife."

Gwen had always been tough. She had been with the Churchhills for a long time. When she came to work here, I never had an issue with her cooking. Since I would get home at all hours of the night, she made dishes for me to heat up.

"Yeah? Well, that sweetness is only on the surface. Underneath she can be a cold-hearted bitch," I snapped at her. Gwen stared back at me. There was no anger in her expression, only the pity I'd seen from her before.

"That's where you're wrong, sir." Gwen turned her back to me and started putting away the leftovers of the manicotti.

Jake stepped into the room, bringing my attention to him. I remembered my first interaction with him. He didn't like me very much in the beginning, but my new mother and father had put me under his care. The stare-down at the limo still made me chuckle.

We both had grown so much over the years. My parents thought that since we were such close in age that it would be good for us. He had become a good friend while also being a great bodyguard.

"TC, sir. I have Sam in your office."

Chapter Fourteen

Aurora

I glanced over my shoulder just as TC and Jake left the kitchen. They made their way down the other hall, which led to TC's bedroom and office. I was sure there was another since Jake lived with us.

When TC entered the kitchen behind me and Gwen had made it known that he was there, my heart sprinted in my chest. I wasn't expecting to see him, and I definitely didn't think just the sight of him would cause my body to react.

He had left his shirt on my floor when he had come into my room. So, I decided to keep it. Not like he would miss it, but now that he saw me wearing it, he might take it back.

The ping from my phone startled me as it pulled me from my thoughts. Chloe's name popped up.

Hey girl! Come shopping with us!

K! Where are you?

We are going to Rodeo Dr.

K see you in a few.

Getting up from my seat, I grabbed my phone and cleaned up after myself.

In my room, I pulled my shirt off and chose some clothes while texting Orson. TC had come home earlier than normal, which was surprising. He normally didn't get home until late.

When I was ready, I headed to the elevator. The doors opened allowing me to board the metal car.

I spotted Chloe and Elizabeth at The Blvd Restaurant and Lounge, one of our favorite restaurants. They both smiled and waved when they noticed me. They had gotten a table outside and already had their drinks.

Taking a seat a waiter came out with another drink.

"I figured you'd want your regular." Elizabeth chuckled as the waiter sat it down.

"Can I get you anything from the menu, ma'am?"

I glanced up at the young man with his book out to take my order.

"Sure, I'd like the Wood Oven Roasted Heritage Pork Prime Rib Chop. Thank you. Oh, and a water. Please."

"Yes, ma'am. It will be out with the others." I nodded to him, and he left our table.

"So, what's with the leggings and turtleneck, Aurora?" Chloe brought my attention from my drink. Her eyebrow cocked with a smile on her face and reached for the neck of the shirt. I moved over trying to keep her from seeing the mark on my neck.

"Well, when I'm invited last minute, it would take me longer to get ready," I quipped as I took a sip of my Tropical Escape.

Chloe giggled and nudged me with her elbow. I smiled at her and sipped on my drink. Trying to keep the grimace from my face. These two had been with me through everything. The last year of high school with TC being the worst of my life.

The day I stopped the shot that would tie the championship soccer game was one of my prouder moments. Both Chloe and Elizabeth were there to help celebrate that win. That was the best day of my life.

"So, what are we going for today?" I asked. The sun was out, warming my body as I sat there. It wasn't a good idea to wear this outfit, but I didn't feel like having that conversation. What would they say if they knew I had fucked my husband. Not only that, but I had allowed him to use my body the way he saw fit.

"I was thinking of getting a new Louis Vuitton. For the Gala," Elizabeth explained as the waiters stopped at our table with our food.

TC

"Sir, I'd be honored to keep an eye on her. But don't you think that it would be wise to let her know that someone would be following her?" Sam's voice reached my ears as I stared out the tinted window of my office.

It would make things easier if she did know, but then that would mean letting her know about the danger that she was in because of my past. That stupid whore in the picture with one of my old comrades couldn't keep her mouth shut when she was drunk. I had to assume she had already told whoever was with her that night everything about Aurora. This was one of the reasons why I hadn't publicly announced that I was married. That and, I didn't want people to see me with other women knowing I was married. It would look bad on the company.

"Right now, Aurora doesn't need to know. I doubt she'll come to any harm," I answered him. He had always been one to have a lot of questions. He and Jake were made differently. Jake was cool and collected at all times, but Sam was only that way when he was out doing his job.

Sam nodded to me before glancing over to Jake. They were a good team. I stood there in my office with them when my phone rang on the desk. My gaze went to my bodyguards before I grabbed the phone. The private number shown on the screen.

"Hello."

"Such an authoritative tone. They really did teach you a thing or two."

"What do you want, Marcus?" I snapped on the phone while Jake and Sam watched me.

"Just wanted to congratulate you on your wife. She's a real beauty."

His comment should have caused me concern, but when I came in here to speak with Sam, Aurora was sitting on our balcony. The vibration from the phone signaling a message made me take it away from my ear. I opened the text to see multiple pictures of Aurora sitting at a restaurant in a turtleneck and leggings with Chloe and Elizabeth.

Shit! When did she leave?

"I'm going to assume from your silence that you received my pictures. I'm surprised you don't have a guard around her like you do your fake mom, dad, and sister. Tsk tsk. What I wouldn't do once I get my hands on her. Hmm?"

"How do you know that she doesn't have a guard with her?" I bluffed glancing at Sam and motioning with my head for him to get to Aurora. He nodded and turned to leave.

"Let's stop bullshitting each other, TC We both know that she doesn't have someone there. I look forward to meeting her in person. Do you think she will like me?" He laughed down the phone. Another photo came through with one of the members of the gang walking in front of her and the other girls. Fuck!

"Are you still there? Did you get my other picture? Wonder what she's hiding underneath those clothes?"

"If you touch her, or try anything with her, I will come back to that shithole of a house and fucking kill you. And then while I'm there, I will burn that motherfucker around your body."

"You know I don't do threats, TC We will be having another conversation again soon."

The line went dead, and I flung the phone. Realizing too late how irrational it was when the device crashed into the wall and shattered.

I leaned on the desk, my hands flat on the surface and took some calming breaths. Jake stood in front of me with his phone in his hand as he stared at me. "Call Sam to find out where he is. If he hasn't left yet, tell him to meet us around the front."

"Yes, sir."

"It's Sam." He sounded out of breath as he answered the phone.

"Have you left the garage yet?"

"No, sir. I'm about to head out." Jake nodded to me, and we both headed to the elevator.

"Pull to the front of the building. TC and I will be down there shortly."

"Yes, sir." The call ended as we stepped onto the metal carriage .

I sat in the Lexus on the other side of the street from the Louis Vuitton store. The girls had been in there for at least an hour, and I hadn't spotted any of my old gang. If Marcus were playing it safe, he wouldn't have picked her up in broad daylight. Jake and Sam sat in the front seats as we waited. I couldn't take it any longer. I flung open the door to the car, making my way across the street with Jake in tow. Where the fuck was Orson?

Jake opened the door, and I stepped into the high-end store. My head on a swivel as I searched for Aurora. I found her standing with Chloe and Elizabeth looking at the newly released purses. Stalking forward, I made a beeline to her. Aurora had covered up all the marks I had left on her last night.

I grabbed her elbow, which brought her attention and fist my way. Before she was able to connect with my chest, my other hand wrapped around her small one. The way her eyes went wide, and her mouth fell open told me she didn't expect it to be me. "TC!"

"Let's go, Aurora." I proceeded to pull her through the shop while she tried to use what little weight she had against me.

"Stop this, you're making a scene!" Aurora begged me, and she finally pulled her arm out of my grip.

I turned and squared up to her. Her grey eyes swirling with something I couldn't quite put my finger on. It wasn't hate that she was trying to express on her face. She shivered as I pressed my body against hers. "If you can't walk out of this store of your own free will, I will throw you over my shoulder in front of everyone in this store."

"You wouldn't dare!" She made sure to enunciate each of her words.

"Try me," I growled as her eyes left mine to glance around the room. Everyone in the store had stopped to stare at us. I couldn't have given a shit. People needed to learn to mind their own business.

"Ugh!" Aurora stomped around me to make her way out of the store. I nodded to Jake, and he followed us as I kept stride for stride with my pissed-off wife.

Sam opened the back door to the sedan allowing Aurora to slip in. I got in on the other side. Aurora had her arms crossed over her chest. She faced away from me to the window with a clear scowl on her face.

As much as Aurora was always on her best behavior, her little tantrum in the store excited me. I had been hoping that she would've held her ground so I could've thrown her over my shoulder. Maybe even spanked her in front of the entire room. But her upbringing got the best of her, and she conceded.

"Jake, make sure to message Orson and let him know that we have Aurora."

"Yes, sir."

When we reached the garage, Aurora was the first one out of the vehicle. I quickly followed her to our private elevator. Jake and Sam hung back as the door closed on us.

"Why are you covering up? Are you ashamed?" I boxed her in with my arms as she stared at my reflection.

"Is that even something I need to answer? I already looked like a whore in my Gala dress in front of the whole store this morning."

I ran my nose up her neck with the thoughts of all my marks on display. One of my hands went up her front while my other grabbed hold of her neck, pulling her flush against my body. Her hands went to mine on her neck as she tried to keep me in her sight.

"Then you're my little whore. No one in this entire city would be ballsy enough to call you a whore to your face. How about I show you some other things that you will like?"

Aurora squirmed against me as her eyes began to flutter. I loosened my grip on her neck, and she let out a sigh.

"Did you like being tied up last night? So that I could do whatever I wanted to your body?"

Aurora did the third surprising thing when she nodded.

Chapter Fifteen

TC

When the doors opened to our penthouse, I grabbed Aurora and flung her over my shoulder. Her hands held herself up on my lower back. Her ass was beside my head, teasing me as I walked us to her room.

I couldn't take it anymore. Slipping my fingers in the waistband of her leggings, I pulled them down below her ass cheeks and bit her.

"TC!" Aurora squealed as she tried to wiggle out of my grip. My cock twitched every time her ass cheek touched my face, and my fingers itched to be buried deep inside her pussy. "Someone is going to see me!"

"No one but me, temptress." I chuckled as I opened the door to her room.

I dropped her on the mattress and glanced up. The red tie from last night's encounter was still tied to the headboard, and I smirked. My fingers grabbed the waist of her leggings and panties, and I ripped them the rest of the way down her legs.

Discarding them to the floor, I pulled her to the edge of the bed. Aurora's chest rose and fell, but her gaze remained on mine. That top needed to be gone. I grabbed the hem of it and tore it open.

"Damn it, TC! I loved this shirt! What is your problem!"

"I don't have a problem. That shirt was in my way."

"Well, you didn't need to rip it. You could've asked for me to take it off." Aurora wriggled out of the arms of the ruined turtleneck—leaving her in her bra. That was about to be gone too.

The sight of her, and all my marks on her skin, made me harder than I could ever imagine. My jacket came off, and I threw it over the edge of the stool at her makeup vanity. Aurora watched my hands as I unbuttoned the fastenings on my shirt. I pulled the shirt from my body and let it fall to the floor on top of her leggings.

Aurora's tongue came out and ran across her lips before she bit her bottom lip. Kneeling, I spread her legs, her eyes never leaving mine. My tongue ran up from her opening to her clit, and the quick intake of her breath made me grin. I had never had a woman respond to my touch as she did. My lips and tongue wrapped around her clit, changing the pressure on it as I sucked.

Her fingers wove their way into my hair, pressing my face tighter into her cunt. Her moans and whimpers urged me on. The crotch area of my pants was so tight, it felt like it was cutting off my circulation. I released her legs, and she wrapped them around my head. Removing my slacks from my body, my cock sprang free from its confines. I grabbed hold of Aurora's hips and picked her up from the bed, letting her ride my face.

"TC!" she groaned softly as her back arched off the mattress, her body begging me to take her with my cock. Aurora's legs tighten as her first orgasm hits her. I lapped up her intoxicating taste, trying my best to keep from losing even a drop. The small bundle of fun was sensitive as I nipped it before bringing her down my body.

"Was that good, temptress? Do you want more?"

Aurora's gaze locked with mine as I rubbed the head of my cock against her soaked entrance. Her hands went to my chest, and she pushed me away. "What? Do you not want my cock inside you?"

"Yes. But you need a condom." Aurora said it so matter-of-factly that I couldn't help but laugh. The glare that she gave me had me chuckling even harder.

"Are you worried you'll get pregnant? I don't think our parents would have an issue with that. We're no longer teenagers," I told her as I pressed her into the bed. Her hand on my bare chest as her grey eyes stayed locked with my blues.

"I'm not worried about getting pregnant. I'm on the shot for that. I just don't want to catch anything from you since you have fucked over half of LA."

"You think I'd fuck them without protection? Are you fucking crazy? Do you know how many of them have tried to get pregnant by me? I didn't roll without a condom that I personally bought or had Jake buy." I grabbed her and pushed her further up the bed. My thoughts gave me the image of her on all fours. Her hands tied with my tie, and her ass in the air.

I pulled her hands up above her head and wrapped the silk around them. I pushed her bra up and away from her tits before turning her over on her stomach.

"On your knees, temptress." Aurora glanced behind her before complying with my demands. When she rested on her forearms with her ass in the air, I couldn't help my groan as her dripping cunt and ass were on full display. "Such a good girl."

I couldn't miss the whimper that escaped her lips. My girl liked the praise. I kneeled behind her, lining the head of my cock to her entrance before thrusting to the hilt inside of her. Aurora was tighter around me than last night but that, was probably because she was swollen inside from where I was pounding her. I wrapped my arm around her waist, my fingers landing on her clit as I thrust inside of her while I applied pressure to her sensitive nub.

"Oh God, I'm so close!" Aurora cried out as she flipped her hair so she could look behind her.

"No, temptress. God doesn't have anything to do with this. This is all me," I answered her as my hand came down on her right ass cheek.

"Mmm!" Aurora's mouth was open as her head rested on the bed. Tears in her eyes as I continued to push her body to the brink. I pulled out and faintly heard her whimper at the loss.

I twisted her onto her back and pushed her closer to the headboard. Sitting between her legs I spread them wide as I spit into my hand and then on her pussy. We were going to find out how much she could take, and how much she liked. Aurora's eyes widened as I rubbed my hand over her entrance and eased three of my fingers into her tight, wet cunt. My other hand was playing with her peaked nipples as I slowly pulled them in and out of her.

Aurora's back arched off the mattress and she groaned. I spit on the fingers that were inside her cunt and then eased my fourth finger inside. "Damn, Aurora. You're such a good girl taking my fingers in your tight cunt. You must have been a porn star in your past life."

Her moans grew louder just as I slipped my hand inside her up to my wrist. Aurora pulled on her restraints while I fisted her and played with her clit with my other hand. "Do you like this? Do you like being stretched? Speak to me, temptress."

"Yes! Just like that!" Aurora's breath was coming in pants as I continued my assault on her cunt and clit. Her walls around my hand tightened, and she arched her back again, but she never let her eyes close. She was a quick learner.

"Come for me, Aurora. Let it all go." I coaxed her as I pulled just enough out and then twisted as I played with her G-spot with my middle finger.

"I'm coming!"

I allowed her to come before carefully easing my hand back out of her. Tasting her on my hand, I had to do what I was thinking of next.

Blanketing her, I stuck two of my cum-coated fingers in her mouth. Aurora's confused expression as my fingers slid down to the back of her tongue. Not quite far enough to make her gag. "Suck them."

Aurora wrapped her lips and tongue around my fingers, sucking and playing with my fingers with her tongue. Damn, I wished it was my cock in her mouth instead of my fingers.

I thrust back into her cunt. My hand had stretched her out just enough not to be as tight as before. She still felt amazing tensing around my cock. Aurora moaned against my fingers, and I forced them further down making her gag which in turn tightened her cunt around me.

Each time she gagged I thought I was going to come. But I kept it at bay until Aurora's orgasm crashed around me. Her moans were what finally brought mine to burst from me.

Untying her hands and removing my fingers from her mouth, I leaned over her. Aurora was panting as she tried to regroup. "You did so good, Aurora. Next time I'm going to teach you some more new things."

Aurora

TC pulled out of me and stood at the edge of my bed. The man was even more gorgeous than when he was a teenager; he had filled out and collected more tattoos. He picked up his pants and slid them up his legs before he fastened them with only the zipper.

My body was spent. TC bent back down, and I noticed the navy-blue color hanging from his hand. His eyes held mine as he brought my underwear to his face and took in a deep breath with the fabric pressed on his nose. TC slipped them into his pocket with a grin. "You smell so good. I think I'll keep these since you have something of mine."

Those were my favorite panties, but I couldn't do anything but lay there. The way TC fucked me and pushed me wasn't like anyone else I had been with. I could see why women wanted to fuck him. He was a beast. He made them feel sated.

The way he took control, and the way I just let him do with my body the way he wanted to unnerved me. What was wrong with me? This wasn't supposed to be happening.

"Those are my favorite ones. Take any of the others." I tried to sit, but my lower body screamed at me. TC chuckled as he came over and sat down beside me. His upper body leaned over me.

"None of the others have your scent on them. Besides, you can always buy more."

I knew the argument about the panties wouldn't get me anywhere. TC's eyes held mine, his other hand coming up to my face. He ran his knuckle over the right side of my face, and I couldn't help the goosebumps that raced across my skin.

"Run a warm bath. It will help with the soreness."

TC stood, grabbed his shirt and jacket, and left me lying there. The intimate encounter over. Struggling to get up, I finally made it to my feet and stumbled to the bathroom. I turned on the faucets and sat on the edge waiting for it to fill up.

What was wrong with me? Why did I keep allowing him to do what he wished with me? When did all this change?

My mind raced with so many questions. He treated me like the plague when he wasn't interested in me, but the second he was horny, I was his play toy.

No matter how much I loved the way he made me feel. Next time would be on my terms. Not his.

Chapter Sixteen

Aurora

I hadn't seen TC in a week. Most of my marks were starting to fade. Well other than the one on my ass cheek. I had even gone to the OBGYN to find out when I should be tested for anything. She wanted to do a pregnancy test on me because I was sexually active again. Which I thought was stupid, surely it would be too early to tell that, but she told me that she didn't want to give me my shot next month if I was. And she would be testing me then too.

But as far as the STD testing, it was too early to test for that. So that would be a test as well at the following appointment. I just didn't understand why he couldn't just wear a condom. We wouldn't be having any babies, and what really threw me for a loop was when he mentioned it so flippantly.

Elizabeth and Chloe had invited me to go swimming at the beach earlier this morning, and going through my closet wasn't helping me find anything I could wear. Each bathing suit bottom I had showed off the mark that TC had left on my ass. It was like he knew just where to place it so I wouldn't be able to cover it up.

A knock brought my attention to my open door. Gwen stood there giving me a curious gaze.

"Hi, Gwen. Is something wrong?"

"Ms. Elizabeth and Chloe are here. Would you like me to send them in here?"

I glanced around the room and then shook my head. There was no way that I could allow them in this room right now. The red tie was still connected to my headboard, and we wouldn't talk about the bathroom door. TC had yet to send someone in to fix it. "Have them sit in the living room, and I'll be right out. Also, Gwen, could you find someone to fix my bathroom door?"

She looked over at the busted door and then cocked an eyebrow at me. "I'll see what I can do. I'll let the ladies know."

"Thank you, Gwen. You're the best."

"You're welcome." Gwen nodded with a smile and left me.

Sighing, I glanced around and spotted my beach skirt. I grabbed it, along with my beach shirt and walked out of the room.

Orson stopped at the beach, and we all exited the car. It was a public beach—nothing like the beach I had been on with the girls on our trip. Making our way down to an empty spot, I couldn't help the feeling that we were being followed.

I felt the same way the whole week when I left the house. Glancing over my shoulder, I couldn't spot anyone that was out of the ordinary.

"Aurora, girl. What's wrong?" Chloe's voice brought my attention back to my friends.

"Nothing." I smiled as we continued, but the nagging feeling of being watched stayed.

We set everything up, and I laid out on my beach towel as I read my Kindle, trying to finish the fantasy book I had started without any interruptions. Chloe and Elizabeth were out in the water. The water was still a little too cold for me, and I needed to keep my tan fresh. It had been a while since I had been out in the sun in a bikini. My tan lines were starting to fade.

I glanced up as someone blocked my sun. The man above me gave me a grin before he squatted down in front of me. He was red-headed, and if I hadn't given the man a second glance, I would've thought he was Alex.

"Can I help you?"

"Yes, are you by chance Mrs. Churchhill?"

"Who's asking?" I countered as I stared into his coal-black eyes. His breath smelled like he hadn't brushed his teeth in years, and the yellow stains on them proved me right as he widened his grin.

"Just tell him that an old friend sends his love." He chuckled as he stood and walked away, disappearing into an alleyway and out of sight.

Sitting up, I realized I didn't even have TC's number. So, what was I going to do? I hadn't seen or heard from him in a week.

"Mrs. Churchhill, are you okay? What did he say to you?" I glanced to the side and recognized Sam beside me. What the fuck was he doing here?

"What are you doing here?" I questioned him as he pulled me to stand. He took out his phone and hit one number. I noticed that he was also carrying his gun in his hands.

"Sir, I spotted him near her... Yes, sir, she wasn't touched... Right away, sir... He wants to speak to you." Sam handed out his phone, and I brought it up to my ear while he watched the surroundings.

"What did the man say to you, Aurora?" TC's husky voice sounded dangerous as he spoke to me. If I didn't know any better, it sounded like he was at an airport.

"Where the hell are you? You leave and don't say anything to me? And then you have Sam following me? What the fuck for, TC?" I was pissed that he had left me after we had fucked. Not like it was any of my business but if we were fucking, he needed to say when his ass was leaving, and when he was coming back.

"I was called away on business, and I didn't think that you would care where I went. You seem to like being home alone. So now back to my question: what did that motherfucker say to you?" The way he was speaking to me made me not want to answer his question, but people were starting to stare. Chloe and Elizabeth were heading over to me, concern painted on their faces.

"He told me to tell you that an old friend sends his love."

"You need to get back to the penthouse now, Aurora, and take your friends with you. If you are not in the house when I get home, I will come to get you. This time, you won't walk on your own two feet." He hung up, and I glared at Sam. This was some bullshit. I had questions. and TC was going to answer them when he got home.

Chloe and Elizabeth's cars came to get them after we had returned to the penthouse, so I was left alone with Sam and Gwen in the living room. The elevator door dinged, and Sam's gun rose. He dropped it as TC and Jake walked into the room. TC nodded and all three of them left us.

"You have questions to answer." I squared my shoulders as TC stalked up to me, his eyes roaming my near-naked body. The coolness of the penthouse had hardened my nipples, making my skin pimple with cold.

"And what questions are those?" I hated that his voice made me melt. It was just like when we first met at the party.

I finally made it to the Churchhill's estate with Chloe and Elizabeth. The day before we had gone dress shopping, and I picked out a Cinderella dress, which I had fallen in love with. The light yellow of the dress made the tan of my skin pop. When I came into the ballroom, I spotted him dancing with the slut of the school. Morgan was grinding all over him, and I rolled my eyes when mine locked with his. Heading over to his parents, I greeted them before we went over to the food table. We sat at a table to eat while everyone was dancing. We were there for a while to allow some of the other dancers to leave the floor. Chloe, Elizabeth, and I went to the dance floor. We were having fun until TC swung me away from my friends.

The way his hard blue eyes stared into my grey ones had me melting in his arms.

"We didn't actually get to meet at the clothing store. My name is TC, and you are?" His voice was everything I had ever dreamed

about, and it sent something through me that I never thought would happen.

"My name is Aurora," I answered him with a curious look, and the smile that he sent my way was like nothing I had ever seen before.

"Pretty name for a pretty girl," he uttered as he turned us around the dance floor.

"Were you not dancing with Morgan?" I couldn't help but stare into his gorgeous blue eyes. If I didn't watch myself, I could get lost in them.

"Are you jealous?" He smirked as we turned one last time.

"No, I was just asking," I responded.

"Good. I'd hate for you to have feelings for me." He laughed as he released my waist and hand, leaving me in the middle of the dance floor. When I glanced around the room, Morgan was laughing hysterically as well as the others behind her.

Holding my composure, I turned to look at my parents and the Churchhills, curtsied, and left with as much of my dignity as I could.

"Why is Sam following me? And who was that guy who approached me while I was trying to relax? And why the fuck can you leave without telling me, but if I leave, you have to know." I placed my hands on my hips and glared at him.

"Sam is there for your protection from the person who spoke to you. And that person is someone from my past who has decided that he needed to show himself. As far as leaving without telling you, I didn't know that was where our relationship was." TC towered over me, but I had no intention of backing down. When I left for my girls' trip, he had to know what I was doing before I left. Well, that shit worked both ways.

"Motherfucker! You made me tell you that I was leaving when you had me pressed up against my door! And we weren't even fucking then! But this time, you fuck me and leave for a week? Fuck you." I turned on my heel and headed to my room. I didn't want to see him right now.

I slammed the door shut and locked it for good measure. TC wasn't going to be getting any pussy tonight, even if he begged at the door like a dog.

TC

I took a deep breath as Aurora headed to her room. As much as I wanted to be with her, right now wasn't the time for me to be balls-deep in her cunt. Aurora looked sexy as hell in that bikini, when I noticed the bite mark on her left ass cheek a smile spread across my lips; it made her that much more intoxicating.

"Sir, we have camera footage of the person of interest walking up to Mrs. Churchhill."

My eyes focused on Sam as he went to hand me the tablet. The next moment, I had him by his throat up against the wall. The tablet landed on the floor.

"Why the fuck did he even get that close to her! What do I pay you for!" The snarl in my tone and the way Sam stared at me told me that I was losing it.

When I came in from the elevator, it took everything in me to hold my temper. Just because we were fucking didn't mean we were anything more than that. Then, her in that fucking bikini made things worse. I wanted to take her right there in that living room. Up against this wall where Sam now struggled to breathe.

"TC, if you want him to answer you, it would be wise to let him go." Jake cut through the fury just before Sam was about to pass out. I let him go, and he slid to the floor, holding his neck gasping in air that he had been deprived of a few seconds earlier.

"I'm sorry, sir. I was watching and making my way over to her to be as close as you told me. But there wasn't any way I could get that close without her recognizing me." Sam's voice was hoarse.

"Now that she knows you are her bodyguard, that man better never get that close to her again, do you hear me?" I squatted down to his level. The fear in his eyes showed me that he understood even before he nodded his head.

Standing, I went into the kitchen to grab some whiskey. Tonight, could've been even worse than what it was. Marcus could have taken her right there and then. What was his plan? He would have been stupid to take her during the day.

But Marcus had never been smart. I was the one that had kept him in check most days. Hell, I was the muscle though I was a lot younger than he was. What was his motive?

Pouring the brown liquor into the glass, I tossed it back without really tasting it. I put more into the glass and replaced the bottle. As I exited the kitchen, I glanced down the hall to Aurora's door. The lights were off, and there was no sound coming from the room.

What was she expecting of me? Hell, what did I expect from myself with her?

Chapter Seventeen

TC

I had been back from my business trip for three days. Aurora had kept her distance and each time I tried her door, it was locked. The frustration I was feeling was being felt by everyone around me but Aurora. Just this morning, I woke up with the hardest erection I had ever woken up with. Even a shower hadn't made any difference.

Wrapping the towel around my waist, I walked out of my room and headed to the kitchen. It was still early for Gwen to be here, and Aurora would still be asleep. I stepped into the kitchen and stopped. Aurora was on her tiptoes reaching for a mug. The shirt that she had stolen from me showing off her bare ass. I snuck up behind her, brushing against her back, and she stiffened as I grabbed the cup she was reaching for. My other hand snaked around her front, pulling her flush against me.

"TC!"

"Yes, temptress." As Aurora turned to face me, the shirt unbuttoned exposing the tops of her tits. Her hands landed on my chest and her palms on my pierced nipples. The smell of her drove me crazy, and her grey eyes stared back into my blues.

"I'd appreciate it if you released me." Aurora's eyes flickered down to the towel and then back up to my face. A blush crept across her cheeks.

"Why?" I tangled my fingers in her hair at the nape of her neck pulling her head back, exposing her throat to me.

"Because I told you to," she panted as her body quivered at the over-extension of her muscles.

"But you don't have panties on. I could take you right here, and no one but us would know." I traced my tongue up her throat to her jaw and then to her ear, making her sigh. She liked this, and I couldn't wait to find other things that she liked.

"We... can't... I'm on my period." Aurora blinked and then smirked as she refocused her eyes with mine.

"Really? And is that supposed to stop me?" I groaned and lifted her to the counter. I'd have to take another shower, but this would be fun. The surprise in her eyes made me chuckle. Whatever men she was with before were nothing like me. I ran my hand between us to her cunt, most of the time women used this excuse when they really weren't, thinking that would keep me from taking them.

I played with her clit before running my fingers further down. Aurora arched into me before I found the string to her tampon. She wasn't lying. "Mmm, I could pull this out. From the way you assumed I'd be turned off by you being on your period, I'm guessing the men you've been with before were. But, temptress, this just means more fun."

My cock was so hard at the thought of being inside of her that I wrapped a finger around the string, ready to pull it out the moment she agreed. I wanted to taste her on my tongue, the sweetness of her orgasm with the copper taste of her period. Aurora's legs had wrapped around my waist.

A gasp brought our attention to the kitchen door. One of the girls Aurora had hired to help Gwen out stood with her hands over her eyes. "I'm so sorry Mr. and Mrs. Churchhill!"

She turned, and the next sound was her footsteps heading to the elevator. Aurora pushed me away from her and stood. Her eyes went to my cock that stood rigid under the towel.

"*This* is the reason we don't do this out in the open. Besides, I don't want you right now."

"I beg to differ, Aurora. Your body betrays you more than you think it does." I smirked at her. She wanted me, and she wanted to know what it felt like to be taken while she was on her period.

"You think you know me, but you don't." She glared at me as she stood there holding my gaze.

"Then let's find out. You're horny. I'm horny, why not let me help resolve that? Unless you want to bring in some toys? Then I'll eat you out, while you play with your clit."

"What is wrong with you? I just told you I'm on my period." Her brow was furrowed, but she was still curious. Her eyes betrayed her. She wanted to be disgusted but she was intrigued.

"There's nothing wrong with me. I told you I didn't care. A little blood doesn't bother me." The more I talked about this with her, the more I wanted her . My cock was leaking, and it was all because of her.

"A little? I just started, there's no little about it." She smirked— her right eyebrow quirking up.

A knock at the kitchen door brought my attention away from Aurora. Jake stood there trying to hide a smirk while his gaze went from me to Aurora. Apparently fucking or eating her out wasn't going to happen this morning.

"I just saw Maggie running to the elevator."

Aurora turned and left the kitchen past Jake as she left to go to her room. Her mug that she wanted sitting on the counter empty; the coffee pot still full.

"Yeah, because she walked in on us," I told him as I headed out of the kitchen, glancing down the hall I noticed that her door was cracked.

"If you go down there, you will be late to an important meeting," Jake said behind me. "Also, the Gala is tomorrow. Your suit is finished, should I get Maggie or Diana to retrieve it for you?"

"Yes. Do I have any more meetings today?"

"Not that I know of, sir. That would be a Lindsey question."

I nodded and turned to my right. Aurora was going to be mine this afternoon.

Aurora

I headed straight to my bathroom to replace the tampon that TC had dislodged. The fire burning at my core from his words unnerved me. How could his mouth on my pussy while I was bleeding be so intriguing? Damn him!

Then, Maggie caught us in the kitchen, my legs wrapped around him. TC's hand between us. She didn't have to imagine much. I felt for her; I had been in her shoes many years ago with him.

I used to think he was one of the most handsome boys at school. But after the party, I steered clear of him. At least I tried to. He and his friends made my last year of school a living hell. The hazing and the pranks were daily after I caught him fucking in the band room.

What made me upset with myself was that I had watched him for a few minutes before I tried to get out of there. And I didn't get lucky enough to creep out of there without a sound. No, I backed into the cymbals, and they and I crashed to the ground.

When TC turned to me, the look he gave me with those cold blue eyes caused me to shiver. I tried to get up without showing him my panties, but I didn't know if I was successful with that. I was ashamed of myself when I had stood there watching him fuck Alexius. The way the muscles in his back moved under his skin had kept my attention like I was hypnotized. Sitting in the first flute chair, I kept my eyes away from Alexius as she walked out of the band room. But TC didn't just leave. No, he came up to me and took hold of my chin.

"Did you like what you saw? If you're a good girl, I'll give you some." The smirk that rested on his lips twisted my stomach. He hadn't buttoned up his shirt and reset his tie to be in line with the dress code.

"I'm good. You can leave now." I didn't want anything to do with him. Jerking my chin from his grip, he laughed out loud as he walked out the door.

Stripping from the shirt, I grabbed some shorts and a tank top. I had been to the dress shop and got my dress for the Gala yesterday. Sam was just three paces behind me. He apparently didn't do what he was instructed before, and he wasn't going to let that happen again.

It sucked that I had started, I was going to have to wear some very thin panties. Chloe had suggested not wearing anything, but that would be a little weird, right? But then again, I could see how angry it would make TC. Tomorrow would be the first time we would be out in public together. If you didn't count him coming into the Louis Vuitton store and basically dragging me out.

He thought that since he was CEO of the biggest logistics company he could do whatever he wanted. I caught my reflection in the floor-length mirror. My skin was red, but I was glad that he hadn't put any marks on my neck.

Grabbing my Kindle from my vanity, I went out to the balcony. Maggie was now in the kitchen, the mug that I had tried to get before TC had come up behind me still sat on the counter. I had known he was behind me even before he pulled me against him. He had his cologne on, but what got me was that he was bare-chested and only had a towel on. It didn't help that I hadn't put on any panties to go get my coffee. TC had always left before then, so I thought I was in the clear.

When TC put me on the counter and played with my clit, I had almost let him take me. Being abstinent this whole time had made me horny, but when Maggie caught us it snapped me out of the euphoria of the moment. I plopped down on the chair I had taken as my own since I had moved in and opened the book on my Kindle. I started this book about an angel/demon hybrid and his Grigori a few days ago. Bravas was hot and was my favorite character. If I thought about it, he sort of reminded me of TC, but only a tiny bit.

"Aurora, did you want anything to eat?" Gwen asked from beside me.

"Please. Anything is fine, Gwen." She smiled and then nodded before leaving.

After Gwen brought me my food, I snuggled down in the lounge chair with my kindle and began reading until my lids grew heavy. Drifting off with my kindle resting on my chest.

I woke up to a tongue against my core and hands wrapped around my thighs. Instinctively, my hands went to the head between my legs. The thoughts in my mind were mush as the pressure changed on my clit, and the vibration of his moan shook my body.

The heat that built down deep in my core had me arching with each change. It felt too good to make him stop. TC lifted his eyes to mine. As much as I wanted to look away, I knew he wouldn't like it.

Those frigid blue eyes actually were warmer than I had ever seen them. Glancing around, I realized we were still on the balcony. I stiffened and tried to sit up. "TC, people are going to see us!"

"And? If they don't want a show they shouldn't be looking right, temptress?" TC raised his face from my pussy, and I didn't miss the tinge of red on his lips. His shirt was half open, displaying the tattoos etched into his skin.

The sun was low in the sky. TC tugged my shorts off and tossed them aside. My heart raced as he climbed up my body. He was a predator settling his hips between my legs. His cock rigid pressed against my core, his pants keeping him from slipping inside me. Why did he have to look this good when he stared at me?

"TC ..." My thoughts were still not making any sense inside of my head. I ran my hands inside of his shirt. His barbelled nipples felt good under my fingers as my hands traced the muscles. He had never allowed me to really touch him like this.

I opened his shirt the rest of the way and then went for the button of his suit pants. TC's eyes never moved from mine as he lay on top of me. They were completely eclipsed by his pupils, and his breath was steady compared to mine. I got them opened and wrapped my hand around his cock, making him hiss.

TC crashed his lips to mine. The copper on his lips and tongue as his fought with mine wasn't as bad as I expected it would be. He hadn't kissed me since we had been married, it was thrilling; sending excitement down my nerves. He grabbed hold of my hips and pulled me up on his lap as he kneeled on the chair.

The cool air caressed my back, one of his hands ran through my hair while the other wrapped around my waist. TC's lips never left mine. As he lifted us both up, I wrapped my legs around his hips. My hands went into his hair as he walked back into the penthouse. I didn't even know whether the staff were still here, but he was all I could think about. And even that was taking a lot out of me.

I wasn't paying any attention to where he was taking me. All I knew was that I wasn't going to have to bring myself to orgasm. TC pushed the door open with his shoulder and kicked it close. My eyes were adjusting to the darkness when he dropped me to the bed. The little bit of light that came from the windows allowed me to watch him shrug out of his shirt.

TC's pants were already at his ankles when he dropped his boxer briefs. He pulled me to the edge of the bed and thrust inside of me. If I hadn't already been dripping wet, it would have been painful. He growled when he bottomed out inside me. That piercing hit just the right spot with each of his thrusts.

Chapter Eighteen
TC

Fuck! Aurora felt so fucking good wrapped around my cock.

Her hands went to my forearms and her whole body tensed with each of my thrusts. She was so wet by the time I got her into my bedroom and onto my bed that sinking into her tight, sticky cunt was a breeze.

She never allowed her gaze to leave mine, and when she started to come, her fingers tightened on my arms. "TC! Fuck! Right there!"

I loved the fact that she screamed my name. There hadn't been a woman I had fucked that could say my name like Aurora did. I pulled out, and the whimper she tried to suppress made me grin.

"Don't worry, temptress. This won't be your only one." I headed over to the bathroom to get a towel. Grabbing one, I took it back to my bed. Aurora was now standing and shifted from foot to foot.

"Why are you up?" I questioned as I tossed the towel on the bed and picked her back up.

"I told you, I'm on my period. I didn't want to stain your bed."

"And I told you that I didn't mind a little blood. What makes you think this is my bed?" I fell on top of her, crashing us both onto the bed. The towel forgotten as I sunk back into her cunt.

"Your smell... it's all around..." Aurora's voice breathy, and her eyes never left mine. Her whimpers and moans spurred me on as she met me thrust for thrust.

I put her legs on my shoulders, one hand pressed around her throat, the other playing with her clit. Aurora tightened her calves around my head as I plundered into her. Hitting her G-spot each time her tits bounced with my thrusts.

"You're such a good girl the way you take all of me, Aurora. I want you to come again for me." Leaning down, I contorted her and crushed my lips to hers. She moaned into my mouth, her orgasm causing her to tighten around my cock.

Pulling the cum from me as she came around me. I allowed her legs to drop to my sides, and my hand released her throat.

The breath she took in told me that I had cut it close. If she wasn't on her period and that shot, there was no way she wouldn't have gotten pregnant before now.

I had never thought how fucking great sex would be without a condom. But fucking her was an addiction I didn't want to break. I wanted her over and over again.

On my bed. Again. The fucking shower. Hell, the fucking hot tub on the balcony.

It wasn't supposed to be like this. But that kiss in front of all those people changed everything.

I stood in the circle of men at the Gala with my father, Aurora's father, Drake, and his father. Sam was in the car with Aurora and her mother, and they were late. I tried not to be too conspicuous searching the crowd and the door each time it opened.

"Looking for someone?" Drake nudged me in my arm, almost spilling my drink on my suit.

"No."

"Looks like Lyla is here, and she has been staring at you this entire time."

I glanced over and spotted the blond eyeing me up and down. She had been one of my flavors of the week, and I hadn't touched her for a long time. She had become clingy and wanted more than sex. I shrugged and glanced over to the doors again just as Aurora came in the door.

And, fuck, if she wasn't gorgeous! I could see now exactly how many of the marks those two seamstresses had seen. Every man and woman in the room stared at her as she stood at the top of the stairs, surveying the crowd.

The skin-tight black dress flowed with her body and the neckline was cut at least three inches below her round tits. Two slits ran up to her hip bones, letting me and every other person in this room know she wasn't wearing anything underneath.

I stood beside the other men as Aurora's eyes locked with mine. Those smoky grey eyes held me in a trance as she started her descent. Her beautiful, tanned legs peeked out with each stride. Aurora's pull-me, chocolate-brown hair cascaded down her back. She was halfway down the stairs when two men went up to her. Each one took her hands and kissed the back of them.

It took everything in me not to plow through the crowd to the three of them. Aurora glanced over to me, her bottom lip between her teeth, before the corner of her lip curled up in a smirk. What was she doing?

Aurora kissed them both on the cheek as she stood there talking to them. What really got under my skin was when she started to flirt with them. The muscles in my jaw bounced as I stared at them.

Fuck it! She was mine!

I finished my glass and thrust it into Drake's hand, and I stormed through the crowd to Aurora and the men. As I got closer to her, I spotted the hickey just under her breast that I had left there last night. She had tried to hide it with makeup, but it was too dark to cover.

Shouldering my way between the two men, I wrapped Aurora's hair around my hand and pulled her flush to my body with my other arm. Her hands went to my chest, and the soft moan that exited her lips excited me. I crashed my lips to hers in a brutal and punishing kiss before pulling away from them. My lips were against her ear, and I nipped the soft lobe. "I don't know what you thought you were doing, but try that again and you will watch those men die at your feet."

The shock on her face was subtle enough that anyone else wouldn't have noticed it. But I knew all her tells. I glared at the men in front of us. They were both pale as they dropped their eyes to the floor.

"We're sorry, Mr. Churchhill. We didn't know she was yours," one sputtered as he backed away, the other kept opening his mouth like a fish before he followed the other man.

"You've kissed me again in front of everyone," Aurora whispered, out of breath against my cheek. "And now everyone is staring!"

"I don't care. If anyone of these motherfuckers thought you were available, they don't now," I growled as I jerked her closer to me. Aurora's chest rose and fell against me, and the people around us slowly began to get back to their conversations.

"TC, let me go, or people are going to see that you have other things on your mind."

"They already know I have other things on my mind. They're not blind, Aurora," I answered her. Letting her step away from me to give herself some space, her grey eyes filled with as much desire as my rigid cock.

I pulled my eyes from hers to search the room. We needed to handle some business and it couldn't wait. Not with her in this fucking dress.

"Tom, why don't you get off the stairs? I'm sure your beautiful wife would like to get off her feet." My eyes landed on Aurora's father as he stood at the bottom of the stairs. He glanced between us. The last time we had spoken, I had told him I wouldn't be able to treat his daughter like a wife. But the way he looked between us, and the light in his eye, told me he didn't believe what I had said that night. Hell, I wouldn't believe it either with the way I was acting.

I grabbed Aurora by the waist as I headed down the stairs back to the circle of people I had been with. One other person had been added to the group. Lyla hung on Drake's arm, pretending that everything that he said was funny. She was one I had been happy to get rid of.

"Oh! TC, I didn't see you! How have you been?" Her squeaky voice brought my attention to her, and Drake rolled his eyes. He liked them quiet and only heard when he was fucking them.

"Lyla. Have you met my wife, Aurora?" I brought Aurora's hand up to my lips and Lyla's eyes moved with her hand. A not-so-subtle glare on her face.

"No, I didn't know that you had gotten married." She was no longer as squeaky as she had been.

"I'm surprised you didn't. It was announced to the world," I quipped and then turned to Aurora. "Would you like to dance?"

"Sure, it was nice to meet you, Lyla." Aurora gave Lyla a small smile before I walked her away from the group to the dance floor.

The people parted to allow us a path to the dance floor. Aurora walked beside me like the queen that she was. The woman was gorgeous, and I didn't even want to think about what she was in the bedroom. I turned her and pulled her flush to my body.

"TC, what are you doing? Why are you acting like this? You have kept me at arm's length, and then I flirt with a couple of guys, and you become all caveman. So, what's the deal?"

Aurora's eyes held mine as she kept a smile on her face for the people around us. She was the reason I was like this.

I had never been this way with another woman, but I couldn't get enough of her. My mind just wouldn't let me think of anyone else. And the way she made me feel when I was fucking her. Damn.

"I'm not doing anything, your mine now."

"What is this? Is this kindergarten? Where it's I licked it, it's mine?" Aurora's pupils were starting to widen.

"More like I fucked it, it's mine." I chuckled. She cocked her head to the side just as I twirled her out and then back into me.

"So, what makes me different from the other women that you have sunk your dick into?"

"You've been the only one I've ever been without a condom with. We've already talked about this. But I can understand if you can't remember—I did blow your mind that night."

Aurora shook her head as she rolled her eyes. But I didn't miss the smile that twitched on her lips. I was learning more and more about her, and I was enjoying it. A hand dropped onto my shoulder, causing me to glance over to its owner.

Jake was beside me, and I stopped our dance.

"What is it, Jake?"

"Marcus' people are here. What do you want to do?"

I quickly looked around, noticing some of the guys I had grown up with in the gang standing around. Some were in wait staff uniforms, while others were in valet uniforms. Emi was standing in a group of girls talking. Her bodyguard beside the group. My mom and dad stood with theirs while they talked with the Emersons and DeLucas. "Keep an eye on them. I see some that I know, but I'm not sure of the others."

"Yes, sir." Jake walked away from us just as the next song started.

Sweeping Aurora back around, I kept my eyes on the men that I knew. If they hadn't changed the code signals, I might be able to find out who else was with them. I spotted Nick, the man who had been with me the night I had been arrested. He smirked at me, but I glared back at him. When they forced my hand, he would be the first to go, then Marcus.

"TC, what's going on?"

I glanced down at Aurora's beautiful grey eyes. This was one reason I hadn't ever wanted to have a wife or someone for the gang to use against me. But now they knew she was a weakness. She was going to hate me until I could handle these fuckers. I didn't want her to know what I was capable of. She wouldn't be able to handle that part of me. That was a fact.

"Nothing for you to worry about."

"Is this about the man that came up to me at the beach?"

Ever since Marcus sent the messenger to the garage I began to carry again. It wasn't something that I had wanted, but it was familiar, and I didn't have a second thought about doing it. The gun was just extra protection just in case something happened to Jake and Sam.

"TC, answer me." Aurora stopped our dance, her hands on the lapels of my jacket. When she wanted to, she could control her surroundings with just a touch of her hand. If I thought about it she was slowly being able to control how I reacted to things around me.

"Yes. And you need to be protected. He now knows what to use against me. I just showed him." I grabbed her hands and led her away from the dance floor. Jake and Sam were a couple of steps behind us as we got to the elevator. As we boarded, I held up my hand to the men following us. They both nodded and turned standing guard as the doors closed.

Chapter Nineteen

Aurora

TC pushed me up against the elevator wall. I had thought we were going somewhere for him to tell me what was going on. But when his hand ran up the slits in the dress, I knew he had other things on his mind. The moan that escaped my lips made TC more out of control. The way he made me feel was alarming, but I loved it. His hand wrapped around to my ass, and the groan that I heard from him excited me.

"You really didn't wear any panties. Were you hoping you'd get fucked here today?" TC's husky voice made me wetter, and his other hand went to my throat. He wasn't as rough, and the only reason I could think was that we were in public.

"If you remember from last night, I'm on my period."

"That's right. You are such a siren." TC's hand flexed tighter around my throat. His cock pressed into my belly. If he took the tampon out now, I wouldn't have anything else to put back in. He crashed his lips to mine as he let go of my neck and hitched my dress up. TC picked me up. And I immediately wrapped my legs around his waist.

I wanted him. Even though it would be messy, and we wouldn't be able to go back to the Gala, I wanted him to sink deep inside me. Our tongues fought with each other like we couldn't get enough of us.

"Take me," I moaned into his lips as we took a breath.

TC never hesitated, his hand went between us and un-zipped his pants. I felt the head and the piercings at my entrance, and my body shivered in anticipation. His finger wrapped around the string that hung out of me, and he pulled, dropping it to the floor. There was never a way to get used to him filling me to the brim. Those piercings got me every time, and he knew it.

"Damn, Aurora. You feel amazing wrapped around me." His lips vibrated with his voice against my neck. I tangled my fingers in his hair spurring him on to thrust deeper in-side me, bringing his mouth tighter to my skin. The feeling of bliss overtook my senses as he pushed my boundaries.

"Right there, TC!"

"I love it when you scream my name. Come for me, Aurora. You know you want to." The growl in his command as I finally let myself go made everything that much more exhilarating. He came with me and bit down on my shoul-der at the base of my neck.

TC pulled out of me and set me on my unsteady feet. I grabbed hold of his shirt, my finger coming into contact with something metal. Staring up at TC, he just stared back at me like he was waiting for me to say something. I pulled back his jacket, and my body went cold as I saw the gun in his shoulder holster. "Why are you wearing this?"

"It doesn't matter, Aurora," he told me as he stepped out of my reach and put himself back into his pants. TC opened the doors, signaling Sam and Jake to join us. I pulled my gaze from TC to try to find the tampon before I noticed the string coming out from under TC's shoe.

"Jake—to the suite."

Jake nodded, and Sam stood beside him in front of us. TC's cum running down my leg along with the blood, had me hyperaware that they would see it. The sticky copper sex smell had me taking a step back. To try to put some distance between me and Jake and Sam.

When the doors opened the guys went out first before TC placed his hand at the small of my back and picked up the tampon from the floor. With every step, more cum and blood made its way to my stiletto heels. Sam opened the door and stepped away as TC and I entered the room.

"You just happen to have a suite in this place?"

"Yes, being the CEO of a big logistics company allows me to have certain things. The same as you." TC turned to face me, and I didn't know what to make of his expression. It confused me because he told me that what was his wasn't mine at the beginning of this arrangement.

"Why are we in this room?"

"Well, I have a blood stain on my pants, you need a tampon, and we both need to clean up. Before we head back down to the Gala."

"Speaking of the Gala. Why are you acting weird, and why the fuck are you carrying that gun?" I propped my hand on my hip, the other pointing at his weapon while I stared at him, waiting for his answer.

"I told you—there are men here that you need to be protected from. If something happens to Jake or Sam, I'm the last line of defense." His voice came out cold and hard, making me shudder. His eyes had turned cold just like they were before all of this. It was like he was someone else. I mean he hadn't changed much, but it was still a change.

"What are you hiding from me? What are you not telling me about these people?"

"Aurora, just get in the shower and rinse off. I need to get another pair of pants." We stared at each other for another minute before I turned on my heel and went to the shower. TC was being insufferable right now.

Why couldn't he just tell me who they were to him? What was the problem with that?

I pulled up my hair to keep it from getting wet. When I heard the door open to the bathroom, TC stood there naked as the day he was born and stepped into the shower with me. I still didn't feel like being near him. There was a part of me that didn't want to know anything more about him, but then there was the other part that was starting to fall for the man I had hated these last nine years.

My eyes roamed his body as he washed. It wasn't fair that men like him got to look like this. The tattoos over his shoulders intrigued me. They looked older than the others.

"When did you get these? The ones over your shoulders?"

"I was young."

My fingers traced the older ink as I tried to figure out what they were. TC turned to face me and pressed me up against the tiled wall. He brought my hands up above my head, and the water dripped off his arms into my dry hair.

"Aurora, there are things that you don't need to know about me. They are in my past, and I'd rather not bring them into my future." His voice wasn't as cold as it had been earlier, but it still held something in it that made me think that whatever happened back then was very bad.

I nodded as I stared into his ice-blues. They left mine to roam my body. TC let go of my hands and grabbed hold of my chin. His grip firm as he brought his lips crashing down on mine. "If we didn't have to go back, I'd fuck you again in the shower. On that couch in the main room. Against the railing on the balcony. Up against every fucking wall in this place, and the penthouse."

"Yeah? Why, after all this time, do you want me so many times?" I needed to know what was in his heart. Even if that meant mine would break with his words. I needed to know.

"Because you're my addiction. I've never had an addiction before. But you, you're mine."

I stayed by TC's side the rest of the time in the Gala-- not that I had a choice. His arm was wrapped tightly around my waist.

His head constantly swiveled. The gun pressed between us so hard that I wondered if it was leaving a mark on my shoulder. I had never been around guns, and being this close to one made me nervous.

Sam and Jake seemed to be closer to us than usual. I had never felt so uncomfortable at a Gala in my life. Lyla kept glaring at me—I could only assume she was one of the women that TC had been with before me.

"TC, I'll be right back." His grip tightened on me bringing my attention to his face. "I've been drinking, and I need to use the bathroom. Are you going to go with me?"

"Sam will go with you. He will sweep the bathroom and then you can go in."

"Are you that paranoid that they have a woman waiting for me in the bathroom? What if there are already women in there?"

He turned to me and placed his hands on either side of my face. Making me look at him. "There is nothing that I would put past them. Sam will sweep the bathroom, then you can enter. He will make sure no one but you is in there."

"Fine." I shook my head and headed to the bathroom, Sam on my heels. Luckily, no one was waiting, and Sam entered the bathroom. A couple of shrieks told me that there were women in the room. I rolled my eyes. This was stupid.

"He must really love you."

I turned to see Lyla walking down the hall toward me. She was beautiful, blond, and wearing a dress that showed more than it covercd. She was his type in a nutshell.

"He doesn't. He's just playing a part for the families and the public," I answered. The fire in her eyes told me that I had to be careful what I said to her.

Lyla's shrill laugh unnerved me.

"He never kissed me or any of the other women he had been with. And he didn't give them a bodyguard either." Lyla came around the other side of me, closer to the bathroom. The venomous smile that graced her lips chilled me to the core.

"What do you want? Do you want him? I'm not keeping him from you or any of the other women."

"That's where you're wrong. He stopped having interest in me and the others after he married you. So, it very much is you that is keeping him from me." Lyla got in my face; the smell of the alcohol on her breath let me know that she had been drinking.

"If that's true, you must not have given him much, since I was the one he hated more than anyone else in this life."

Lyla's hand swung toward me, but I pushed her hard against the wall. My hand wrapped around her throat. "I don't care who you are or whether you have been with my husband. The next time you see me, you better cross the street to the other sidewalk. If you don't, and you try to do anything to me, I will make sure you tremble each time you see me."

The door opened, and Sam came out with the other women from the bathroom. I gave Lyla another shove into the wall and walked into the bathroom.

When I came out of the stall, I froze. TC stood up against the door, his eyes roaming me as if he were looking for something. After the initial shock, I went to the sink and washed my hands.

"So, Sam isn't good enough now?" I waved my hand at the paper towel dispenser and tore the paper to dry my hands.

"He's adequate enough. But he thought it would be best for me to come and collect you." TC's eyes kept roaming as the corner of his lips lifted. "Apparently, you have a fighting side."

"Is that what you want to see? Me fighting over you with one of your sluts?" I propped a hand on my hip when he stalked forward.

"You don't have to fight for me, temptress. You already have me. Don't you see that? Did my confession in the shower not tell you that?" TC backed me into the wall. The cold tiles made goosebumps race down my skin.

"TC, you know once the newness of this wears off that you won't want me like this anymore." My hands went to his chest to try to keep him away. I didn't think that he was thinking straight with the whiskey in his system. "TC, I think it's time to go home."

"Yes, it is. Because I'm going to take you against every wall there, and then you're going to be on your knees while you suck my cock like a good girl."

Chapter Twenty

TC

The buzz that I was feeling wasn't from the liquor that I had consumed tonight. It was Aurora and that sinful dress she had on. Those pull-me curls in her hair and when she looked at me with those fuck me grey eyes. Damn it was a whole other ball game.

I didn't know if I would be able to wait to take her until we got home. With the way she stared at me, it took everything in me to keep from locking the women's bathroom door and fucking her again. But with everything else going on, I figured I'd curb my appetite until we were safely home.

She was waiting for me to do something. Her mouth opened slightly as she panted, and her hands kept our bodies connected ever so lightly. Mmm. Bringing my finger up to her chin, I lifted it a little more.

It was her eyes that had me from the start. From the time I saw her in that suit store all those years ago. They drew me to her like a moth to a flame.

I walked into that uppity little suit store with Laura and Emi. My life changed for the second time that week when I locked eyes with that grey-eyed beauty.

She had blushed, making her whole face turn a gorgeous shade of pink. I didn't even listen to what Laura had been saying. Hell,

I didn't even know she was talking to Aurora's mom until Emi elbowed me in the ribs.

"Tom, I was trying to introduce you to Aurora and her mother, Mrs. Emerson. They are very close friends of ours."

I stuck out my hand to shake hers, and when that soft hand slid into mine, I almost groaned. I had never felt skin that soft before, and I had to wonder what she thought of mine. Was it rough? Hard? Scratchy? I didn't know because I had never worried about it before.

"TC people call me TC"

Aurora giggled before she introduced herself.

My heart hammered against my chest wall as I stared at her. When they left, I glanced over to the windows and tracked her across the road. Her chocolate-brown hair was down almost to her ass. I finally looked at my reflection in the glass and shuddered.

How could she even find me attractive like this? My hair was down to my shoulders, and I looked boney. Nothing like she was used to seeing, I'm sure. But for some reason she was flirting with me.

Aurora was used to my hard, punishing kisses that left her gasping for air. But this one. This one needed to be different. She knew deep down that she was mine, even though she kept saying that I would get bored of her.

Fuck, I think the night she moaned my name was when I subconsciously knew. I was never going to let her go, and anyone who thought they could take her from me would never see the light of day again.

Those plush soft lips against mine as I kissed her, enticing me to take more of her. I wanted to tease her as I pressed my tongue to her lips, and they opened to allow me in.

I had never wanted to taste someone like this. The softness of her caress on my face did shit to me that no other woman's touch had.

"We need to leave; I need you."

"Mmmm." Aurora's body squirmed in front me. As much as I wanted to take her here in this bathroom, I needed her at home.

Taking her by the hand, I took one last look into her dilated eyes before leading her out of the bathroom. Sam and Jake were two steps behind us as we made our way to the front door.

People were leaving anyway, and I wanted to get Aurora away from Marcus' gang members. Glancing around, I didn't see my sister or Drake. But my sister's bodyguard wasn't around either. My father and mother were still talking with the DeLucas and Emersons—they would be there for a while.

Heading out the door, I sent Sam to get the car. I didn't trust that all the valets were actual people who worked for the event. Nick could've planted a bomb if he wanted, and I knew Sam would check the car before bringing it around.

I glanced over to my right when someone bumped into me. Nick was coming toward me when Jake put himself between us. My old gang member smirked before he crossed his arms. "Damn, I knew you were all smoke. Now you have a security blanket. You never had the balls to be with us for life."

"Nick, you know all the shit you are saying is bullshit," I countered as I held Aurora behind me. Her hand wrapped in my jacket.

"Then why don't you do something, pussy? Don't want to scare the slut behind you?" The contempt in his tone pissed me off, along with him calling Aurora a slut.

If we weren't in the middle of downtown and around some of my clients, I would've already put a bullet in between his brown eyes. My left-hand itched to reach up and pull the Glock from underneath my jacket.

When the time came, he would be gone. I pulled open my jacket—just enough for him to see the concealed weapon in its holster. He glanced down and then back up to me, and I momentarily saw the fear in his eyes.

"If I see you or any of the others in that gang in a dark alley. You won't come back out," I snarled as Sam brought the car up to the curb. Jake took Aurora from me, and I stalked forward backing Nick against one of the columns. "You can let Marcus know if he tries to do anything to anybody in my family, no one will find his body."

The shiver that ran through Nick's body excited me. I shoulder-barged him as I went down to the car and stepped in. Jake snapped the door closed and got in the passenger seat up front.

It had been years since I had allowed my brain to fall into that type of darkness, but it felt good. I didn't know if I should allow that to happen again. But if any of them tried anything, I'd make good on my promise.

"TC, was that man from your past?"

Aurora's voice brought me out of the darkness that I was spiraling down. Her grey eyes held the fear I knew I would see if I showed her my past self.

"Yes, he is. But don't worry about him. Or the other one. I won't let them hurt you, and if they do then it will be the last thing they do." I grabbed her hand and brought it to my lips. Our eyes connected, and I couldn't help but take her lips with mine.

The way her lips felt on mine as my hand slid into her hair at the nape of her neck made me hard. Her hand slipped into my lap, playing with my cock inside of my slacks. Using my other hand, I trailed it up her thigh and pulled the dress up around her hips while I coaxed her into my lap.

Jake pulled the curtain between the front and back seats. It would hide Aurora, but not her sounds of pleasure. Aurora slipped her tongue in my mouth as she ground her naked pussy onto my lap. The sweet taste of the wine that she had been drinking assaulted my tastebuds. The soft vibrations of her moans made me groan as I bucked against her.

Aurora's hands went to my belt and then the button of my pants. Yanking them open, she took hold of my thick cock. I hissed while her hand stroked me from tip to base. She ran her soft fingers over my piercings. I needed to be inside her.

"Stop playing, temptress, and slip that beautiful wet pussy over my cock." I grabbed hold of her hair, pulling it back and making her arch her back.

She moaned as she gripped my cock tighter. "You forget there is something blocking us."

"There won't be much longer." I chuckled, and I took hold of the string and yanked it out.

Guiding Aurora over me, there was no way I could keep the groan from escaping my lips. Shit! She always felt amazing wrapped around my cock. I held her tight in the arch as she drove her cunt down the length of my dick.

"Fuck! Aurora, what are you doing to me?" I groaned as a soft whimper left her lips.

She had never ridden me the entire time we had been married. I used my other hand to pull the top of the dress down letting her tits out. They were beautiful and natural with slightly darker nipples peeking through.

Letting go of her hair, I covered her nipple with my mouth sucking and nipping it. Aurora moaned out loud and I continued my assault on the one. My hands on her hips guided her deeper and harder against me.

"TC! You're going to make me come!"

I came up from her breast with a grin. She was so wet that the squelch our bodies made as we ground together filled the car. "That's my goal, temptress. If you keep using that cunt of yours to clamp down around me, I won't last much longer myself."

The look she gave me would have done me in if I had let her continue to control the pace. Reaching around her I flipped us on the backseat while loosening my tie. I wrapped her hands in the silk and tightened it around her wrists.

I tied the other end to the door and glanced down. Aurora's pupils almost eclipsed her irises, and she was panting. Fuck, she was beautiful!

Taking my time, I slowed the pace. Aurora whimpered as she tried to meet me. To take me in deeper. She arched off the seat while pulling on the tie.

"TC, I want to come!"

"I know you do, temptress. But I'm in control now, and I don't think I'm going to let you just yet."

Aurora groaned, and I continued my lazy pace—getting her worked up because once we got on that elevator and into the penthouse the entire complex was going to hear her.

At this slow speed, it took all I had not to bust a nut. I hated getting off before her. I wanted her to get her pleasure first.

The car came to a stop, and the blush crept up her cheeks. She was clearly anxious that Jake and Sam were going to open the door and see the best of her. Their doors opened, and Jake knocked on the back window. He knew me all too well.

"One moment, Jake." I pulled out of her and undid the tie before putting my bloody cock back in my slacks.

Aurora quickly sat up and readjusted her dress. Her hair was disheveled, and her makeup was smudged. I pulled her to me and kissed her, smearing her lipstick even more.

I opened the door and held out my hand for Aurora. She slipped her hand in mine and stepped out. I allowed her to walk a couple of steps in front of me before pulling her into my arms and putting her over my shoulder.

"TC!"

"Yes, temptress?" Aurora's dress hung between her thighs, showing off the back of her tanned legs. Her hands were at the small of my back as she attempted to hold herself up.

One of the other tenants walked past us and shook her head. She was a bitch anyway. I pressed the call button for the elevator and waited as Aurora squirmed on my shoulder.

"Look, you're showing everything I have to anyone walking by. Please, just let me down!" Aurora pleaded as the doors opened, and Jake shook his head when he entered the elevator with us.

"Jake doesn't look, and Sam won't ever look at you— he's your bodyguard. As far as any of the old fuckers that live here in this building, they can look. But if they think they can touch what is mine then they will have a hand missing," I answered her before smacking her on the ass. The sound of my hand connecting with her flesh echoed in the elevator.

She moaned with it, making me spank her again. Each one had my cock throbbing in my slacks. Damn, I needed her in my room, and on her knees. She was about to know what I was capable of in the bedroom.

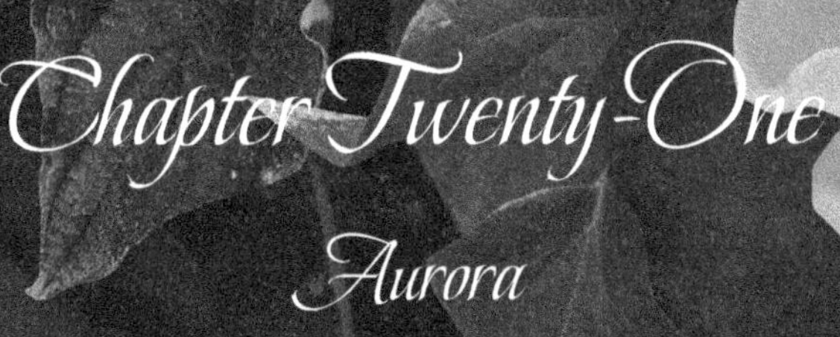

Chapter Twenty-One

Aurora

TC carried me past Sam and to his room. I was confident that what he had uttered wasn't a threat but a promise. The blood from my period was soaking into my dress, but TC didn't care as he continued his steady pace. The door opened, and I knew that he had us in his room.

Placing me on my feet, his hands pushed the shoulders of the dress off, allowing my breasts to show. TC's pupils were so dilated I couldn't tell where the blues of his eyes were. His hands followed my curves along with his eyes. I glanced down and realized that he hadn't buckled his belt or buttoned up. The only thing that was up was the zipper.

"TC, let's go to the shower?" I was already a mess, and there was no doubt that he was too.

"Is that where you want me to take you?"

I nodded, and he shed his shirt and jacket to the floor. The thud of the gun startled me as it hit the wooden floor. I didn't think I could ever get used to a gun being around me.

"Don't worry, temptress. The safety is on." TC grabbed the dress and jerked it the rest of the way down. The groan as he allowed his eyes to roam my naked body once more caused goosebumps to erupt down my body. "I didn't notice in the other shower, but did you shave for me?"

Dammit, Chloe! I was hoping that he wouldn't notice. She had been adamant that I needed to shave, and that he would love it. Hell, I didn't even know why I had listened to her. I couldn't let my emotions get the better of me.

"Maybe."

The growl that came from him reminded me of a feral animal. He pulled me up into his arms and walked us to the bathroom. I had never been in his shower before. Last night was the first time I had ever been in his room. I wrapped my arms around his neck and pulled myself close to him. His mouth landed on my neck, and his teeth nipped the side he was kissing.

I couldn't help the moan that slipped from between my lips. He shouldered the bathroom door open and sat me on the counter. The cold tile woke me up more as TC dropped the pants and his boxer briefs.

He was already hard, and the steel piercings reflected the fluorescent light from the bathroom. His cock was already stained with my blood. He turned on the shower, adjusting the temperature before turning back to me.

His chest was covered in tattoos but the three that I really noticed were two skulls on his pecs with devil horns with a dagger running up his sternum. The hilt curved in on itself towards the blade, stones adorned the hilt. It was beautiful and dangerous all at once. TC was a bad boy in a suit. He was something I had said I would stay away from. But our parents had other plans. When I first saw him in the suit store, I was intrigued.

When Laura walked in with Emi, I was excited. My family and hers were more family than friends. My mother had gone to school with her mom, and the same with my dad. But when he walked in behind them with the bodyguard behind him, my heart sped up.

He was like no boy I had ever seen. His dirty blond hair was down to his shoulders, hiding part of his face. But those blue eyes made me want to gravitate to him. After I was able to pull myself back to what was going on, I realized that my mother was introducing me to him.

"T.C,. they call me TC" His hand shot out, and I giggled as I slipped my hand in his. I couldn't help but wonder why I was being so girly.

"Aurora." His hand was calloused. Something else that I wasn't used to when shaking a man's hand. But it was warm, and it caused goosebumps to race up my arm.

I barely caught the invitation to his introduction party, which was exciting because I could actually get to know him before school. He was going to be attending Oceanside with me. My mother said her goodbyes to Laura, and I grinned at him as I left the store.

This was a good way to ask for a new dress for the party. The windows to the suit store were dark on the outside—keeping people from being able to see in from the outside. This was the only store that carried the private school's uniform, so only the kids from Oceanside had this designer's clothing.

"Aurora, we will need to get a dress for the upcoming party."

"Yes, Mother." I smiled and pulled out my phone to text Chloe and Elizabeth. They had been my friends since grade school and had been through all the heartache that was Dakota. Now, I was hoping to be friends with the Churchhill's new son.

"What are you thinking about, temptress?" His breath fanned over my face as he ran kisses along my jaw.

I shook my head to his question. But what really ran through my mind was that damn party. Would this have gone differently if he hadn't met Morgan first? Would this have been easier to deal with? I mean there were some marriages that were like this and they turned out fine.

"There has to be something going on. Are you thinking about me inside you making you come against the tile shower?" Fuck if he continued to talk to me like this I'd be coming on this counter.

He grabbed me up by my ass and took me inside the shower. The spray came from the ceiling, melting away the curls in my hair. TC's lips were attached to mine as our tongues fought with each other. My nails dug into his shoulders, and he entered me to the hilt.

"Fuck, Aurora!"

My legs wrapped around his waist as he plundered my pussy. It was like he was claiming me with each thrust. I was most definitely going to be sore after this.

"TC! I'm coming! Right there, don't stop!" There was no stopping the orgasm that seized my body. He continued his assault on me as he allowed me to ride out my high. TC came right after I did, his grunts and groans making me ready for the next round.

"Aurora," TC panted my name before he crashed his lips back on mine. This was the most he had kissed me since we were married.

He put me down, and the shower washed the blood from his front. He grabbed a loofah, adding body wash to it as he ran it across my body. When he reached my core, his eyes held mine while he washed it clean. I couldn't help the whimper that escaped me when his finger brushed along my entrance.

I rinsed off and stepped back out of the water to allow him to get under the spray. I started out of the door when his hand wrapped around my elbow.

"Where are you going?" Water ran down his face and his body as he brought me back into the shower with him.

"I need to dry off and go to bed." My hands brushed over his pierced nipples as his left hand went into my wet hair. "TC."

"Yes, temptress?" His lips brushed against mine as he spoke. "I don't think you need to be in your bed tonight. I haven't finished with you yet."

It was a good thing that I was getting the shot. Because as much as he came inside of me, there would be no doubt that I would be pregnant when I wasn't on my period. Luckily, next week would be my appointment to get my next one.

"I still need a tampon. TC, are you not tired?" I tried to get him to let me go, but the way his lips barely caressed mine sent shivers down my spine.

"I'm never tired if I can fuck you." Sighing, I pushed at his chest, and he let me go.

Stepping out of the steamy shower, I grabbed a fluffy grey towel and wrapped it around my body. I took another and used it to wrap around my hair. TC turned off the water and came out as I was leaving the bathroom.

I couldn't stay in his room tonight. He had kept me in here last night, but it couldn't happen again. TC was heading out of the bathroom as I snapped his door shut. My heart was hammering, but I still walked toward my room.

Heading over to my dresser, I pulled out some panties and a tank top. I turned to go to my bathroom when I ran into TC

"Temptress, all you had to say was that you wanted me in here with you. You don't have to run." He leaned on the door frame with a smirk on his face. His towel hung low over his hips. Droplets of water still clung to him, showing off the line of hair leading to his cock, which was already hard underneath.

"It's not that. I need tonight to myself. Okay?" As much as I wanted to lay in his arms, I needed to think about what had happened. Between the sex in the shower and the men that were from his past. And then the sex in the car—I was being smothered.

"Okay." He came up to me, and I thought for sure that he was going to throw me over his shoulder and take me back to his room. It's not like I would have fought him because part of me wanted him to do that. To become a caveman and show me that he actually wanted me. TC kissed the top of my head and exited my room.

I slid down my wall with a sigh. My head lay on my knees as I quietly sobbed for a few moments before getting back to my feet and heading to my bathroom to get a tampon. My mind was so jumbled.

I was sitting at the island the following morning drinking my tea, Gwen came in to start breakfast. She smiled at me as she pulled out the pans to start. I glanced over my shoulder at TC's door and turned back to my tea.

"He had a meeting to get to this morning, Aurora."

"Huh?" I never used this word before when I replied to someone. Gwen chuckled and then turned to me as she wiped her hands on her apron.

"He's not here. Mr. Churchhill left early this morning for his meeting." Gwen answered me again, a soft grin on her lips.

"Oh. Okay." I swirled my tea in the cup with my spoon, thinking how things were between us.

"What would you like this morning?" Gwen asked me as she turned back around to go to the fridge.

"French toast?" I glanced up at her, and she smiled at me over her shoulder.

"You got it. It's a beautiful morning, why don't you go out on the balcony?"

"Yeah, I think I will." I picked up my tea and left her in the kitchen.

I went to one of the other chairs. The lounge chair was still too fresh in my mind. I stared out over the buildings as I watched the birds go about their routines.

The clouds were sporadic, allowing the sun to shine through. Giving the world light on this side of the planet. Why couldn't things have been different?

What was I going to do? There was a word for this right? For this feeling I had for my husband. I don't think I'd call it love. Maybe lust? It must be lust because that's all it was for him. Because he would never be able to reciprocate anything else.

Chapter Twenty-Two

TC

Leaving Aurora in her room last night was hard. Something was wrong, and it wasn't just the alcohol telling me that it was. I had never second-guessed myself, and it felt weird that I was.

I sat at the head of the table drumming my fingers on the wooden surface. While the Chief Financial Officer spoke on how much money we were bringing in versus how much we were spending. Considering we were making billions on international shipments, he didn't have much to bitch about how much the employees were getting paid.

"I vote that we do not give a raise this year."

I glanced up from my hand and stared at him for a moment before turning my attention to the other board members. They were sweating bullets, given that each one of them thought that they could outplay me since I had been given this position.

"And why is that, Frank?" His eyes widened as did the other board member's eyes around the table.

"Well, we are overspending in that area."

I nodded my head, and he seemed to relax at that motion. "So then, if you want to cut wages, why don't I cut yours instead? You have two incomes, right?"

"Mr. Churchhill, sir. I have a family too."

"So do the people you want to withhold a raise for. My father has always treated every employee here like family, and that is what I intend to continue to do." I stood making the CFO sit as I walked around the table. Drake had a shit-eating grin on his face.

"Just because I'm the owner and CEO does not mean that I know nothing about the financial side of this company. I know that we have billions in the savings account that is used for wages. I also know that what you are telling me about the outgoing money is bullshit. I didn't go to school to have you and anyone else run all over me." I came up behind Frank and patted his shoulders. Getting down to his level, I looked around the table. My icy blue eyes stared into each man's eyes to get my point across. "So, when you want to bring up not giving the employees raises like they have been given every year, just remember that I can cut yours in half to let you see how they live."

Frank nodded and then pulled all his papers together. Like a lot of the men here, he thought that because I was young and a little inexperienced, I wouldn't know their schemes. But what they didn't know was that I had experience—only in a totally different way.

"This meeting is adjourned. Have a wonderful day, gentleman," I announced and walked over to the big window. Men stood from their seats as I stood gazing out over LA.

Somewhere down there, Marcus was planning something. But at this moment, I couldn't allow it to mess with my mind. Aurora, on the other hand, she was my main concern right now.

"You really had it in for him today, bud." Drake came up and stood beside me with his hands in his pockets. There was tension radiating from him.

"What's up? Is there something on your mind?" I turned to him and noticed the grin before it faded as he turned to me.

"What do you think about Emi dating?"

"She's old enough to date. But he better not hurt her 'cause I'll put him in an unmarked grave if he does." I didn't know where Drake was coming from, but he better watch himself. "Is she dating someone?"

He shrugged before punching me in the arm. "You know I'm right there with you."

"I'm going to head out early. Are you good here?" I turned to my best friend. He wasn't something I had ever thought I'd have in my life. Just like I didn't think my feelings toward Aurora would change.

But she was changing them. And I didn't know if that was going to fuck me over or help me. The alcohol I had I drunk at the Gala had me off my game— I had showed the gang too much.

"You know I have you, man. I saw you with the wife. You looked good together. Looks like I'll finally have my way with the ladies."

"Go for it, but make sure you keep your eyes open. The people from my past are watching you too." I clapped him on his shoulder and left him in the boardroom.

The look in Aurora's eyes still haunted me from last night. I needed to know she was okay. Opening up the door to my office, I went to my desk and sat down for a moment.

I pulled out my phone and messaged Sam.

When Jake and I entered the penthouse, Aurora was on the balcony still, and Sam was standing just beside her watching. Loosening my tie, I made my way to her. My steps sure and precise on the hardwood floor.

Sam nodded when he saw me and headed back in. Aurora never lifted her gaze from the city. Sitting down on the lounge chair, I waited for her to acknowledge me.

"Is there something wrong, Aurora?" I asked her after she didn't turn to me.

When she turned her gaze to mine, her grey eyes were dimmer than they had been. I also didn't miss the tears in her eyes that had yet to fall. "Can you not talk to me?"

"What's to talk about, TC?" She was calm, a little too calm for my liking. I noticed that her eyes went to my right. To where the gun was holstered between my body and arm.

"Is it the gun? Is that what all this is?" I stood in front of her making her look up at me. God damn, how I loved this position. She would look even better with her lips around my cock.

"No, TC It's not the gun. I mean it's a little bit about the gun, but that's not everything. Before you went to live with the Churchhills, you were someone else. But you haven't shared that with me, and you tell me to trust you about these people who you are carrying *that* around for." Aurora's voice quivered as she held my gaze. "Sam is following me around, which I haven't ever had before. And what is this?" She motioned between us just as the first tears started to fall. I pulled her to her feet, cupping her face with my hands, making her keep her eyes on me.

"Aurora, I told you about the gun. Me and it are the last line of defense if something happens to Jake and Sam. These people it is for are bad people, and if Sam isn't with you then they would hurt you to get to me."

"I don't understand. Why? I'm nothing to you. Everything that happened at the Gala was for the parents and the people there. We were a united front." The look of desperation on her face mixed with something else I couldn't pinpoint at the moment. Fuck, why couldn't things like this be easy? Why did I get so close to her when this should have been just an arrangement? Because it was those grey fucking eyes and that voice as she moaned my name.

"Is that what you think? Was my confession in the shower not enough? Woman I've never kissed anyone while not fucking them, and even then, it was minimal. I've never been bare with anyone but you. What else do you want me to say?" I ran my hand through my hair. She was getting under my skin.

What else did she need?

"TC, your actions are all the same. You sleep with a woman, and then get bored of her and go on to the next one. I can't allow you to do this to me anymore." Her voice trembled as she stood and brushed past me.

"What am I doing to you?" I asked her as she continued a few steps forward.

I grabbed her arm and pulled her to me. Crashing my lips to hers, she melted into me before she put her hand on my chest and pushed away. Just like in the shower. She wanted this, but she was keeping her distance. What else did I have to do to make her realize my affection for her?

Her hand came up to her lips, and she turned and left me on the balcony. Picking up the glass on the table, I threw it across the balcony shattering it against the wall. God damnit!

I glanced over my shoulder and spotted Gwen. She had her arms crossed over her chest and tapped her foot. Taking a deep breath, I tried to fix my hair before I walked in.

What did she want from me? I'd shown her more attention than I had ever shown another woman. What more could I do to show her I couldn't go on without her?

"TC, you need to do something or you're going to lose that woman. And it won't be because of that gang of yours in your past." Gwen hit me with the wooden spoon just like she always did when I did something she didn't like.

"I'm trying. I don't understand what you or she wants from me! Damn it!"

Instead of heading to her room like I was going to, I went into mine and slammed the door. I know real grown up, right?

I lay on my bed tossing and turning again. Just like the other night, I fucking needed Aurora right here with me. Getting up, I headed for my door and then the kitchen.

A strong drink was calling my name, and even then, I didn't know whether I'd be able to sleep. I walked into the kitchen and spotted Aurora sitting at the table. Her gaze went down before landing back to her glass.

"Can't sleep?" I asked her, pouring a glass of my favorite whiskey.

"Apparently, and apparently, you can't either."

"We need to talk." I placed the bottle onto the counter beside me while leaning against the marble top.

"I have nothing to say to you." Aurora didn't even glance up from the paper she was writing on.

"Well, I think you do. You have an issue, and as a couple, we need to talk about these things." I pushed off the counter and went to the table she was sitting at. "What are you writing?"

She glanced up at me as I came around behind her. Aurora wasn't writing anything other than doodling on the lined paper. I took the pen from her, along with the paper, causing her to turn her grey eyes completely to me as I took a step away from her.

She came up to me and reached up to grab the paper from my hand. I didn't miss the fact that she was still wearing my shirt from the first time I had come into her room and rocked her world. Bringing my face to hers, she continued to try to get the paper while I kissed her, which made her freeze. I broke the kiss, and she backed away from me.

The shirt covered her, but I knew she wasn't wearing panties. That was her thing; she didn't like to wear anything in bed. Hell, I didn't even want her in the shirt. Placing the paper and pen on the island, I stalked up to her, pinning her against the wall.

"TC, you really need to stop." Aurora's hands went to my bare chest. Her palms landed on my nipples, and she looked up at me.

"What am I doing, temptress? I just came in here to get a drink, and then I found you here. In my shirt, no less, and no panties," I answered her as I ran kisses down her jawline and neck. The shiver from her excited me even further, making me harder with the thought of her in nothing but this shirt. Her pert nipples grazed my upper abs, a tell-tale sign that she was just as excited about me being this close to her.

"You don't know if I have panties on or not." Her voice came out in a rush, so I ran my hands down her body and to her naked ass cheeks. I lifted her up and pressed her harder into the wall.

"Oh, temptress. You know I know you don't have any on." I wanted to sink my cock into her and fuck her so hard that she wouldn't be able to walk tomorrow.

Chapter Twenty-Three

Aurora

Waking up in TC's arms wasn't the plan when he picked me up and carried me back to his room. If anything, I just wanted to feel him one last time. To think that we were just an ordinary couple.

When it came to him, there was nothing stopping him from taking what he wanted. And I wasn't going to stop him. But I needed time away from him, so I could think without him being in my face.

I couldn't let him continue to use me as he saw fit when he didn't have the same feelings I had. This wasn't supposed to happen—me falling in love with him. But those teenage feelings I had for him didn't seem to understand that what he did and what he actually felt were two different things.

Taking his arm, I moved it away from me and got out of bed. As I stood, TC groaned and turned onto his back. My heart hammered in my chest while I stood there waiting for his soft breathing to regulate again. I glanced around to try to find the shirt I had been wearing, only to not be able to find it.

My bags were packed, and I had been sitting at the kitchen table trying to write him a letter explaining that I wasn't going to be staying here. But every time I tried, it sounded awful. So, he wouldn't be getting a note. I would have Orson return here to let him know that I needed time away.

I didn't know how mad he would be, but he would have to understand. He didn't want this, even if I was starting to fall for his charm. Slipping out of the room, I cracked the door and padded my way back to my room.

It was a good thing that no one was here. Otherwise, they'd be seeing me naked. Damn him and throwing our clothes everywhere as he pulled them off. I liked that shirt. Pulling out some shorts and a tank top, I found my phone and texted Orson.

Orson answered me a few minutes later. Grabbing my bags, I snuck my way through the penthouse and into the elevator. The ding caused my heart to race, and I started to sweat. I had forgotten about the sound.

The doors opened, and I hurried forward with my bags. I pressed the parking garage button. The sound of the elevator doors clanging shut was music to my ears as the box took me to the waiting car below.

My mind started to argue with me that I should just go back and get in bed with TC and try to talk to him. But then the other part of me was urging me not to listen. I was just going to get hurt in the long run.

Finally, I made it to the garage, Orson was there to get my bags. His smile didn't reach his eyes, and I had a feeling that he was hoping that we would fall in love with each other. What he didn't understand was that I was the only one falling, and that TC was just using me for sex.

He took my luggage, put it in the back of the car, and opened the door to allow me to get in. I took a deep breath and slid into the backseat.

Orson got in the driver's seat and took me away from TC. My heart broke the further away we drove, but I needed to clear my head, and the only way I could do that was to be away from him.

"Miss Aurora, are you sure we don't need to have Sam with you?" Orson's voice brought me out of my thoughts, and I looked up into his gaze in the rearview mirror.

"No, I'll be fine on my own." I didn't miss the sigh from Orson before I moved my gaze to the window to my left. If I didn't tell anyone where I was going, then I wouldn't need to have a bodyguard to protect me from the men that TC was entangled with. At least that's what I believed, and if Sam was with me. TC would have a way of finding me. Orson could tell him if he wanted to, but with as long as he had been with our family, I hoped that he wouldn't.

We drove through the city to Elizabeth's home. I had initially wanted to go to my parents, but they loved TC so much I think they would talk me into going back to him sooner than I needed to. Or really wanted to. I mean if it were up to my heart, I wouldn't have left.

The bright streetlights flashed by as Orson continued down the LA streets. If this had been the bad part of town, I would have probably been afraid without TC or Sam. Sighing, I couldn't help wanting to get to Elizabeth's home and take a load off my mind.

Orson pulled up to the gate and punched in the number to open the metal barrier that kept me from getting to one of my best friends. Stopping at the front steps, Orson got out and opened my door before getting my bags from the trunk. Elizabeth rushed out of the house and pulled me into a hug.

"Thank you so much for letting me stay. I just need some time." I hugged her back, but I didn't feel the weight that I was expecting to lift with being with her.

"Girl, you know that you or Chloe are welcome here anytime for however long you need." She pulled away, and we strolled into the house.

Orson brought in my bags and set them in the foyer. Elizabeth stopped, turning to my driver with a smile. "I'll get the staff onto that Orson. Thank you."

Orson looked over at me and nodded. The pleading in his eyes as he stood there told me he was trying to get me to return with him. I couldn't until I knew that my mind and my heart were in the same rhythm. "Please take care of him, Orson."

The older gentleman sighed and then bowed before he turned and left out of the front doors. I didn't like that he was upset, but I needed some time away.

Staying with Elizabeth was just what I needed to be able to clear my head, but I still couldn't figure out whether I could live with all the secrets that TC kept from me. If he would just be honest with me, that was all I wanted, but he just continued to keep me in the dark, and it wasn't like I was more than an easy fuck. He had plenty of women who easily gave themselves to him and I didn't need to be that.

I'm sure that with me gone for these few days that he had gone back to fucking those women. I sat looking into the mirror while I got ready for the day. We were going to meet up with Chloe and go to the movies. I was still making sure not to go around by myself.

Chloe was blabbering about some guy that she had met the other day. I still found it funny that she was talking about a man after she had just gotten out of a relationship with another one. She wasn't one who I would peg to be married to anyone. But here she was, talking about how in love she already was.

"Chloe, are you ever going to settle down? I mean hell you've been in love with every man that you've dated." Elizabeth slapped her arm as she pulled into the parking lot.

I opened the Jeep's door and got out. Chloe and Elizabeth exited the vehicle still arguing about Chloe's love life. They made me smile just like they had done when we were girls. Shaking my head, I continued in front of them to the movie theater.

They continued to argue in front of the cashier, who was trying to get their attention to see their tickets. I pressed through and showed the woman on the other side of the counter my phone. She motioned us forward, and I went up to the food counter to get a drink. My grandmother had brought me to the movies so much that I started to hate popcorn. While I sipped on my large drink, Chloe and Elizabeth ordered popcorn and drinks. As much as I loved that I was finally getting to see this movie, I was concerned that it would be night by the time it ended.

Damn, TC and his cautiousness. I didn't think I would ever be my carefree self again. Turning with my friends, we headed into the theater and into our seats. Something about this just didn't seem right. I had made the decision to leave to clear my head, but something was out of the ordinary tonight.

I sat in the darkness of the theater watching a sappy love story because Chloe had been in her feelings when she got the tickets. Sipping on the extra-large drink, cut the movie short for me. I got up and went into the bathroom. Well, part of it was the need to use the bathroom; the other part was I had to get out of that movie. It was bringing back all the feelings I had bottled up for TC.

Why did my heart have to start this whenever I see a movie or a couple walking down the road? This whole thing had been a mistake in doing this. I knew that now but there was no way that TC would take me back after I left. He didn't have any feelings for me. If he did then he would have made an effort to find me.

Standing there in the bathroom, I stared at the reflection that gazed back at me. I didn't think that I would ever see this person again. The woman with the grey eyes and chocolate hair stared back at me with a deadness in her eyes again. Why was she back? I left TC to get my joy back, but apparently, I hadn't found it.

I turned on the water and cupped my hands to splash my face, trying to get myself together. Why did all of it have to be like this? Why couldn't it have been what we had said in that drawing room? The way we hashed it out that night at our betrothal. None of this uncertainty would have happened. We would have been fine if how things had stayed as they were supposed to.

As I gazed into the mirror one last time, I spotted a masked person behind me. I gasped loudly, but couldn't get the scream out that was stuck in my throat. Turning from the mirror, I faced the man who stood silently behind me. My mind raced as I tried to figure out a way to get out of this bathroom, but he was between me and my escape.

"What do you want?" My voice came out more commanding than I thought it would. However, the man didn't flinch.

His eyes stayed on me as mine continued to look around. Desperate to find something to help me. My phone was in my pocket, but there was no way I could get to it and make a call before he reached me. The only thing I could do was turn it on and hope that someone would be able to find it.

He never answered me before he rushed me.

I woke up the next morning and reached over. My hand landed on the cold sheets that Aurora had been on last night. Sitting up, I looked around the room, trying to listen for the shower to be running. Everything was quiet though, and I stood to find my boxer briefs. I pulled them up and glanced around again. "Aurora?"

Walking out of the bedroom, I spotted Gwen. She stood in the doorway facing the inside of the kitchen. It wasn't something she normally did. I made my way up to her and spotted Orson sitting at the kitchen table that Aurora had been sitting last night.

"What's going on? Anyone seen Aurora?" I glanced between them both, and Orson started to shake. His hands folded in front of him turning whiter than normal.

"Aurora left earlier this morning. She made me take her away. Said that she needed to figure things out." The sob that came from Orson beside me confused me more.

Why did she leave? Did she not know how much danger she was in now? Of course not. Because I hadn't told her what she was in danger from. Just that she was in danger from some men from my past. Now, she was out of my protection. She didn't even take Sam with her.

"Where did she go?" Knowing her, she told Orson not to tell me. Aurora wouldn't just leave and then allow him to tell me where she went.

Orson glanced up at me and shook his head. Just like her to make him keep his mouth shut. I leaned against the wall and crashed the back of my head into the wall. "FUCK!"

Gwen flinched and went to the oven. I left them both in the kitchen, walking through the house to figure out how to find my wife. If she was found by Marcus and his gang, she wouldn't last long. Heading to my bedroom, I found my phone and messaged Sam and Jake.

> I need you in my office in the next twenty minutes.

> Sam: Yes, boss.

> Jake: Be there before then.

I got dressed and went to my office. There wasn't much time to figure out where she was and to get Sam over to her or at least close to her. Then, I could get her back and bring her home. I couldn't allow Marcus and the gang to get to her. If they did there was no telling what they would do to her or would make me do with her in their possession.

A knock came upon the door before Jake entered with Sam following him. Jake came up to the desk and sat, while Sam sat in the other chair. I stared between them both before speaking to them both.

"We have a problem. Aurora has gone. We need to find her before Marcus does."

"How did she leave? Have you tried to track her phone?" Jake sat forward as he pulled out his phone.

"I've tried to call her. It's been turned off." I shook my head, my hand coming up to my face.

"That would be the smart move for her, but we can ping her last known location before she turned it off." Sam began typing on his phone.

They both worked through whatever they had on their phones. It was crazy how much I trusted these two men with my life and those around me. The coldness that had come over my body had my stomach in knots. There was no way I could delay in finding her. I couldn't lose her to them.

"Damn it! She's smart. She turned off her phone before she left here."

"Who took her? She's not just going to jump in a cab." Jake stood, his hand wrapped around his jaw as he thought.

"Orson took her wherever she is. She instructed him to not tell me or anyone her whereabouts." I glanced between the two men, and they nodded.

"Have you checked with her two friends? They may know. What about her parents?"

I shook my head. Aurora wouldn't go to her parents. They would just send her back to me. Now, one of her friends. They would hide her. But what did she tell them? No, they wouldn't care why she was coming to stay.

"Call her friends. See if she is there with them. She wouldn't go to her parents," I answered them, sitting back to try and think of what needed to be done.

They both nodded, and each one called one of Aurora's friends.

The past few days brought me lower than I ever thought I could be. I had never felt this way. Sam and Jake couldn't find Aurora, and her friends weren't much help since they didn't know where she was. I found that to be a little suspicious; they normally knew where she was.

Drake was having to deal with the company, and luckily, my father nor my mother had found out that Aurora was not with me. Sam has been at Chloe's house keeping watch to see if she showed up and was tailing her if she left. Jake had another man watching Elizabeth's home which is proving to be a problem.

Elizabeth hardly went out and when she did it's always in a blacked-out SUV. Jake's man tails them, but whoever is driving was good. He always shook Jake's man off.

"TC, you need to take a shower. You are starting to stink." Jake's voice brought me out of my thoughts.

He had always been very blunt with me, which was probably the reason that I had grown to like him. Jake was promoted to head of my security when I was passed the company, at my request. I didn't want my father's guys, even though they had more experience than Jake. I trusted this man with my life.

"I don't stink that bad. Do you have anything to report?" My eye twitched, which was due to the lack of sleep I'd had over these weeks.

"Nothing yet. sir. I have my phone to intercept her signal when she turns it back on." Jake stared at me. He had that look that he gave me when I was being stubborn. Which was most days. "Sir, with all due respect. You do stink. I suggest you take a shower. Do you think Mrs. Churchhill is going to want to touch you with you looking the way you do?"

I glared at him, but he didn't budge. There was nothing I could really do to the man. He had practically grown up with me, and he knew all my shit. Even when I thought I had him fooled, he would surprise me. Rising from my chair, I grabbed the bottle of my favorite whiskey and stumbled my way to my bedroom.

Jake stepped in front of me and held out his hand. I cocked my head at him before he motioned with his eyes to the bottle in my hand. My eyes followed his, and I noticed that it only had a quarter of the golden liquid left. Jake went to grab it from me when I tipped it back and downed the rest. I normally never drank a whole bottle in a month.

But in the two weeks that she was gone, I had gone through this new bottle. Pushing the glass bottle into Jake's chest, I went into my bedroom. The place was a mess, it wasn't like it used to be. I had tried to find something, anything to tell me where she had gone that first day. But there was nothing.

I walked over the clothes and the broken mess of the room to the shower. When I found Aurora, she would hate the way this place looked. Not like she stayed in here much. I couldn't bring myself to go to her room. There would be no way I would be able to handle the emptiness of that room now.

Standing in the bathroom, my gaze fell on my face in the mirror. I didn't know who he was. He didn't look like the man I was supposed to be. His cheekbones were far too prominent, and his eyes were sunken in. And let's not talk about the bags under his eyes. The blue eyes that stared back at me were no longer mine.

I took in a deep breath and then pulled off my clothes. Jake had been right. I didn't just stink, but I was a fucking mess. This wasn't going to find Aurora. I was going to have to get out there myself and find her. Just like when I went on a hunt for people for Marcus, I was going to have to get back into that person.

The shower really woke me up, and it had me almost back to myself. I stepped out of my room in jeans and a tight-fiting shirt. If I was going to find Aurora, I was going to have to look the part. That meant no suits and flashy cars. I grabbed a jacket and threw it on to hide my gun.

Jake was going to be upset with me, but this was how I was going to find her. If I didn't find her, I wouldn't be able to go on. She was my addiction, and she couldn't even see it. I went into the kitchen and spotted some muffins on the island. Grabbing one, I peeled away the paper surrounding it and took a bite out of it.

I have to admit that it was probably the most amazing muffin I'd had. But that could also be that I had almost starved myself trying to stay awake. Gwen always made amazing muffins. Heading back out of the kitchen, Jake stood by the elevator in jeans and a sweater.

"What do you think you are doing?" I asked as I walked past him to the elevator.

"You know I'm not going to let you go out by yourself. Especially when you are not yet sober." Jake answered me as he stepped into the elevator with me.

Sighing, I pressed the garage button and stepped back to the wall. I was still a little unsteady on my feet, which hadn't happened in a very long time. If Jake was going to be my wingman, that was okay with me.

We sat in a stolen car as I waited for the one man who would be able to tell me everything. Jake sat in the passenger seat, keeping watch with me. I didn't think he would be okay with stealing a car, even one that was on its last legs.

I glanced over at him as he stared down at his phone. He was always checking it to see if Aurora had turned hers on. If this guy didn't show, then he wouldn't today. This guy had a way of being wherever he wanted to be. He had always been like that.

"Who is this person you are looking for? Is he still alive?" I glanced over to Jake. He could be right. There was no telling what happened on these streets on a daily basis. I could be chasing the wrong lead. But it was the only place for me to start.

We waited for most of the day in the car. The more time that we spent in this hot-ass fucking car, I regretted the decision to be here. And that's when I saw him coming out of the alleyway. My hand went to the door when Jake's hand went to my forearm. I turned my gaze to Jake, and he pulled his phone up for me to see it. A green dot flashed on his screen, and my heart raced as I stared at it.

"Did her phone just turn on?"

Chapter Twenty-Five

TC

I glanced over to Jake, and he nodded. Turning my gaze back to the man in front of me, I spotted Nick with him. The greasy little bastard walked around like he owned the place. I was going to need more answers than just that damn phone coming on. I exited the piece-of-shit car and strolled over to where Nick and the other man stood.

Pulling my gun out from its holster, I grabbed Nick's elbow and pressed the barrel of my Glock into his back. Jake was beside me, his hand on the butt of his gun. Nick's body tensed in front of me, and I chuckled. "Look who's scared of a has-been now."

"TC? What the fuck are you doing here?" Nick growled as he struggled to be released from my grasp. I tightened my grip and pulled him closer to me.

"I'm here to get information. And you're going to give it to me." I jerked him away from the other man who I was sitting around waiting for. Steering him to the broken-down car, I gave him to Jake who zip-tied his hands together.

"Haven't seen you in years, boy." I turned to the old man, and he eyed me up and down. He would always call me 'boy' when I came to him for information about people. "You don't look like you just came out of prison. Look too good for that."

"Yeah, I'm surprised they didn't tell you I was dead. Hell, I'm surprised you aren't dead yet. I was hoping to blend in today." I grinned at him, his balding head shining in the sun.

The old man guffawed and slapped his knee. He always had a weird sense of humor. "Naw, boy. You can't just roll up in a beater and then step out in jeans that looks like they haven't been worn and a T-shirt."

"Well, like you said. It's been a while since I've been here. You stay alive, you hear me, old man?" I clapped him on the shoulder a couple of times and made my way back to the shithole of a car and Jake.

I would probably never see this man again in my life. Even though he was on the streets, he was a good man. He was always the person who was easy to talk with. Most nights when I was younger, I'd seek him out just for the stories that he told. I would start to believe that I could be like some of the people he talked about.

Getting back into the car and starting it, I pulled it away from the curb. Nick sat struggling in the back with the zip ties. I took us to one of the old warehouses I now owned on the other side of town. Pulling up to the old building, I got out, pulled the back door open, and grabbed Nick by his elbow.

"Get your hands off me, you fucking traitor. I won't tell you a damn thing!" He tried to pull out of my grip as I walked him in the door to the building. Jake stepped in front of me and opened the metal door.

I pushed Nick into the building, and he stumbled forward landing on his face because his hands were behind his back. "God damn it, TC, you broke my nose!"

"If you don't tell me what I want to hear, you will have more than your nose broken," I growled at him, pulling him up to his feet. He spat blood at my feet as I pushed him further into the warehouse.

Jake walked behind me through the old building in silence. People had told me that I needed to get rid of this place as it was doing nothing but sitting and becoming run-down. I refused since this building had been in my father's family since the beginning of Churchhill Logistics.

"TC, what are you thinking about doing?"

"I'm going to interrogate him. He should know where Marcus has Aurora," I answered as I shoved Nick into the chair. Jake handed me more zip ties, and I tied Nick's ankles to the legs of the chair and then his arms to the spokes on the back of it.

"I'm not gonna tell you shit!" I glanced over at him and noticed the blood was starting to dry on his face from colliding with the concrete floor.

The grin that spread across my face stilled his mumbling. Kneeling down, I got in his face staring back at him, my grin widening. "You see, that's where you are wrong. Marcus didn't tell you what other things I was good at? Did he?"

Fear flashed in his eyes as I slipped further down into the darkness. A darkness that I had kept at bay all these years. If that was the price I had to pay to find Aurora, that was fine with me.

"Jake, I'm sure we passed by some mechanic's tools. Do you think you could grab me a wrench?" I never looked back at my bodyguard. Jake's footsteps left us to find the wrench I had asked for.

Pulling the knife from my shoe, I ran it over Nick's thigh. Slicing through the thin material of his jeans. I tipped the blade deeper into his thigh. Loving the feel and sound of the blade slicing through his skin and muscle.

Nick's scream reverberated off the empty walls, but I didn't let up. I pressed the blade deeper into his flesh. The blade squelched as it sliced through the sinew and muscles as Nick continued to scream. My blade hit the bone, and I twisted the knife. Nick's body went limp, and I pulled the blade out of his thigh. Blood welled up from the wound and into his jeans.

"What have you done?" Jake's voice pulled me out of my thoughts as the blood dripped down the blade. The tip of it must have broken off when I twisted the knife.

"Showing him what he would have to deal with if he doesn't give me the information that I want." I wiped the blood on my jeans and took the wrench from Jake.

"TC, maybe you should take this slower? I mean are you sure about this?" Jake's stoic gaze stared back at me.

"I'm one hundred percent sure about this. And no, I'm not taking it slow with him. If you knew all the things that he has done to women, you wouldn't be saying that," I growled pulling up a chair and sitting in front of Nick. "If you can't stomach it, leave because this man will not be coming out of that chair alive."

"I'm not going to leave you. I took an oath to your father to stay by your side."

I didn't expect him to leave. He wasn't going, and I wasn't going to push him out. Jake stood behind me while I waited for Nick to wake up. It was going to warm my heart to punish him for all those women. I never liked it when Marcus allowed him to do things to the women.

"Ah. There he is." I stood as Nick started to wake up. Jake had put a tourniquet on his leg. I would have just let him bleed out, but Jake had a point. There wouldn't be a way to get information from him if I let him die.

Nick groaned and opened his eyes. His face was ashen as he tried to stare back at me. Using the wrench, I lifted his head. "Did you have a good sleep?"

I waited for him to wake up completely. There was no time for him to pass out again. I needed the information that he had, and I needed it now. "So, this is how this is going to happen. You are going to give me all the information that you have on the whereabouts of my wife."

"She's with Marcus. He is going to make her not so pretty for you. When he was planning to take her, he said he was going to cut her up in little pieces and send them back to you." Nick laughed, but I was sure that it was mostly due to the loss of blood.

"Yeah, and where is he keeping her? And who is he going to get to do the dirty work, huh? You're with me." I plunged the broken-tipped knife into his other leg, and he groaned. I got up from my chair and went over to Jake.

"He has others. Ones that will take her while they do it too. Even if you kill me, your woman won't be far behind me." He laughed as I stalked forward again. If he and Marcus thought that they were going to touch her and then live to tell this, they were sadly mistaken. The rage that filled me when he told me what they had planned for Aurora made the darkness deep inside me surge forward.

Bringing the wrench back, I swung the metal tool across his head. Each time harder than the last. The blood sprayed from his head as I beat him with the wrench all over my face and my shirt. I didn't come back up until I knew that he was dead. It felt good to take his life with my hands. Like I had wanted when I was younger.

"Let's dispose of him and find out how to get a hold of Marcus. That way we can get Aurora back." Jake's hand came to my shoulder and stilled my left arm.

What was left of Nick's head and brains dropped to the floor at his and my feet. It had been a long time since I had let my emotions take over when I was interrogating someone. My heart drummed as I stared down at all the mess I had caused.

I stood there as Jake wrapped Nick's body in a tarp. When he finished, I helped him take him over to the water and to weigh him down with anchors. Making sure the chains held, we put him into the water and watched him sink.

"Time to call Marcus and find out what he wants."

Sitting in the car, I called Marcus from Nick's cellphone. I knew if I wanted to get him to answer quickly, I would need to use this phone. He would want to make me worry about Aurora if I used my phone.

"Nick, it's about time you called me. Where have you been? I need you at the house in thirty minutes." Marcus' voice came from the other end of the phone.

I chuckled to myself before taking a breath in. "Well, I don't think he will be making it to the house. He's gone for a swim."

"TC, I guess you know that I have your pretty little wife. She's been sitting around waiting for you. She's doing just fine without you." He laughed over the phone. It wasn't too convincing. He wasn't sure of himself. Like he always was, he always needed someone beside him to make him more confident.

"Let me just tell you, if you harm one hair on her head. I will put a bullet between your coal-black eyes. Now tell me where I am going to get my wife back?"

Marcus was silent on the phone for a moment, and I gave it to him. He was probably scrambling to figure out what he was going to do. Because he knew that I wasn't a person to be played.

"The warehouse tomorrow, twelve noon."

"I'll see you then. Oh, and Marcus, I wasn't playing when I told you that I would put a bullet between your eyes. She had better be at that warehouse in the shape that you took her in."

Marcus hung up the phone just as Jake got in the car. Starting the old vehicle, I backed it away from the building and pulled out onto the road. Tomorrow was going to be the last day that Marcus was going to breathe oxygen. One way or another.

He had taken what was mine, and now, he was going to pay for touching her. Let alone doing whatever he had done to her since he had taken her.

Chapter Twenty-Six

Aurora

My whole body felt heavy as I tried to open my eyes. When I tried to move my arms, they wouldn't budge and strained my shoulders when I struggled in the restraints. Everything felt fuzzy, and my vision was blurry. Whatever that man gave me put me out, and I mean out.

The cold chilled me to my bones, but I continued to force myself awake. Did they have me in a freezer? If so, I'd end up dying from hypothermia. Shaking my head a little to make myself wake up, I felt a calloused finger briefly touch my cheek, making me stop to try to figure out who it was.

Someone's hand ran down my face, and for a moment, I thought it was TC's. The combination of cigarette smoke and body odor made it easier to realize that the touch was from someone else. Finally prizing my eyes open, I was met with dark black eyes and red hair. Fuck! I remembered this man!

When he smiled, the familiar yellow teeth and atrocious smell assaulted my nose, bringing me back to the day I had seen him on the beach. My heart accelerated when his eyes moved from my face further down. The way his lust-filled eyes stared at me filled me with disgust as I pulled at my arms; struggling to get out of my restraints and putting more pressure on my shoulders.

The burn of the ropes on my wrists made me flinch each time I moved them. I removed my gaze from the maniac in front of me to my surroundings. The walls were concrete blocks and had very little lightning making me think I was in some kind of basement. No wonder my skin prickled. There was no heat in this place at all, and if I was going to try to escape, I would need to know where I was so I could alert someone.

But there were no windows, so the only light in the place was the single fluorescent bulb above me. I didn't know how I was going to be able to even get out of here, much less tell someone where this maniac was holding. Not like TC would care. He only wanted this marriage to be able to keep his company.

"Who are you looking for? He's not here yet." Even his voice disgusted me, making my skin crawl with the way he continued to touch and rub on me. "When TC gets here, I plan on showing him just what happens when he doesn't keep his toys locked up."

"He won't come for me. You kidnapped the wrong person." I sneered at him when I brought my gaze back to his. Whoever this person was, I couldn't understand why someone would want to follow his orders.

"That's what you think. You know he's not the white knight you may think he is. He's not been the man that he is now. He used to kill people; did you know that?" He didn't realize that I had never thought of TC as a white knight even when we were teenagers. He'd always had that darkness and ice behind his eyes when I would catch him looking at something behind me.

"Exactly, so why kidnap someone who he can easily replace? I think you've just dug yourself a hole to fill," I answered him. Ignoring the comment about TC killing people. Did I think he could? Maybe? All I knew was that he came from a bad past, so he could have done what this man was saying, possibly even more. Did I think that he would hurt me? No, but that wasn't because I thought he could love me.

"He will come. I know TC. He and I go way back." He slapped me across my face and walked away up the wooden stairs to my left, leaving my cheek numb. I had never been slapped before by a man or a woman. It took everything in me to keep the tears from streaming down my face. On the landing, he shut the door behind him, turning off the light, plunging me into darkness, tied up and in the dark.

As much as I knew that TC wouldn't come for me, I could only pray that I was wrong, and he would rescue me. Right now, he was my only hope of surviving this. But if he knew I had left, how would he know if I was here? My phone had dropped in the bathroom at the theater; I didn't even know whether it ever turned on.

The numbness in my arms started to run up to my shoulders. My lips were chapped, and my throat was on fire. I was hungry, and I didn't know how long I had been here to even figure out when I had last eaten. My stomach grumbled as I sat there, and my bladder begged to be relieved.

It was dark as I opened my eyes, and it seemed colder than I had noticed before. If he wanted to trade me for whatever he thought he could get from TC, he was doing a bad job of trying to keep me alive to finish the deal. If I was being honest, I didn't think I would ever see my parents, my friends, Orson, or Gwen ever again.

I didn't know what to do as I sat there waiting for whatever to happen to me. The door on the landing opened and a light blazed on. A woman walked down the stairs with what looked like a bag in her hand. From her haggard appearance, I was sure that she was on something.

"Time to eat. Have to make sure the little princess looks okay when her knight comes to rescue her. Make sure she's as fat as she was when we got her." The way her singsong voice got under my skin made me want to gouge her eyes out. And the roll of her eyes pissed me off even more.

She had makeup all over her face, and her long black hair looked as if it hadn't been brushed in weeks. The woman had way too much perfume on if that was what you would call it. It was as if she had taken a bath in it. The knife that she pulled from her waist glinted off the fluorescent light, and she cut the rope that was binding me.

As soon as my hands were free, the blood rushed to my fingers as I massaged them with the other hand. The black-haired woman thrust the bag into my chest. "Well hurry up! I don't have all day!"

I glared at her, but it wasn't like she even noticed as she plopped in a chair close to the stairs. She took out a bottle and poured something white onto her hand. The woman then proceeded to snort whatever it was into her nose.

Shaking my head, I opened up the brown bag and found a few burned fries and a half-eaten sandwich. I went for the fries because there was no way that I was going to eat the sandwich. The fries were cold and so salty that I could hardly choke them down as there was nothing to wash them down.

I stood from the chair and went up to her. She looked up at me with a hazy gaze and appeared to be looking right through me. She was no longer here, let alone this conversation. If I didn't find a bathroom soon, I'm sure I was going to piss myself. "Where's the bathroom?"

She turned and pointed to a five-gallon bucket in the corner. I turned back to her, shocked at what I was going to have to use. My bladder, however, didn't care where we were going to relieve ourselves because it was now screaming at me to go. Heading over to the bucket, I glanced around and saw that there was nothing to wipe myself with.

I remembered seeing some napkins in the bag, so I went over to the bag and grabbed them all. If I knew them, they would have taken the bag away with what was left. Placing the napkins on the milk crate beside me, I relieved myself into the bucket.

"Hurry up. I have things I need to do, and you need to be tied back up." The woman glared at me, and I spotted something white on her nose.

If I could get her high enough, I might just be able to make it out of here. Not like I would know where here I was but if I were to make it out of this basement it would be a good start. My stomach growled, I was still hungry but I wasn't going to eat that sandwich, I was thirsty and maybe that would help with the hunger.

"Do you think I could have something to drink?" I questioned her as she dipped her head to her hand and snorted.

She rolled her eyes, stood, grabbed the bag, and ran up the stairs. My heart raced—she hadn't tied me back up. I took my time to look around the room to get my bearings, which the asshole didn't let me do. The place was a mess. Boxes, buckets, and broken furniture were scattered everywhere.

It looked as if this was where they threw their trash. My eyes continued around the basement, and I noted that there were boxes stacked haphazardly in the corner. Before I could make my way to them, the door opened at the top of the stairs, and the woman came back down the stairs with a bottle in her hand.

She shoved the bottle in my hand and sat back down in her rickety chair. Turning the water over in my hands, I checked to see if they had tampered with the bottle. I didn't need to be drugged if I could help it. I twisted the cap and heard the crack as the seal came loose from the bottle, which made me feel better drinking it.

I chugged the water, some of it spilling out of the sides of my mouth and dripping onto the dirty shirt, which I had put on for the theater. I sighed, and my gaze went around the room again to see if there was a trash can anywhere. Finally, walking back to the table I sat the bottle there. The woman stood up with zip ties in her hands. "Sit down already. This whole thing is stupid. I don't know why Marcus has to do this fucking shit."

This woman tightened them as far as they would go and made sure that I couldn't move anything she thought would be a problem. The problem for me was that I would probably lose the circulation in my hands if she didn't come back sooner rather than later. Which would mean that I would end up losing my hands.

She practically ran up the stairs and sent me back into total darkness. I tried to get comfortable so that I could sleep for a little bit before anyone else got any smart ideas. There would be no fighting anyone off if they decided to come down here to do what they wanted with me. I was even more defenseless now.

I wondered what Elizabeth and Chloe were doing. Time here didn't have any meaning since there was no way that I could figure it out. All I could do was hope that maybe my friends looked for me, and when they couldn't find me called my dad. If these assholes wanted money, we could give it to them, and I wouldn't have to worry about being saved by TC.

When Jake and I reached the theater, the cops were already around the building. I had gone home, showered, and changed into a suit before heading over to where Aurora's phone had been turned on. Jake opened my door to let me out of the back, and I headed over to the cops. Being CEO of the largest logistics company normally got me more information than the ordinary person. Normally.

"Sir, you are not allowed beyond this point." A young officer stopped me at the barricade.

"I believe my wife is the one you have been called about. I need to speak to her friends." Jake pulled out his security badge, and the young officer turned around to get his captain.

"Mr. Churchhill, right this way the girls are a little shaken. We will do everything we can to find your wife. Is there anyone that you could think of that would want to take her?" the older, pot-bellied captain asked me. I knew this would be one of the questions that he would ask me, and I wasn't going to tell him who it was.

Because he wouldn't be the one to get to Marcus and put him behind bars. I would kill that motherfucker and then dispose of his body. No one would even mourn him or look for him. I shook my head, "No, but I trust that you'll find whoever is responsible. I'd like a moment with my wife's friends."

"Yes, sir." He nodded and left us alone.

Turning my gaze back to Elizabeth and Chloe, they were sitting on the bench with a blanket covering them both. They were huddled together, and I kneeled in front of them. Neither one looked at me because they both knew they had lied to me about where Aurora was all this time.

"So, do you both know how much danger you have put your best friend in?"

They both shook their heads and still wouldn't look up. I sighed and rolled my eyes. I would never get them to talk to me. "Look, where is her phone?"

"The cops took it. She had the phone off the entire time that she was staying with me. She needed to clear her head, and being in that penthouse with you wasn't letting her do it," Elizabeth said, finally pulling her gaze from her feet and star back at me.

"Then she knew that I would be tracking her. That's why she turned it back on." Elizabeth and Chloe nodded. I ran my hand through my hair and down my face. They were worried about their friend, and I was the only one that knew who had her. "Don't worry. I'll be getting her back soon. When I do find the person who did this, he will never do anything like it again."

Elizabeth and Chloe glanced at each other and then turned back to me and nodded. I lifted my chin at them continuing, "What I need you both to do now is tell them nothing about what was just said. You got that? I don't need cops fucking up being able to get Aurora back alive. Okay?"

They nodded again, and I stood, straightening my jacket. I motioned for Jake to come to me. I made sure that the cops were preoccupied with other things before turning my gaze to him. "We need a plan. I need Sam with us. Once we get back to the penthouse, I will fill you and Sam in on what we need to do."

"You know I have your back."

"Make sure that someone takes them home and have them stay with them until I take care of Marcus."

"Of course, sir." Jake nodded before sending out a text to the guys he trusted.

Jake was only a few seconds before he turned back to me. I couldn't believe that Marcus would take Aurora in the open like this. He was getting impatient, and he was starting to make mistakes. Taking her in public was the second biggest mistake of his life. And if he had hurt her, he would hurt in the same way.

A cop approached the girls to start questioning them. I had no doubt that they would follow my instructions. They wanted their friend back, and I was the only one that would be able to do that. As good as the LA police force was, I didn't trust them to get my wife back in one piece.

"Ready to go? Sam should be getting to the penthouse." Jake's voice cut through my thoughts.

"Yes, let's get a plan, and then tomorrow, we will put an end to Marcus and his crew. I'm sure he will have people there with him. He never was one to be brave enough to come alone."

"So, we are going to this warehouse tomorrow, and then what? Will he really bring her to this warehouse?" Sam was pacing my office, while Jake sat in the chair in front of my desk.

Jake had already seen the tip of my darkness when I interrogated Nick, and yet he didn't treat me any differently than he had before. Perhaps he knew what I was capable of when he took the job. Only to be now reminded of what my file said about me.

I'm sure he had read up on me, otherwise, he wouldn't have been so hard on me when we were first introduced. *I had gotten dressed in the shorts and shirt that Laura laid out on my bed that morning. After taking a much-needed shower, I walked down the staircase and spotted Laura and Emi by the door waiting for me. Laura was talking to one of the maids while Emi ran up to me and jumped into my arms.*

Emi smiled up at me before shocking me even more by kissing me on the cheek. She wrapped her hands around my neck, her grin widening to meet her eyes. "We are going shopping! Are you ready to go? Momma said you needed school clothes and a haircut."

Well, she wasn't wrong about my hair. It was longer than I had ever had it, and it was starting to give me a headache. Not to mention that I had noticed just how much shampoo I had used to get it clean.

I gave Emi a grin as I took us to Laura. This woman had opened her home to me, and her daughter was excited to have a brother. But did they know about my past? I'm sure that the director from the orphanage would have told her. I mean, some of the things that I had done weren't even on paper because I had never been caught for doing them, which was a good thing No one needed to know just how bad I was. Especially Emi, who had already captured my heart. I never thought that I would go soft in just a short amount of time. But Emi had that power about her. She lightened the mood around her with her smile.

"Well, are you kids ready? We're going to take you to get fitted for your school clothes, and then we will get some lunch before getting your haircut." Laura smiled and motioned for me to follow her out the front doors.

I nodded. Fitting for school clothes? What kind of school would require clothes that had to be fitted?

We all stepped out onto the porch and waited. I glanced around trying to figure out why we were waiting. When they had come to pick me up, they had driven themselves. Then, I noticed the white SUV limo coming up the cobbled driveway. The damn thing was loaded, and when it pulled up in front of us, a guy in a suit got out from the passenger side.

He looked like one of those bodyguards that famous people had following them around. I watched as he walked to the very back door and opened it. Laura motioned for me to follow her, and when we got to the man, I could tell he was a few years older than me.

"Jake, good morning! When did you get back?" Laura stood in front of him and smiled.

"Yesterday, Mrs. Churchhill. Mr. Churchhill instructed me I had been assigned." Jake cut his eyes at me. I could tell that he didn't trust me, and I wondered whether the man of the house didn't trust me.

Jake was an imposing figure with his jet-black hair and green eyes. Something about him made me think he had been in the military or probably been at his job for a while. Laura turned to me and smiled. "Jake, this is Tom. He's the one you will be guarding. Tom, this is Jake, he will be your bodyguard."

He nodded to me and then helped Laura into the limo. I sat Emi down, and she crawled in, leaving me with Jake. I could tell he was sizing me as I was him, trying to figure out if we would be getting along, or if he was going to try to be my parent. "If you behave, we might be able to be friends. Otherwise, I'll just be another person in your life who you will have to tolerate."

Glaring at the man in front of me, I finally got in the vehicle, sitting opposite Laura and Emi. They both smiled at me. I grinned back at them and watched Jake close the door and make his way back up front.

"Mrs. Churchhill, where are we going first?" a soft-spoken older voice asked through the speakers.

"The clothes shop first, Mr. Walker. We need to get clothes for Tom and then make our way to get clothes for Emi," Laura answered. She turned to me and continued, "So, Tom, I know this will probably be a bit of a change for you. But the school you are going to be attending has a few rules about dress code and appearance. So, we are going to be getting some casual suits for you to wear and formal suits— those will need to be fitted. After we get Emi's clothes, we will need to get your hair cut and since it's a little long we can do a few things with it."

"Suits? And a bodyguard? I don't see a need for a bodyguard. I'm no one, and not a single person in this world would care about me. Don't you think this is a little much since I just came off the street? I mean, how do you know I'm a good fit for your family?" I asked her bluntly. This whole situation was a little weird to me —why would a family of their caliber want someone like me?

"Tom, you are no longer a simple person. You are a Churchhill. Do you not realize the danger you will be in? We own a multi-billion-dollar company. So, you need the best education we can give you. Because, you see, one day, we hope you will take over the company." Laura smiled.

I frowned at her. I couldn't run a company like that; hell, I could barely take care of myself when I lived out on the streets. For what I did for Marcus, I didn't need to be presentable. All I had to do was show up and take care of whoever he wanted iced.

"Why not Emi? Is she not the rightful person to take over?" I questioned her glancing over at the small girl, who smiled, beside Laura.

"This is true, she is the rightful person, but due to her being so young and us being older, we need to be able to keep the company in the family." Laura patted Emi's hand.

I shook my head and leaned back against the seat. This was so crazy; this was not something I would have dreamed of for myself. I ran my hand through my hair before turning my gaze back to Laura. "Is that why you adopted me? To become your successor?"

"No! My parents adopted you because I wanted a brother," Emi answered me and moved over beside me. She rested her head against my arm as she stared up at me.

"No, Tom, like Emi said. We wanted another child, but we are too old to have another safely, and Emi wanted an older brother, so that's how we came to adopt you."

The limo stopped, and I looked out, spotting a building that showcased suits of different designs. The door opened, and Laura and Emi exited. I followed them out with Jake three steps behind me. This was going to take some getting used to.

"Yes, Sam, he will bring her to the warehouse. He is a narcissist and will want to show off what he did or didn't do. We will have to be prepared. He will most likely have people out in the open. What you will have to watch for are the people in the shadows," I answered him from the window. My thoughts not fully on the conversation that I was supposed to be having to save Aurora.

"Then we need to make sure we have extra magazines and an extra gun. That way, we won't have to struggle with whoever is in that warehouse," Jake added, looking between Sam and me.

"All right then, let's get to bed, tomorrow will be eventful." My phone rang in my pocket as they left the room. Drake's name flashed on the screen, and I accepted the call.

Chapter Twenty-Eight

Aurora

The light came back on like it did every time someone came down the stairs to let me out of my restraints. While it blinded me, I could tell that there were two of them this time. As my vision came back to me from the blinding light, I noticed the red-haired, pixie-cut woman with the other woman.

I could no longer feel my arms as she had made the zip ties a little too tight the last time. The other woman with her was very familiar and didn't look like she belonged in this type of place. When she turned, I recognized her from the restaurant I had gone to with Elizabeth and Chloe before our girls' trip.

"Look, Haylee, she needs a shower. Marcus is taking her to the warehouse, but she needs to look halfway decent, and right now, she looks like you." The red-haired woman shook the other.

She looked to be high again. I didn't know how she was still standing. The redhead sighed and took the knife from Haylee.

When she turned to me, I was sure she recognized me, her eyes narrowed before she released my hands. She stepped back and placed another brown bag on the table behind me. "There's food in the bag, and here's some water."

The blood rushed back to my hands, and I hoped that I would be able to use them soon. No one here was going to feed me, so I needed to be able to do it myself. The tingling in my hands answered me as I continued to try and move my hands and fingers.

Red was still trying to get Haylee up, and I didn't know if she was going to be able to or not. She was slumped against the wall, with her chin resting on her chest and her arms to her side. I reached for the bag and opened it.

The sandwich was whole and still wrapped in its paper. Onion rings were also in the bag, making my stomach growl. The last time I had eaten seemed to be hours ago. I pulled out the sandwich and stuffed an onion ring in my mouth.

While I was stuffing my face with the food, Red had gotten Haylee up, which was surprising, I was sure she was a goner. I opened my bottle of water and chugged it before heading over to my bucket to relieve my bladder.

This thing had started to stink, but I doubted there would be anyone who would be taking it out of here. Finishing up, I went back to the two women in the basement. I hadn't seen the maniac since the first day I was here, but that was fine by me.

"Haylee bring her up quickly. She needs to get washed up before Marcus gets here," Red told the stoned woman and waited for her to nod.

I stood there as Red jogged up the stairs and out of the door. Haylee stood on wobbly feet and grabbed my arm, steering me up the stairs and out of the basement. My heart started to race—I was finally able to get out of that basement. I had been in that chair for so long my limbs were screaming at me with all the exertion.

We continued down the run-down hall. She seemed to be running as she pulled me, and I was having a hard time keeping up with her, which seemed wrong since she was stumbling every other step.

"Can you please slow down?" I didn't like that I was practically begging her.

The woman looked over her shoulder at me without a care in the world, stopped, and then pushed me into a door. The door caved in on itself to reveal the nastiest bathroom I had ever seen.. Granted, the toilet had mold on it and was stained, the shower wasn't much better; they clearly hadn't been cleaned in years.

"Hurry up and take a shower. I don't have all day." Rolling my eyes, I stepped out of my nasty clothes. I decided not to press my luck and make a big deal about the door not being closed. She had basically torn it down when she pushed me into it.

Stepping in the shower, I realized that even though I had turned on the hot water faucet it was ice cold. They probably didn't even know that their water heater wasn't working, or they made sure I got a broken shower. There was no way I was going to be able to get warm. My whole body was quivering under the glacial water.

Quickly showering, I stepped out and noticed that I didn't have a towel or any other clothes. "Do you have any other clothes? Or a towel?"

"What does this look like? The Ritz-Carlton? Put those clothes on and get out here." She was staggering on her feet more and more the longer she stood there.

I found a hair tie on the floor. Normally, I wasn't one to use just any hair tie, but with my hair wet, it would make my already-nasty clothes soaked. Getting back into my clothes, they stuck to me like a second layer of skin as they soaked up the water on my body. I wrapped my hair up into a bun, the water dripping down my neck, making my clothes even wetter somehow.

The woman came into the bathroom and pulled me out by the arm. She made me uneasy as I followed her down the hall. This house's walls had holes in it and we wouldn't talk about the roach that crawled over my foot as I made my way with this crazy bitch.

"Haylee! Why isn't she tied up? Are you trying to let her escape?" Marcus's familiar voice caught my attention, and a man came up behind me and tied my arms behind me. I groaned as my shoulders were pulled tight again.

"Sorry, boss," Haylee slurred, stumbling over to the man with rotting teeth.

"Are you fucked-up? What the fuck!" Marcus slapped her, and she fell on her ass in front of me.

Her hand went to her cheek, and the tears that welled in her eyes almost made me feel sorry for her. Almost. In the short time that she has been with me, I had already grown not to like her.

The man behind me pushed me out of the house and down to the rusted, old car. The outside of the house didn't look any better than the inside. Whoever these guys were, they weren't very good bad guys. Even I knew I should have been blindfolded or something, at least that's what happened in the books that I'd read.

I was pushed into the car, and the huge man slid in next to me. As I went to move over, Marcus got in on the other side. I was squashed in this tiny car, and my hands were starting to go numb again. Another man sat in the front and pulled off when he had been given the command to.

They were very bad bad guys. I could find my way back to their house and to mine if I wanted to. I just had to figure out how to get away from these stupid men. And they'd gotten mad at the woman for not having me tied up. I scoffed in my head, hell, at least she'd kept me in the dark most of the time I had been at that fucking hell hole.

We continued down the road to an oceanside abandoned warehouse. Well, at least they got the abandoned warehouse right. As soon as he parked, I was being dragged out of the car by my bun, which rung out more of the water that was still in my hair.

"Ow, you fucker!" I screamed at him. He didn't give a shit that he was almost pulling my hair out of my scalp.

We walked over to the door, and Marcus went in first, and we followed. The man who had me by my hair grabbed some tape that was on a table. He sat me in a chair and taped my mouth shut. Marcus turned to me and grabbed my chin. "Mmm, TC will be here in a few minutes. I can't wait to show him what you look like. It took him long enough to find you."

I could do nothing but glare at him. My heart raced as the man taped my ankles to the legs of the chair and then my tied hands to the back. But I couldn't think about that right now. All I could think about was the thought that TC was actually coming for me.

The man dragged the chair to a column and walked out to the middle of the room with Marcus. Everything was dark and quiet as I stared around the inside of the building. Why would they bring me here? Well of course they would, it would be easier to kill me here and dump me in the ocean.

Besides they would probably have a fight if TC was coming to get me.

Doors slamming informed us that someone was outside the building, and I couldn't help but think that it was TC. A bright light raced across the concrete floor as the door opened and three imposing figures walked through. My vision had taken its time adjusting to the light for it to have to readjust to the darkness once more.

Three sets of footsteps came toward us. I didn't want to believe that he had actually come because this was just an arrangement. But I was overjoyed that he had and he brought Sam and Jake with him— it would have been a dumb move if he'd come alone.

"All right, Marcus. I'm here. Now, where is Aurora?" It had been weeks since his baritone timbre graced my ears, and even knowing that I was in trouble, his tone made me wet.

TC was in jeans and a tight-fitting T-shirt with a light jacket over the top. I wondered if he had his gun with him? TC didn't move his head, but I could see his eyes searching for something. *Was he searching for me?*

"I want you dead at my feet like the scum you are. If you can't help your old family out, you don't need this for yourself," Marcus yelled from across the room. I struggled in my bindings, trying to get free to tell him not to do this.

"You never did like when someone had more than you, which was why you had me take out most of your competitors. You couldn't even beat those men because you were fucking weak."

Marcus pulled his gun from his pants and his two lackeys did the same. Jake and Sam brought up theirs in return. TC leisurely pulled his from under his jacket and aimed it at

Marcus. I didn't miss the tremble in Marcus' arm. Was he afraid of TC?

"Marcus, we both know that you were never a good shot. Now tell me: where is my wife?" The growl in TC's voice shook even me, but the sound of the gun coming off its safety sealed the fear inside me.

Chapter Twenty-Nine

Aurora

I sat in the shadows as I watched TC, Sam, and Jake stand-off with the three in front of them. Even though I had seen the gun in TC's possession, I had never seen him have it pointed at someone. His eyes were as cold as the arctic air with the gun pointed at Marcus.

If I were ever afraid of my husband, it should have been at this moment. The way he stood so still and unblinking was like he had done this before. Knowing that he had a rough past, a part of me thought that he probably had.

"You have 'til the count of three to tell me where my wife is or I'll shoot you where you stand. One…" TC began to count, and Marcus shifted, hesitating on what he should do. "Two…"

Marcus lowered his gun and raised his hands, the gun slung around his thumb. Was it that easy? Did Marcus fear him that much? I tried to continue to move my hands to try to loosen the tape so that I could take the tape off my mouth; to call out to TC; to tell him that I was here; and that we needed to go home.

Marcus turned and winked to the man on the left, causing my unease to skyrocket. What was he going to do? Someone had come behind me and cut my arms and legs loose from the chair. Where did they come from? There were only three people in the car with me.

Whoever the person was, they roughly pulled me up and something sharp and cold came to my neck. Marcus turned back around and faced TC as I was pushed forward into the brighter part of the warehouse. TC's eyes flickered toward me, but they didn't stay on me long as they went back to Marcus.

TC's jaw hardened, and the muscle twitched underneath his skin. I hadn't noticed it before, but he had dark circles under his eyes, and his cheekbones were more prominent. Like he hadn't slept well since I had left. The other two didn't move from their position as the standoff continued.

"Here she is. I think I took okay care of her while you were trying to find her." Marcus laughed as he looked to either side of him at the men standing beside him. They both chuckled but stopped when TC's eyes snapped to each of them.

"If you think that the state that she is in is taking care of her, you thought wrong. Now, let her go," TC practically growled at Marcus, his gun still trained on his chest.

"*Tsk Tsk.* No, you see, you have nothing to bargain with."

"What do you want, Marcus? There's always something that you want," TC ground out through his clenched teeth.

"Well, you can start by wiring me some of that money that you have made. Let's say 50 percent."

My heart fell into my stomach. He wanted half of TC's fortune he had made for himself? And for what? So he could blow it? It wasn't like he was going to fix that house up. I struggled in the man's arms and the sharpness of the knife dug into my neck. TC glanced back over to me, and for a moment, I thought I saw something else in those cold blue eyes.

"Don't think you are going to shoot your way out, you see if you kill me, he kills her, and then what are you going to do?" Marcus laughed maniacally, and the man behind me chuckled, too.

TC was going to have to give him the money. That is if he would ever spend that amount on me. TC turned back to me in what felt like slow motion, pulling the gun in my direction and fired. The wind from the bullet whirled past me, and something hot and wet splattered on the back of my head and into my hair.

Sam and Jake fired at the two men in front of them. Before I crouched down, I saw the bullet that hit TC, from Marcus' gun. Covering my ears from all the loud gunfire, I tried to get as low to the ground as possible. Opening my eyes, I spotted TC running further into the warehouse after Marcus. All my thoughts were on TC and how I needed him to be okay. Sam and Jake came over to me and pulled me up, almost carrying me out the door and away from the muffled gunshots. Jake pulled the gag from my mouth, and I gasped in a deep breath.

"Jake, what about TC? You need to get back in there to help him." I couldn't help the tears streaming down my cheeks when neither one of the men made a move to go back into the building. They were his bodyguards. Why were they not going back in to help him?

"He will be fine. See he's coming out already," Jake answered me. My eyes darted over to the building and to TC coming out with Marcus in front of him.

TC had the gun pointed at Marcus' greasy black hair as he led him to me, Sam, and Jake. Blood gushed from his nose, and his clothes were torn. TC didn't seem out of breath though, and he stopped the maniac in front of me.

"Kneel." Marcus did as TC ordered before growling, "Now, beg for Aurora's forgiveness."

Blood dripped from Marcus' face and arms as he bowed his head in front of me. It stopped in front of his knees and my feet. TC held the gun to his head and shoved him with its barrel when he didn't comply.

"I'm sorry. Please, I'm so sorry." Marcus rushed out as he bent forward.

"For?" TC growled again, as he pressed the gun harder into his head.

"I'm sorry for treating you the way I did and kidnapping you. Please, forgive me!" Marcus wailed as he glanced up at me.

I didn't know what to do other than nod. Glancing up at TC, the wildness in his eyes made my heart race at the realization of what he was going to do.

"TC, don't do that in front of—" Jake started too late as TC pulled the trigger.

The shot and the splatter of blood on my shoes turned my stomach, but what turned it even more was the fact that I wasn't really that disgusted by the violence. Marcus' body landed in front of me, and that's when I noticed all the blood on TC.

At first, I wanted to be afraid of the man standing in front of me. But in hindsight, I couldn't. He had come to rescue me. Something I didn't think that he would do. TC holstered the gun and moved forward.

"Are you okay? They didn't hurt you too badly, did they?" His hands ran over my face and then down to my body.

It was like he was searching me while he patted me down. The blood on his hands smeared over my already-dirty clothes, making me look like I had war paint on my face.

"TC, I'm fine. Other than being really hungry." I brought my hand up to his on my face.

TC's eyes snapped to my wrists, and the growl that escaped him sent a shiver down my back.

"Who did this to you?" He grabbed my hands, staring down at the red angry welts that ran around my wrists. His eyes were ice cold as they came back up to stare into my grey orbs.

"You killed him. He is lying at our feet in a pool of blood." I stepped forward, and he took a step back, trying to undress me in front of Jake and Sam. "TC! I'm fine. Let's go and get something to eat."

"No, you are going to the hospital to be checked out." TC grabbed my hand and pulled me to the car and opened the door.

I got in thinking that they would probably question this if we went to the hospital like this. Right? TC shut the door and went over to Jake and Sam. Sam came over and entered the driver's side door while Jake dragged Marcus' body over to the water. What were they going to do? Were they really going to do what I thought they were going to do? They went to the other side of the building and didn't return for a long time.

When they came around the corner, TC had taken his light jacket off and both guns out in the open, one black and the other one gold. The way he strolled back up to the car with Jake made me squirm in my seat. If I hadn't been kidnapped and almost starved, I'd have wanted to jump him right now in the back of this vehicle.

My arms screamed at me when I pulled myself up to stare over Sam's shoulder at TC. That man risked his life to find me and then get me back from a man he once knew.

"He has been worried about you since you left. I've never seen him like this in the four years that I've worked with him. Mr. Churchhill was distraught when he couldn't find you," Sam disclosed to me before TC and Jake got back to the car.

Did he really worry about me like Sam said? TC entered the back seat with me, while Jake closed the door and got in the passenger door.

"To the hospital, Sam."

"TC, I don't need to go to the hospital. I need food." I turned to face him, and his eyes stared back at me.

"You will go to the hospital, and Sam will go get whatever you want to eat. Jake will be with us to protect you along with me." TC's hand went to my face, his calloused fingers tracing my cheekbones and down my neck. I had never seen him look at me like he was as his eyes followed his finger.

"Fine. But won't they ask questions? About the blood on my skin and clothes?" TC touching me, excited my nervous system along with the endorphins in my brain.

"No, because I'm going to tell them that I found you like this after someone took you. And also, because the doctor knows Sam. She used to serve with him." TC continued to stare at me like he would never see me again.

"Okay." I pulled away from him, even though I craved his touch. It was like I couldn't decide if I wanted him near me or not.

TC didn't move toward me, allowing me to have my space, but he kept his hand on my knee. The ride to the hospital was silent but not awkward. Sam stopped the vehicle in front of the emergency department doors, and TC stepped out of the car and helped me out.

Once I was out, TC picked me up and carried me into the hospital. The adrenaline that was keeping me upright quickly drained from my body, and I laid my head against his shoulder. I couldn't hear what TC was saying to the person in front of him as I slid into the most comfortable sleep I had had in a while.

Chapter Thirty

TC

I sat in the chair beside Aurora's bed waiting for her to wake up. The cops had shown up to talk with her, but I refused to let them come into the room. I was sure that she hadn't gotten much sleep while she was at Marcus' piece-of-shit house.

The nurses drew blood from her and then started saline to help get her rehydrated. I was pissed at myself. I should have known that he had her at the house. He was too stupid to take her anywhere else. If I had gone there rather than interrogating Nick, I would have found her sooner and then burned the place down around him.

When I had Marcus on his knees begging for her forgiveness, I let go of the man that the Churchhills had raised and became the killer that I used to be. The darkness consumed me so much that when Aurora nodded, I pulled the trigger without even hearing Jake warning me not to in front of Aurora.

My eyes went to Aurora, and the neglect of her clothes, and the sharpness of her cheekbones. It made me want to kill Marcus all over again. If I'd had time, I would have made him starve like he had let Aurora. However, the other part of me wanted her to know that she would never have to deal with him again.

Sighing, I leaned down and placed my head on the back of her hand. Just having her here beside me calmed me. Once all the adrenaline was gone, would she be afraid of me? I knew that I owed her an explanation about my past and what I used to do in Marcus' gang.

The only thing I feared was her leaving me, but if that was what she wanted to do, who was I to keep her by my side? Hell, I basically married her to keep my company because I was too worried about pressing the issue and not getting to keep what I had worked so hard for. Now, I didn't know what I was going to do when she woke up.

A knock on the door brought my attention to the door and a nurse came in with reddish brown hair. She had very little makeup on, but that didn't take away her beauty. I was sure I had seen her here the night before when she was hooking up Aurora to the IVs.

"My name is Kali; I'll be your nurse again tonight. Has anything changed with Mrs. Churchhill? Anything I can get you?" Kali came over to Aurora's IV and checked them and the bags hanging on the poles.

"She is still sleeping. Does she need to be woken up to eat?" I had been worried about her not eating since she got here.

"No, sir. What we can do is insert a feeding tube. I know you mentioned that she hadn't been fed regularly when she was kidnapped. This way, we can make sure she is getting nutrients that she needs until she wakes up." She turned to me and smiled. Kali was a very knowledgeable nurse.

"Thank you. When do you think you can get that going?"

"I'll call the attending doctor and get a verbal order, and I'll be back in a few." I nodded and laid my head back on Aurora's hand, watching her breathe as she slept.

The doctor said that she wasn't in a coma, but with the little sleep that she'd had he wasn't going to wake her up. Other than being a little malnourished and bruised from the too-tight bindings, she was fine.

"Who are you?" Kali's voice asked as she stood between Drake and the rest of the room.

"Well, sweetheart, I would be the best friend of that big fucker over there." He was teasing her, but Kali's posture didn't change.

"He's fine. That lug-head is my friend." Kali stepped around him, and Drake made his way over to us.

"Hey, man. How's things going over here?" Drake picked up a chair and put it beside mine. I was surprised that he didn't slide it.

"She's still sleeping. The doctor thinks her body is exhausted from the whole ordeal. So, since it has been twenty-four hours, we are going to put a feeding tube in to be able to feed her." I didn't like the look that Drake gave me, but it was better than what Aurora's parents had given me.

My father and mother had to take them out of the hospital room so as not to wake up Aurora. They had come again earlier today and spent time with her. I had stepped out to call Drake to make sure the company didn't burn down. Not that I didn't trust him, but I needed to talk about something other than what was going on in that shrinking four-walled room.

"Well, at least she's getting rest. You know you can take as much time as you need. I have this while you handle this."

"I know. It's just hard to know what she is going to do once she wakes up. Those guys really did a number on her," I answered him. When he came up to me and asked to help get

Aurora, I didn't quite understand. Until he told me about his family ties. He was a beast when we had both hunted down Marcus in that warehouse. He had cut him and had him on the ground with an already broken nose.

I couldn't believe he was really who he said he was. I had been in and out of the underground gambling ring—collecting money and other things from the underlings. But then again, if I had been smart enough to read the Latin name of the building I would have figured it out.

"I can believe it. Like I said, I have your back—now and always." Drake raked his hand through his hair, he only did that when he was nervous about something or thinking about asking something. "What do you think about me dating Emi?"

"I'd tell you just like I told you in my office—if you hurt her no one will find your body." I snapped my eyes over to him. I meant what I said; that girl wasn't my biological sister, but she picked me from all the others, and she was now my family.

"I can tell you that I will never hurt her. It has taken me a long time to work up the courage to ask you. I love her." Drake stared back at me, and I couldn't understand how he could just say those words, especially coming from the background he had.

"I believe you, Drake, and I would happily call you my brother. But like I said, don't hurt her."

Aurora's hand tightened in my hand taking my attention back to her. Drake kept still beside me, and her eyes opened . My heart sped up as the grey of her eyes turned to look at me. She didn't flinch when she saw me. I couldn't allow myself to question what that meant.

"Are you okay? Are you hurting? Are you hungry?" I rambled, standing and then sitting on the bed with her.

"I'll go get that nurse." I barely heard Drake as he walked out of the room to get Kali.

"I'm fine. How long have I been here?" Aurora's voice was soft, and she tried to sit up.

"We've been here for twenty-four hours. Are you hungry?" I wanted to make sure we could get her something to eat, but would she actually be able to eat an entire meal?

"Yes, a little."

"Drake has gone to go get the nurse. She will be here soon, and we'll get you something." My hand itched to touch her face and hair, but that wasn't what I was like before this. Would she think I was crazy?

"Okay. TC?" The tone in her voice chilled me. Was she going to tell me to leave and never come back? Fuck.

"Yes, temptress."

"Thank you for coming to get me. I was so scared I would never see anyone again." The tears welling up in her eyes stilled my racing heart and made it plummet.

"I'd do it again if it meant I would be able to see you and be near you again."

"I missed you. You probably think I'm crazy, but I really did."

"I don't think you are crazy..." Kali burst into the room with her stethoscope and a salt-and-pepper-haired man. Drake came in and leaned against the wall by the windows. I kissed the back of her hand and stood, allowing them to check her out. I would talk with her once they finished what they needed to do.

"Aurora, follow my light. How are you feeling? Anything hurting?" the man asked, flicking the small light from one eye to the other.

"I'm hungry, and I'm sore, but I'm not in pain."

Kali had strapped a cuff to her arm and was taking her blood pressure. Before checking her heart rate manually, even though Aurora was connected to a monitor.

"Kali, get Mrs. Churchhill something small and easy to swallow. I don't want her to throw anything up."

"Okay, Dr. Simmons." Kali left and was back with some jello within minutes. She sat the cup on the tray table beside the bed and turned back to the man.

"Try the jello, and if you keep that down we will get you something else, okay? Just call Kali, she will get you whatever you want." The man patted Aurora's arm and walked out of the room.

Kali had stayed to enter things into the computer. I went back to her and grabbed the jello and the spoon. Opening the container, I spooned out some of the orange dessert and fed it slowly to my wife. I was thankful she was accepting of my help.

"TC, do you want me to inform your parents so they can let the Emersons know?" I had almost forgotten that Drake was still here.

"No, I'll call them in the morning. They can come visit her then." I didn't want to share her just yet. Gwen had been blowing up my phone since I told her that we had found her, wanting to know how she was and whether she would be coming back to the penthouse.

"Okay well, I'll leave and let you both have some alone time. Well as much alone time as you can have here." Drake laughed as he headed back out of the door.

If I didn't need him to help me run my company, I'd kill him for his sarcastic-ass, but he did know how to bring me out of a bad mood. I didn't think I would ever like that man when I met him. Shaking my head, I turned back to Aurora to see her smiling.

"You think he's funny? I thought you hated him?" I chuckled, which brought Aurora's eyes up to me from the last bite I was feeding her.

"I used to hate both of you. You more than him. I didn't know what I had done to make you treat me the way you did at your party," Aurora answered me before she slurped the jello from the silver spoon.

"Aurora, I really don't have a good reason for what I did to you in front of all those people. After I did it, I regretted it every day after that."

Chapter Thirty-One

TC

"I thought when we met in Spencer and Taylor that we had a connection. It was like you changed when you met Morgan." Aurora stared back at me with curious eyes.

I didn't even know what to tell her because my thoughts had ceased to exist as I stared at her. What was I going to tell her —at that point in my life, I was trying to fit in with her circle? I had never been that close to girls like her and Morgan. So, in my mind, I thought that to stay in that circle, I would need to be the way they were.

I was standing in the foyer with my parents and Emi, greeting guests as they walked past us into the formal room the Churchhills used for parties. It might as well be a ballroom. The only person I was looking forward to seeing was that gorgeous chocolate-brown-haired girl, Aurora.

She had been on my mind since that day in that store. When I was trying on suits, I had imagined standing there with her in that mirror. Aurora in a dress that suited her figure, and her arm through mine.

But now, I waited to find out if she would even show. Some of my father's board members showed up with some of their daughters. That was when I spotted a blond in her tight light-green dress and green eyes. She smiled at me with a wink as she continued into the room.

Aurora had not shown up. Maybe she didn't really like me and had just been nice when she smiled back at me in the store. I mean, who would want to be near someone like me? "Tom, why don't you go mingle with the kids that have come? We will come to get you when it's time to introduce you formally." Laura smiled at me as she placed her soft hand against my cheek and nodded toward the room.

"Okay. Thank you for all of this," I told her as I stepped forward. They followed me inside and went to the people who were their friends.

I made my way to the drinks table and grabbed some iced tea before turning and scanning the crowd on the dance floor. Some people who were my age sat at the tables watching the room—I could only assume to find me.

The blond from earlier walked up to me, a sexy smile on her face. I couldn't help the smirk that came up on my face. Her eyes roamed my body, and there was the lust in those big green eyes. They weren't as hypnotizing as the grey ones I had seen in the clothes store, though.

"Hi, my name is Morgan," the blond introduced herself to me, "You are a lot more handsome than what everyone is saying about you."

That excited me. If the students were already talking about me, there would be no problem being able to have my choice of girls. I had never been one to keep one girl for long when I was living with Marcus. There was one who could potentially take me off the market, but she wasn't here.

"Really? I haven't even stepped foot in school yet, but I'm already on everyone's lips?" I asked her with a grin. Morgan squirmed under my gaze and grinned back at me.

"Oh yes. I felt it necessary to introduce myself before any other girl caught your eye," Morgan expressed as she fingered my tie.

I raised my eyebrows at her with a smirk. Well, she was a few days too late in that regard. Morgan took my smirk as an invitation to grab my hand and pull me to the dance floor. I sat my glass down at a table full of students watching my every move.

As I danced with Morgan, the doors opened, and Aurora came into the room. Our eyes made contact, and she smiled until she noticed who was dancing with me, and her face fell. Aurora went over to my parents. I watched as she and her friends stopped in front of them and talked for a moment.

I ground my hips against Morgan's backside, my hands gripping tightly on her hips. Aurora was beautiful, and I wanted to know whether she would be jealous of me dancing with another girl. Her eyes continued to flick over to me, and I thought I saw a little bit of sadness in them before she turned with her friends and went to the table that held all the food.

Morgan pulled me over to the table I had sat my drink down on and introduced me to all her friends and the guys who were dating some of them. Sitting down at the table, I continued to watch Aurora and her friends. I couldn't take my eyes off her in that beautiful blue dress.

"I swear, Aurora thinks just because her daddy is the CEO of his company she can get whatever she wants. I'd love to bring her down a peg or two." Morgan's whiny voice interrupted my thoughts.

I could use that as an excuse to get close to her and dance with her. To touch her skin again, and if I could take us further away from this group of rich assholes. I might be able to steal a kiss.

"I'll do it." I stood and went over to her as she danced with her friends.

My heart was racing as I took her in my arms. Laura had taught me how to dance, and it had made me nervous touching my mom on the lower part of her back. But this felt right as I spun us away from her friends. I smirked at her as she realized who had taken her away.

Aurora gasped, and I pulled her closer. I needed her as close as I could get her. We made a small circle, her perfume intoxicating me. To make it seem like we had just met, I introduced myself, "So, I don't think we met. My name is TC, and you are?"

"My name is Aurora," she answered me with a curious look. Fuck, her voice was music to my ears. I could listen to her speak for the rest of my life.

"Pretty name for a pretty girl," I whispered in her ear, and I caught Morgan glaring at me as I continued to try to get closer to her.

Glancing around, I tried to find an opening to move us further away from the dumb blond I had gotten acquainted with. But there was no way to move through the crowd that had gathered around us. Fuck, this was going to be bad.

"Were you not dancing with Morgan?" Her question made this whole predicament even worse, but I could hear a jealous tone in her voice, so dancing with her did what I wanted it to.

"Are you jealous?" I smirked at her. My heart was hammering as I spun her around again.

"No, I was just asking."

"Good, I'd hate for you to have feelings for me," I broadcasted to the people near us. I laughed and left her in the middle of the dance floor.

Hopefully, I would be able to make it up to her at some point because this wasn't how I wanted it to happen. Morgan was laughing hysterically as well as the others behind her. The sickness that I felt as I left her and then spotted my parents' faces along with Aurora's mother's. I knew that I was going to be in trouble when everyone left.

I glanced back at Aurora in the hospital bed. Despair coated my insides as I tried to find the right words.

"Would you believe me that it hadn't been my intention to leave you on that dance floor? I used the bullshit comment that Morgan said to dance with you, but I wanted to take you further into the room and possibly steal a kiss." I couldn't hold her grey eyes anymore, and I dropped mine to the cup and spoon in my hand.

Aurora lifted my head; fresh tears running down her cheeks. "You mean that?"

I nodded. It was the only thing I could do. My voice had stopped working after I had answered her. "I wanted to apologize, but you kept away from me, and it started to make me mad—not only at you but at myself too. Because if I hadn't been the way I had at that party we could've been friends."

"I'm sorry too. About the picture. I shouldn't have done that. I'm sure I hurt Laura just as much as I hurt you." Aurora placed her hand on my cheek and leaned forward, placing a soft kiss on my lips.

"Aurora, I need to know what is going through your mind about yesterday." I stared at her, and I tried to figure out what she was thinking. Aurora pulled her hand from my face and placed it in her lap.

"At first, when I saw you holding the gun, I was afraid of you but then when the man had me from behind with the knife.

I wasn't half as afraid of you as him." Aurora's hands fidgeted in her lap, but she kept her gaze from me.

"Okay, but what about by the car? With Sam and Jake?" Jake had told me that I shouldn't have done what I did, but I had anyway. I needed to know what she thought about me now. How she saw me when I had killed a man in front of her for hurting her.

"I wasn't afraid. I was glad that you killed him." She looked up at me with confusion yet determination in her eyes. "Does that make me a bad person?"

I moved over to her and pulled her close. Making sure not to tug on her IV lines. I kissed the top of her head as she finally cried into my chest. "No, it doesn't make you a bad person. When you get to go home. I'll tell you about my past. All of it; I won't keep you in the dark anymore."

"TC, I would like that. But know that who you were before you were adopted isn't completely you anymore. You are a blend of those two people."

"I know, but I really want you to know me, and then you can make a decision if you want a divorce or not," I offered to her because I didn't want her to be bound to me if she didn't want to be.

"I don't have to make that decision later. I don't want a divorce. Being away from you made me realize that I don't want to ever be away from you again. And even if you can't ever tell me, I can. I love you, TC," Aurora told me as she held my hand. "I love you; the good you; the bad you; and anything in between."

"Aurora..." I didn't have any words for what she had just revealed to me. How could someone actually love me? For Aurora—not knowing about my past, and only seeing a glimpse of it near the warehouse—I was surprised that she wasn't telling me to get away from her or screaming in terror.

A knock came on the door again and the man who was with Kali earlier today came in. He came up to the bed and sighed.

"Good evening, my name is Dr. Simmons. I'm the attending doctor working under Dr. Santos today. I apologize for not introducing myself earlier, but since you had woken up, I wanted to make sure that you were medically sound. As long as Mrs. Churchhill continues to eat well, she will be able to go home by the end of the week."

I stood from my seat on Aurora's bed and held out my hand. Sam had once again been an asset to me. If it hadn't been for him, we would have been questioned about the blood on both of us. And if they would have run it, they would have known it wasn't mine or hers.

Chapter Thirty-Two

Aurora

It was amazing to be able to go back home. I had been in the hospital for a week and a half because it had been hard to eat the entire meals they brought me when I started to eat three times a day. So, Dr. Santos decided to keep me for a few more days, just to make sure that I was able to keep things down.

"Do you have everything?" TC's voice came from the door as I packed up the P.J.s that he had brought me to the hospital. They had made my life a little easier, along with visits from my parents and my friends. It didn't seem like I was in a hospital wearing regular clothes and having people visit me. Chloe might have brought me things that I shouldn't have had, too.

"Yes, I'm pretty sure I do," I answered him. He had been with me the entire time I had been here. Never once did he leave my side; he had Drake take care of the company until he was able to go back.

I didn't know that he could be like this. I hadn't ever seen him like this with the girls he dated in school. TC's arms wrapped around me, and his scent crept up my nose while I breathed him in.

"I'm glad we can finally be alone."

I turned in his arms, and he quickly pulled me flush to his body. My hands linked behind his neck as he laid his forehead against mine. I was able to relax in his arms like I hadn't ever been able to before.

"TC, do you think if I hadn't been late to your party things would have been different with us?"

"Yes, but it should have been different even with it playing out like it had. But my parents hadn't had me long, so some of my old life seeped through. Like I said, I didn't want to..." TC sighed as he kissed my cheek and grabbed me up into his arms. He crashed his lips onto mine, and I couldn't help the moan that he elicited from me. "I want to get home. It's been too long since I had you wrapped around my cock."

"Then tell Jake and Sam to move their asses and get my stuff so we can go home," I told him, slipping my hand between us and palming the bulge in his jeans. As gorgeous as he was in his suit, I loved him in jeans and T-shirt. It showed off his tattooed arms and pierced nipples.

"Oh, you temptress. Don't tease me with a good time if you're not well enough to keep up," TC groaned into my ear as he nipped my earlobe.

"Oh, I think I can keep up."

TC sat me down on the bed beside my suitcase and pulled out his phone. His fingers flew over the screen, and I couldn't help but giggle at his excitement. I didn't ever think a man would be so excited to get me home and have me; much less the man in front of me.

"They are on their way up. Temptress, you don't know what I've been wanting to do to you and watching you do what I've been having wet dreams about." The feral look in TC's blue eyes excited me, and I was one hundred percent sure my panties were drenched.

"Yeah? Are you going to tell me what you want me to do? Or are you just going to show me?"

TC took a deep breath before sliding himself in between my thighs and taking hold of my chin right under my jaw, making me look up at him in his eyes. I shivered under his gaze, and my nipples pebbled in my bra. "You don't know what you do to me when you talk to me like this."

"Do you like it?" My tongue ran over my lower lip, and his eyes flickered down to watch.

A knock echoed into the open room, and TC groaned as his lids slid over his orbs. He took a couple of deep breaths before he turned to whoever was in the doorway.

"Sir, we have the car up front. Would you like us to get the bags?" Jake's voice floated over to me. I hopped down from the bed and grabbed TC's hand before he could respond.

"Yes please, Jake." He nodded to me, and he and Sam grabbed my bags as I tugged TC out of the room.

It wasn't fair that he could play when I needed him so badly. He chuckled as he finally came flush with me. Kali waved at me, and I waved back. She had been great while I was here, and I hoped that she would be happy with whatever decision she made. She was too kind to have to deal with what she was dealing with.

TC pressed the button for the elevators and pulled me close to his side. I waited beside him on pins and needles. To say it wasn't torture being beside him and not being able to jump him right then would be a lie. The doors opened and let us all in. TC pulled me to the back and ran his nose up my neck and to my ear. "Don't worry, temptress, it will be just us today. I gave Gwen the day off, and after Jake and Sam bring your stuff up, they will be gone, too."

A shiver ran down my spine at his promise. My mind was playing things over and over that he might want to do. But the thought of him tying me up again had me a little nervous while I sat there with him. Trying to search his face to get any hit of what he had planned.

"Are you trying to figure out what we are going to be doing?" TC whispered in my ear. His breath fanning over it from his voice made me wetter. There was no way that I'd be able to sit in the car without leaving a damp spot on the seat.

"Maybe?" I answered him. I reached my hand down and palmed his cock through his jeans, and the stifled hiss was audible.

"Temptress, you keep acting like this, and we won't make it to the penthouse."

"Is that a promise or a threat?" I pressed as I glanced up through my lashes.

The elevator doors opened before he could answer me, and Jake and Sam exited. It was TC's turn to pull me out and behind the guards. We couldn't get into the car soon enough. TC opened my door, and I slid into the back while he followed behind me.

TC's hand went to my thigh as Jake and Sam shut the trunk and got into the car. I was glad that my parents hadn't come to help take me home, if they had, we wouldn't have any time once we reached the penthouse on our own. I was excited to find out what was going to happen.

"Are you not so confident now that we are in the car?" TC leaned over and whispered in my ear.

"I don't know what you're talking about. I'm just as confident as I was in the hospital room and the elevator." I answered him while holding his gaze.

TC grinned, and I didn't know if it was a good grin or something I should be worried about. His hand moved up my thigh, closer to my sex, making me squirm in the seat. I had to try to hold back the moan that wanted to make itself known.

"We will see when I get you in our room." He pressed a chaste kiss to my lips.

I cocked my head with a raised eyebrow. *Our room?* We had never shared a room together, other than him coming in and fucking me in my room and then taking me into his. What did he do while I was gone?

"What do you mean 'our room?'" I asked, and he chuckled.

"You will see." I didn't like the glint in his eyes. It had never been there before, and I didn't know how to take it.

We reached our building, and Jake drove into the card-restricted garage, stopping at the elevator to allow TC and I to exit the car and head on up to the penthouse. He pulled me into it and pressed the penthouse button. My body hummed with excitement as the floors flew past and brought us closer to our home.

When the doors opened, the place looked completely different. It no longer had things that TC wanted on the walls, and the furniture had been changed. The only person that I could imagine helping TC with this was Gwen.

"What have you done here?" I turned to TC, who leaned against the wall with his arms thrown over his shoulders and his hands clasped behind his neck.

"I figured I'd make you feel more at home. It's the least I can do after everything that happened because of me." He walked up to me and lifted me into his arms. "Come with me, temptress. I have something else to show you that will excite you so much more."

I wrapped my legs around him, and he took us to his side of the penthouse. TC walked through the open doors of the room with long strides and a grin on his lips. He sat me down, and I turned to look at the difference that had been made in this room as well.

The doors had been changed to barn doors, and my things had been moved to one side of the room. As I continued to stare at the room, I spotted something I didn't ever think I would see hanging anywhere in this house. The photo that the photographer had captured of our swoon worthy kiss was hanging on the wall on TC's side.

If I was being honest, the picture was gorgeous. She had done a wonderful job of getting it just right. My rings shone brightly as my hand rested on his chest with my head. That whole thing had changed both him and me.

I turned to him, and he was there in front of me. His thumbs caressing my cheeks as his other eight fingers slid into my hair. I couldn't help shedding some tears, this was probably going to be the closest I was going to get to an 'I love you,' which was all right by me, because there was no way I would know how he had been raised until he told me.

"You know, I didn't even know if I would ever see these pictures. I wanted to get away from you so badly that night." I ran my hands up his arms and rested them on his biceps.

"I didn't know if it was the whiskey I had consumed or you that made me kiss you the way I did. But I'm glad I did because otherwise, it could have been years before we came to be something like this." He was being so gentle with me, unlike how he normally was when we were alone.

"Yeah? You shocked me when you did. I think that in the back of my mind that was when I started using you to be able to get myself off." I pulled my lip between my teeth and looked up at him.

"How long had you been thinking of me while you were using your fingers and toy?" TC wrapped one hand into my hair and then pulled me closer to his body with his other. He was already hard again as we stood in the middle of our room. I had hoped that he wouldn't have noticed my admission.

"Long before you caught me."

Fuck! When Aurora confessed to thinking about me when she was playing with herself, I nearly ripped the clothes that she had on and took her in the middle of our room. Lifting her up by her ass, I walked us over to our bed and laid her on the mattress.

Aurora's eyes were already hooded as I climbed over her and scooted her into the center of the king-sized bed. Her hands had traveled down my abs to the button on my jeans, and I caged her with my arms and legs. She unbuttoned them and ran her fingertips along the edge of my boxer/briefs.

I waited for her to make the first move because as much as I wanted to ravage her right now, I couldn't hurt her any more than what she had been through. She hadn't talked about what had gone on in that house, but I knew what could have happened.

Aurora's eyes left my eyes and went to my cock, which was still sitting inside my underwear. Her hands relieved me of the confining garment, and one went around me as the other grabbed my balls. I groaned at her touch, which brought her eyes back up to mine. Fuck, I needed to be inside her like my life depended on it.

"Aurora, are you sure you are okay with this? If you're not, we can wait." If she had said she wasn't ready, I would be okay with that.

"I'm fine, TC. If you are wondering whether they did anything to me sexually, they didn't," she answered me before planting a needy kiss on my lips and pulling me further on top of her.

I gripped the hem of her shirt, pulled it over her head, and flung it to the floor. Aurora was perfect. I got an eyeful of her plump breasts in her cute little bra, pulling the cup down below her left breast, I took hold of her nipple and began to nip and suck on it.

Aurora arched off the bed, and her hands went to my back. Her nails bit into the skin of my shoulder blades with a moan on her lips. I pulled off her nipple and brought her up onto my lap to be able to unclip her bra. The need to have her naked and wanting underneath me had me struggling to remove it.

"Here let me." She reached around and undid the clip and the infuriating thing came down her arms and then fell to the floor.

"Fuck, Aurora, lie back and let me get these bottoms off." Aurora laid back, and I pulled her bottoms off and flung them to the floor with the rest of the clothes. She was already wet when I slipped a finger into her pussy.

I grabbed her back up into my lap. Aurora hovered over my cock before she slid her wet cunt around my throbbing cock. She moaned as she sheathed me to the hilt. It had been so long since I'd had her, and this felt amazing as I helped her ride me.

Aurora's pussy pulsed around me, and the whimpers that escaped her mouth when I hit her G-spot edged me closer to my own orgasm. I didn't know how long I was going to last with her circling her hips each time she came down.

Changing our position, I kneeled and pulled her legs up and onto my shoulders, so I could get a full view of her tits and cunt. Aurora's hands went into her hair above her, further putting herself on display for me. "What are you doing to me, temptress?"

"I'm not doing anything that you don't love," Aurora cooed, trailing her hands down her body.

God damn her and the way she teased me. She ran one hand up her leg, and the other to her clit. Ever since I had watched her that first night, I loved seeing her touch herself and I was disappointed that I hadn't let her in a while.

"Are you going to be a good girl and make that pussy of yours come all over my cock? Are you making that clit feel good, temptress?" I moved ever so slowly inside of her tight, wet pussy. She moaned as I continued my slow thrusts.

"Yes, please… faster." Her fingers on her clit moved faster as she got closer to her climax. I could tell that she was getting closer when she started to match my thrusts with her own.

"Do you want to come, temptress? I can do that; all you have to do is beg." Aurora's eyes closed tightly as she nodded. I chuckled and crashed into her making her open those beautiful grey eyes. "That's not begging, temptress. I need you to tell me—use that voice of yours to plead with me to give you what you want."

"TC, please… make me come… I want to come all over your cock." Aurora locked her gaze with mine at her last comment. Her voice dipped into that sultry tone that I loved to hear.

Fuck, I covered her in an instant. Aurora's legs hung on my arms as I brought her to her orgasm. Her fingernails dug into my back, and her body tensed and spasmed under me. It took everything in me to not come with her.

I pulled out of her cunt and rose from the bed, backing into the middle of the room. Aurora stayed on the bed as she came down from her high, but her eyes stayed on me. I motioned for her to come to me with a finger.

Aurora got up from the bed with shaky legs, but she stood with her head held high. My hand wrapped around my cock as she padded over to me. That mouth of hers hung slightly open, begging me to shove my cock in it. "On your knees, temptress."

She raised an eyebrow before lowering herself to her knees. Aurora's hands rested on her thighs, staring up at me. I grabbed her hair, and she arched her back. "I want you to take my cock into your mouth. Do you want to suck my cock for me?"

"Yes." Aurora's hands wrapped around my cock before she placed the tip of it into her mouth.

God damn! She slipped it further into her mouth, and when she allowed the head of it to pass down her throat, I thought I was done. I pulled out to the tip and then thrust into her mouth, making her gag, and spit started to coat my length.

I fucked her mouth, the gagging sounds that she made encouraged me to go faster. Spittle ran down her chin as she looked up at me. Fuck those eyes. I pulled from her mouth and came all over her face. Aurora used her fingers to wipe my cum off her face, and she sucked it from her fingers before swallowing it. I brought her up in my arms and crashed my lips to hers before picking her up and taking her over to the shower.

"You did so good, temptress." The blush that crept up her cheeks made me grin as I guided her under the stream of water.

"Really?"

"Yes," I answered her as I washed her hair.

Aurora's hand rested on my waist while I continued to soap up her hair with my fingers and massage it into her scalp. She groaned as my hands got to the back of her neck. Aurora would get her reward, and it would start now.

I grabbed the body wash and pumped some into my hands before lathering it onto her body. When I reached her thighs, they quivered as my hands reached her cunt. Fuck, I wanted to bury my face into that beautiful mound of hers.

"TC." I glanced up and realized that her eyes were half-closed, and her breath was coming quickly.

"Yes, temptress?"

"What are you doing to me?" I laughed as I came back up and rinsed my hands before grabbing her face.

"I'm rewarding you. You were phenomenal, and I can't wait to take you again. But I have other plans for us later."

"Oh really? And what are they?" Aurora pressed herself closer to me. Her tits rubbing on my abs. She shocked me by taking one of my pierced nipples in her mouth and circling her tongue over it.

"You are about to get punished if you continue this," I answered her with a groan.

I hadn't ever let someone touch my nipples, but fuck, when she did it, I was hardening again. Taking her face with my hands again, I brought her gaze back up to me, and she popped off with a line of drool connecting us until I took her mouth with mine.

"We have things we need to talk about before I take you somewhere special," I told her when I pulled away from her intoxicating mouth.

"Okay."

I quickly showered and then toweled us both off. Aurora went to walk ahead of me, but I grabbed her back up into my arms.

"TC! I can walk, you know."

"I know, temptress. But you will probably never walk around this place ever again," I answered her before depositing her on the bed.

"Why? Because I left during the night?" Her tone of her voice told me she regretted leaving.

"No, because I want to touch you for the rest of my life," I replied before laying down beside her and pulling her against me.

Aurora snuggled into my side, her head lying on my chest. I never would have thought I would feel like this toward her, especially after everything that had happened in our past. But it seemed that things tended to work out when they were supposed to.

"Aurora, I do need to tell you what my life was like before the Churchhills." I glanced down at her as I tipped her face up to mine. She nodded, and I took a deep breath. "What you saw at the warehouse was just the tip of what I used to be. Things used to be hard for me. My parents left me on the street when I was seven, and I never saw them again. I did everything I could to survive, When I had just turned thirteen, I got picked up by Marcus and his gang."

Aurora sat up and stared down at me.

"Even though I had stolen things in those six years, I had never seen what people did to each other until I went to live with Marcus. The things that I did to earn my place in that house were horrible .

"I've tortured people to get information from them, and not all of them were bad people. I've learned how much a body can take before it blacks out. There are probably hundreds of bodies in that ocean that no one knows are there."

Her hand covered my hand, which hid my face from hers, and pulled it away so that our eyes locked.

"And if you didn't know any of that, do you think that the cops would have been able to find me If they had found me, do you think that Marcus would have stayed behind bars?" The pleading on her face brought back the darkness that had surged up when I saw her and then put a bullet in his head. "TC, you saved me. They didn't have to come after you because they left you when you needed them."

"I would kill him again if that meant you would be safe."

TC helped me into the black Bugatti. He shut my door and rounded the car, getting in on the driver's side. After shifting it into drive, we pulled out of the parking spot and out of the garage. All the times that we had rode in a car together, Jake or Sam had driven.

"I thought these cars were automatics?" I knew very little about cars, but I did know that these cars were only made in automatic trans or semi-automatic—thanks to me having to listen to Sam talk about them when he first became my bodyguard.

"That's true, you must have had a crash course from Sam. I had this bad boy made with a manual." TC turned his gaze to me and winked before taking his gaze back to the road.

Being in his car without Sam and Jake was new to me. I had never been alone with him in this car before, and it purred as he shifted gears and maneuvered it through the streets. The seat was soft, and I almost felt relaxed enough to take a nap, but my curiosity of where we were going kept me awake.

"So, are you going to tell me where you're taking me?" I asked as he turned the car down a back road. He looked to me with his eyebrow raised and shook his head before changing the car's gear.

"Nope, I'm not going to tell you. I told you it was a surprise." he tsked as he slowed the car again, turning on his blinker and pulling onto a dirt road.

I was afraid that he was going to hurt the underside of his car with how bumpy the road was. Sitting back, I watched the scenery pass by the window before he came to a stop. I glanced around but didn't see anything special. TC smirked at me before getting out of the car and coming over to my side.

TC opened my door and held out his hand; I took it, and he helped me out of the low car. He led me over to the edge of the cliff and pointed out. I followed his direction and couldn't help the gasp that came from me.

The sun was setting over the city, and it made LA look amazing. I glanced beside me, and he was standing there with a grin on his lips with his arm wrapped around my waist. Shaking my head, I turned fully to gaze at him; he was still watching the sun go down below the horizon.

"TC, why did you bring me here?" I asked; the wind whipped my hair to the side, and I tried to contain it so it wouldn't hit him in the face.

"Ever since I met you in that clothing store, I wanted to bring you here—maybe even have our first kiss here. But fate had a different route for us. This was the place I would come to when the killing and the torture got too much, and I needed a break." He stared at me with his blue eyes, and they were no longer icy when I stared into their depths.

"You wanted to bring me here? Why...You didn't even know me then," I answered him as I played with my hair. My heart was flying as his gaze left my eyes and went to my lips.

The wind whipped my hair up again, sending a slight chill through me. I had left my jacket in the car in TC's haste to get me out of the vehicle. He took off his jacket and draped it around my shoulders smiling at me in a way I hadn't noticed before..

There was no way that someone couldn't be attracted to him. His eyes pulled me into their depths, and when his lips touched my skin, it was divine. I shivered again, and he pulled me into his body, wrapping his arms around my shoulders. Not too tightly, though, so that I could still look at him.

TC's eyes went to my lips again, and I stepped further into his embrace when they touched mine. It was sensual but calming; it was nothing like what I was used to with him. I went slightly light-headed from the lack of oxygen, though I couldn't push him away.

I wanted more, but he pulled away, leaving me gasping to catch my breath. My gaze held his as a smile crossed my lips.

"I think if we had been together all this time, our parents wouldn't have been so worried about making us marry each other."

"Yeah, but at this point, I don't think I would want to change anything. What if we did date then, and we ended up not being compatible?" TC's hands cupped my face and held me still.

"That's true."

"Come on, let's go home. I need to have you again."

TC pulled up in front of the barrier and scanned his key to get in. He quickly parked the car and sat in his seat before he glanced over at me. I unbuckled my belt and climbed over into his lap. His hands landed on my hips.

"What do you think you are doing, temptress?" TC groaned as I ground my pussy on his lap, causing his length to grow in his jeans.

"I"d never been fucked in a car before the time we left the Gala."

"Really? Before me, what kind of sex had you had?" I had figured that he wouldn't want to know.

"Nothing like what we have been having. If I'm being honest with you, and it won't go to your head, you're the only guy that has made me orgasm." The shock on his face quickly turned to a smirk. TC raised his eyebrows, then unbuttoned his jeans, and pulled out his cock.

"Well, we need to make sure you have more car fucking, and not just when you need to be quiet because of the drivers. I like the fact that I showed you what it feels like to come."

"I didn't say that I'd never had an orgasm. I just said that you were the first guy to get me there," I corrected him, pulling up the skirt I was wearing and straddling him. It had been a good idea to wear this.

If anyone were being nosey, they wouldn't have seen anything other than us kissing. TC held his cock up as I slid down his thick girth. I wasn't about to tell him he was the biggest I had been with. He hissed as I settled onto his lap.

"You know you are perfect," TC uttered next to my lips, his hand threading into my hair. I was far from perfect, but when he told me things like that it made me feel alive.

I ground into him with my hands resting on his shoulders. TC made me arch in his lap with a tug of my hair. Hitting the right spot inside of my pussy as I bounced in his lap. It was like he knew just where I needed him to be to come.

"TC, I'm coming... Don't stop."

"You're going to make me come like this, temptress. Fuck, are you close?" His voice was strained, and his brows were furrowed as he gritted out his words.

"Yes..."

"Tell me when you are. I want to come with you," he groaned as I continued to grind myself against him. I used to never be able to get into guys talking to me during sex, it used to kill my mood, but when he spoke to me like that it made me wetter.

"Fuck, TC, yes please... Come with me... I'm there!"

He followed my plea, tears raced down my cheeks, nails gripping onto his shoulders. TC's hold on my hair tightened as he unloaded everything into me. He stilled as I came down from my high. Our eyes never leaving each others. TC loosened his grip on my hair and pulled my face to his. I loved when he kissed me.

"I'm going to leak everything out when I get up. How are we going to get out of the car?" Because I could already feel it seeping around his cock.

"When were you going to tell me you weren't wearing any panties?" The smirk on his face made me blush and pull my bottom lip between my teeth. "Were you expecting us to fuck in my car?"

"I didn't think anything about it. Besides, I thought you would like it." I shrugged as I went to move. TC gripped my hips, keeping me on his lap.

"So, what you are going to do is open this driver-side door and then get up. That way I can put my cock back in my pants while I watch the cum run down your legs." TC grinned, and I rolled my eyes before opening the door and getting off him.

I pulled the skirt down back over my hips. "Fuck, not that fast!"

I laughed as he gave me an incredulous glare, and I sent him a cheeky wink.

"Come on. I think I heard the elevator."

TC took his time putting himself up. I didn't think he really cared if someone saw us fucking in his car. Hell, there was no telling where he had been with women before. He finally exited the car just as some of our cum dribbled past my knees.

Kneeling in front of me, his hand went to the back of my thighs, and he glanced up and ran his tongue up my right thigh, collecting the cum. TC swallowed it and then ran it up my left thigh before standing and crushing his lips to mine. He forced his tongue between my lips and deposited the mix of our cum into my mouth. I swallowed it as he pecked my lips.

"Young people and their public affection. Some are more discreet. Then there are others like them who should be behind closed doors."

"You're right, Darlene. This was never appropriate back in our day!"

TC chuckled and pushed me away from the elevator's door, closing it.

"I think we need to piss them off more, what do you think?" I cocked my head as he squatted and grabbed me and threw me over his shoulder.

"TC!"

The little old ladies gasped as he walked with me on his shoulder past them. I smiled and waved at them. They both scoffed and turned to continue to their vehicle. I couldn't help but laugh at them— they probably would have fainted if they had seen us in the car.

"Seems like you had some fun with that. I think I will keep you like this all the way to the penthouse." TC slapped me on the ass and groaned.

"Well, they could keep their thoughts to themselves," I answered him as I tried to keep my hand from slipping off his lower back.

The elevator stopped, and TC walked out into our home. It was weird to think of it as my home now, even though I had been living here for a while. TC took us straight to our bedroom and he sat me down.

"I've learned that people never do that, temptress. They will always have something to say about what you do or say." He turned me around and slapped me on the ass again. "Go get in the shower. I'm going to find something to snack on."

I watched him walk out of the room before shedding the clothes I was in, leaving a trail to the bathroom. The car sex was good, but I was hoping that he would join me in the shower. If there was one place I wanted to fuck in it was the shower.

Chapter Thirty-Five

TC

I pulled open the grey cabinets and took down the crystal wine glasses. Setting them on the marble countertop I went to the stainless-steel fridge and took out the fruit tray that Gwen had prepared. She knew what fruit Aurora loved, which was something that I intended to learn for myself—along with many other things that I needed to find out about my wife.

My phone rang, and I pulled it out of my back pocket. It was an unknown number. I was always getting numbers calling that I didn't know, but they didn't normally hide the number. This was a little strange, I half thought about not answering, but something told me that I needed to. "Hello?"

"Mr. Churchhill, my boss wants to schedule a meeting with you," an older voice said through the phone.

"You will need to call in the morning and speak to my assistant, Lindsey. She will get your boss on the schedule," I answered. No one had my number unless they were already working with me and even then, they normally didn't call me this late at night. Who would have given my number to this person? I knew it wasn't Lindsey.

"I don't think you understand, Mr. Churchhill. My boss isn't someone that can just walk into your company."

"Who is your boss?" His answer was going to tell me whether I was in deep shit or if just on edge.

"I think you know who he is, TC. Your previous captain has been under him for years, and now he is missing. The boss needs to have a meeting with you."

Fuck! I was in deep shit.

"Okay. What would fit his schedule?" If there was one person I didn't want to piss off even more, it was this man. He could wipe out my entire family, and no one would know what had happened.

"That's what I thought you would say. He wants to meet with you in two weeks, he has a funeral to conduct before-hand. I'll be in touch." The phone disconnected, and all I could do was try to calm my now rapid breathing.

If it was anything that urgent, he would have wanted to see me immediately. Meeting him in two weeks would give me time to try to get my family out of the country. Until I could figure out what he wanted from me. Hell, he could be wanting to get rid of me at this meeting for taking out Marcus. In his eyes, it could be a power play.

Fuck.

Bringing my phone back to my face. I scanned my contacts for Drake's name. It rang twice before he picked up.

"Hey, man, what's up?"

"I'm going to need you to help me get my family out of here for the next two weeks." I rested my head against the counter, and the phone to my ear.

"Okay....? What's wrong?" Drake's concerned voice came through the speaker with.

"The main boss Marcus was under had his underboss call me. He wants to meet me in two weeks. I need to make sure that he isn't going to off my family," I answered him, I had never felt this defeated in my life. Aurora was just now back in my life, and now this shit had happened.

"Dude, I doubt sending them anywhere is going to help. If he wants to off you all, he will find them. On the day you meet him, take both Jake and Sam. If I go, you just might be killed. I'll keep the others safe," Drake explained to me as a door shut on the other side of the line.

"I should have been thinking. If I had been, I would have gone to him first to get the go-ahead to take Marcus out. It wasn't like he was making the boss any money." I slammed my hand on the counter, and the wine glasses shuddered.

"But that's not the issue though, is it? And we don't know what the issue *is* right now."

His words made sense—even if I had gone to him and he had rejected me killing Marcus , and I did, I would have been in even worse trouble. It had always been drilled in my head to ask for forgiveness rather than permission.

"Okay, we just need to have them all in one spot. I guess we'll have dinner at your place, so they won't think anything about it. The boss doesn't know about you.." I stood from the counter and looked around the kitchen. I was going to have to be on my game that night; otherwise, the boss would have me killed, and there was no way I was going to go out without a fight.

"That's fine. I'll invite my parents too. Is that okay?" A giggle sounded through the phone, and Drake shushed them, making them giggle more.

"That's fine—as long as you think they won't get hurt." I couldn't live with myself if someone got hurt because of this shit I had caused.

"Did you forget who my family is?"

"No, but I don't want to cause anyone to lose their lives." When he told me that his family was part of the Italian Mafia, I thought he was kidding, but as I looked deeper into the name, it was proven true. I just didn't understand why his father would want to help run a logistics company.

"They will be fine. I have tons of security around my place."

"All right, we will talk more. I'm sure Aurora is out of the shower by now."

"Okay, boss. See you Monday?"

"Yeah." I hung up the phone and turned to find Aurora in the doorway to the kitchen.

Her arms crossed over her chest and an 'I just caught the end of that conversation and want to know what was going on' look on her face . I had promised her that I wouldn't keep anything from her from then on, so there was nothing I could do other than let her know what was going on.

"What was all of that?" There was clear anxiety in her voice.

"Can you come sit? I'll tell you everything."

After I filled her in about what was going on, Aurora was quiet as she sat in front of me. The only thing I could think was running around her head was that she needed to get away from me to stay safe.

"So, you're telling me that there is someone here in LA who has more power than Marcus?" Her eyes told me that she was afraid.

"Yes, there is always someone that has more power than someone else. And apparently, I made the top one mad."

"Will he want to kill you because you killed Marcus?"

"I don't know yet. I won't know anything until I meet with him. But that's the worst-case scenario."

Aurora stood and paced around the kitchen. This wasn't what I wanted when I brought her back to the house. I wanted to be able to come home and relax with her, and not have to deal with more of this mess.

"So, do I need to make funeral arrangements?"

"It wouldn't hurt. I mean, I hope that he doesn't want to kill me as he is waiting to meet with me. But then again, he could be lulling me into a false sense of security." I stood and walked up to her. She had been through a lot in the past couple of weeks. "Aurora, I will be taking Jake and Sam with me. And I'll try my hardest to come back to you."

"You better—-if you make me a widow now that we have been through this, I'll kill you again when I meet you in the afterlife." She hit me in the chest before burying her face into it.

"Aurora, whatever happens in that meeting I will get back to you. I promise you that," I answered her and pulled her face up to mine.

Between the puffiness of her eyes and the tears in her lashes, Aurora was just as beautiful when she was smiling as she was now. I pressed a kiss to her wet lips; the salt from her tears mingled with the sweetness of the lip balm she was wearing.

Aurora grabbed hold of my shirt as she took the kiss deeper. I didn't understand how someone like her could even be worried that I wouldn't come back, or even want me to come back to her. But here she was pulling me closer in our kitchen. I broke our kiss and brought her eyes back to mine.

"Let's take this fruit and wine back in the bed. That way we can stop thinking about this right now." I moved away from her, grabbed the tray of fruit, and handed Aurora the wine glasses.

Taking out the 1982 Château Lafite Rothschild from the wine rack, I followed her through the house and into our bedroom. The phone call from the underboss had screwed me. I had planned to be back in the room before she got out of the shower. I sat the tray down on the bed, and the bottle of wine on the side table.

Aurora climbed into the bed and I followed her. I moved the tray closer to us and snapped off a grape. Handing her the fruit, I popped open the wine and poured each of us a glass. Aurora better be glad that I even had wine after her stunt in the club before we were married. Because I would love to see how she acted after that much in her system.

"TC, why are we doing this?"

"Because we are going to start over, and we are going to do this thing right." Aurora held my gaze as I handed her the glass of wine.

"You really mean that?" She searched my face and I placed the wine on my bedside table.

"Yes, I will make sure that I make up for what I've done and what I've not done as your husband." I raised my glass in a toast and tapped it against Aurora's. "To spending the rest of our lives together."

Aurora giggled and then shook her head. "To spending the rest of our lives together."

I woke up with a leg thrown over my hips and fingers tracing my chest. Opening my right eye, Aurora was awake and watching her fingers as they followed the lines on my chest. "You know it's easier to see them if you are on top."

"Did I wake you?" Aurora's breath fanned over my nipples, making them hard. Harder than they normally were since I had them pierced.

"No, but I was hoping that maybe you could take care of what's currently resting on your knee." I smirked before cocking an eyebrow at her.

"Really? Didn't you have enough last night?" Aurora giggled, sitting and straddling me. Her already wet pussy rubbed against the underneath of my cock.

"I will never have enough of you," I told her. Aurora's hands went to my chest causing the cover to slide off her body. My hands went to her hips and gripped them tightly as I locked eyes with her in the early morning glow.

Aurora was gorgeous, and I was stupid to have been the way I was, but it wasn't just me. She hadn't wanted this either. Now, though, she had told me that she loved me. Love wasn't something that I was accustomed to, and I really didn't know if what I felt for her was love.

Chapter Thirty-Six

Aurora

Orson drove me to Churchhill Logistics. I was having lunch with TC, and this would be the first time I had been on the top floor. Today was a bright day, and the weather was starting to get a little warmer. Orson pulled up to the curb of the tall building, and one of the valets opened my door and helped me out.

"Thank you,"

"Mrs. Churchhill, right this way." Sam motioned for me to follow him into the building. TC still made sure that he was near me if I wasn't with him.

It felt as if what happened two weeks ago was a dream that I was starting to forget. Now that Marcus was gone, I could breathe. I didn't know what would have happened if TC had allowed him to live. The cool air from the building's A/C unit chilled me as we entered the revolving door. Sam was two steps behind me, and we headed over to the private elevator to get us to the top floor.

As we headed up, Sam stood in front of me while I relaxed at the back of the elevator. I glanced over to the side, and my reflection stared back at me. Since I had been eating again, my face had started to fill out, and the bruises from the warehouse were all but gone. The woman that stared back at me was a totally different one than the one who started this journey.

"Mrs. Churchhill, we are on the floor." Sam's voice brought me out of my thoughts. It was different, when we were not in public, he would call me Aurora just like he would call my husband TC, but in places like this, he and Jake made sure to keep things business.

Sam led me down the semi-busy hall. I noticed that there were only a few people up here with TC and Drake. We passed a couple of women at small desks in front of office doors, and they watched me pass. It wasn't like I wasn't used to the stares. Sam came to a stop at the last door and knocked.

The desk in front of the office was empty. Whoever sat here was a very organized person; everything was neatly placed in order. Sam tapped me on the shoulder, and we entered the room.

I was shocked at how open and bright the place was. A woman was standing beside TC handing him folders when Sam and I came in. She looked up and smiled. The gorgeous redhead had to be his secretary. She was in a pencil skirt and a white blouse, buttoned almost to the top. Her hair was in a clip with not a single strand was out of place.

"Thank you, Mr. Churchhill. And yours and Mrs. Church-hill's lunch should be arriving soon." She took back the last folder she had given him and strolled around the desk. From how tall she looked beside TC, I thought that she had been wearing heels. But instead, she was wearing flats.

"Thank you, Lindsey." TC stood from his chair, and Lind-sey nodded to me with a smile as she passed me. I walked forward to his desk as came around the oak desk. "You look gorgeous. Did you get all dressed up to come here?"

"You told me we were going to have lunch together, so I didn't want to look a total slob. I didn't know we would be having lunch in your office though." I glanced around again at what was in the room. Some of this had to be from when his father was here. I didn't think he would like any of this.

"Well, lunch here will be better for the both of us. Besides, why go out when I can have it catered to me?" TC chuckled, pulling me against him. My hands went instinctively to his chest, and his left hand went to cup my cheek.

I thought I heard the office door shut, but I didn't turn to see. TC held my gaze before his lips met mine. I stood on my tiptoes and gripped his lapels to pull him closer. TC wrapped his arms around my body bringing me flush to his body.

"Never thought I'd see this."

I broke the kiss and turned to see Drake walking into the room like he owned the place. He plopped down on the couch. His dark eyes flickered between us before TC's hand went to the small of my back and steered me over to the couch.

"Drake, is there something that I can help you with?" TC sat and guided me down beside him.

Crossing my legs, I tried to hide the fact that I wasn't wearing any underwear, and TC's hand went to the edge of the dress on top of my knee. Drake's eyes went to his hand, and the smirk that crossed his face was dirty.

"I was just wondering if you had heard from our wonderful bossman?" Drake leaned back into the couch and rested his arms on the back of the seat.

"Not yet, but I'm sure I'll hear from him soon. What have you found out from your side? Didn't you say that you have ties to family?" I glanced between them both. TC didn't move his gaze from his friend.

"Still working on that part. My father is supposed to be setting up a meeting for me and him to talk about things. Once I know something you will know." Drake took a deep breath and rose from the couch. A knock brought all our attention to the door.

"Mr. Churchhill, your lunch is here." Lindsey's head snuck through the door.

"Tell them to bring it in."

"You ordered me food too?" Drake slapped his hands together as the delivery guy walked in with bags. Which held the deliciousness of something that made my stomach growl.

"No, asshole. This is my lunch with my wife. I'm sure you can make it back before I'm finished." TC stood and guided Drake from our position on the couches, leading him to the door.

The man who brought the food began to set things out on the table in front of me. Wherever he had gotten this from, the food looked amazing. TC came back just as the man placed the last bowl of food. He pulled out his wallet and gave the man a tip.

"Well, this looks good, what do you think?" TC sat beside me, grabbed a plate, and handed it to me.

Broiled chicken with some type of cheese and diced tomatoes,. beside it were fancy green beans and loaded mashed potatoes. TC grabbed a plate that had what I assumed was a steak and loaded potato. Salad sat in a large bowl and serving spoons were next to it.

"It looks amazing. I don't think I've eaten food like this." I cut into the chicken and popped a bite into my mouth. The moan that exited my lips brought TC's hard gaze to me. His pupils already taking over his irises.

"I didn't think you could sound like that other than when I was balls deep into your pussy." I didn't miss the husky tone in his voice. He cut a bite from his steak and lifted it to my lips.

I shook my head, never having had a steak that wasn't cooked medium-well or more before. He finally put it in his mouth and then brought my face to his and moved the bite into mine. TC held my jaw and watched me as I chewed the morsel.

The steak was juicy and nothing like what I had before. The explosion of flavor eclipsed the chicken I was eating. Covering my mouth with my hand, I glanced up at TC

"This is really good!" I mumbled around the food before I swallowed.

"See, you always have to try something before you can say that you don't like it." TC chuckled as he took a bite of his meal.

We finished up the meal and had the most delicious dessert. I couldn't say that it was the best because Gretchen's bakery had that. Setting down my plate, I looked over at him and noticed that there was some chocolate on the side of his mouth. I leaned over and sucked it from his face.

TC pulled me onto his lap and slammed his lips to mine. His cock was already hard in his pants . His hands ran up underneath my dress, and a groan vibrated from my lips as he reached my bare ass. TC pulled from the kiss, a smirk gracing his lips, and his eyebrow cocked up.

"Were you wanting your tight cunt filled with my cock, temptress?" TC's pupils were eclipsed as he played with my ass cheeks. Kneading and pinching me as he ground me on his lap.

"We can't here. Someone could walk in or hear us." His lips went to my throat nipping and sucking at the tender spots that he had found.

"God damn, temptress. Are you going to make me wait until I get home to take you?" His teeth ran over my collarbone when one of his hands tangled into my hair.

"Yes. I want you to make me scream." My bottom lip went between my teeth as I locked eyes with him.

"Then I guess Drake will have to deal with the rest of the day. We are going home, and I'm going to sink my cock into this wet cunt that's making a mess on my pants." TC's hand that had been in my hair went to my throat, which tightened just a little, as his other hand went between us.

His middle finger pressed inside me. Making a come-here motion against the roof of my pussy. I swallowed the moan that begged to escape from me. TC chuckled while adding two more fingers. "Temptress, why are you denying me what I want to hear?"

"Because your secretary is out front, and so are Jake and Sam," I panted while trying to keep my voice low.

"I know you're making excuses. Jake and Sam have already heard you, but if you don't want Lindsey to hear you, let's go. Because I need to hear you." TC stood, and I wrapped my legs around his waist. I thought he was going to take me out of the office to go home.

But he brought me over to his desk and laid me down, throwing things to the floor. TC pulled my dress up and bent over me. His breath caressed my clit before his mouth covered it.

My hands went to his hair, and I couldn't stop the moan that erupted from my lips when he moved on my clit. He was making me even wetter than I already was, and at this point, I needed to come so badly.

"TC, please, I need to come." He continued to alter the pressure on my clit and then inserted two fingers making me arch on the desk. He slowly thrust them in and out of me in time with the change of pressure. "Yes, right there! Fuck, right there!"

TC popped off and took his fingers from my pussy and stepped back leaving me on the desk. My eyes locked to his as he ran his tongue over the fingers he had inside me.

"Oh, temptress, you are going to have to wait until we get home."

The shock on her face made me grin. As much as I wanted to give her the orgasm she was so close to, I wanted to hear her screaming my name, and having her do that in this room would embarrass her later . I sucked her arousal from my fingers, and fuck, if she didn't taste as good as I knew she would.

Aurora kept her legs spread wide, and that beautiful cunt glistened with her arousal. I knew she was trying to get me to come back to what I was doing. But I needed her at home. Stepping back between her legs, I reached for her hand and helped her up.

"Come on, temptress, I may just play with that bare cunt in the car but you are going to have to wait to have that orgasm for when I get you home." I wanted to try something with her. Something I never tried with anyone else.

"You're cruel, TC" Aurora rose and rearranged her dress and then her hair.

"Only sometimes, temptress." I grabbed her jaw and pressed my lips to hers.

A knock came on the door, and Jake stuck his head in. Aurora pulled her hair up in a messy bun. Jake came all the way into the room, when he noticed the items from my desk all over the floor. He cocked an eyebrow. "Sir, do I need to get the cleaning staff in here."

"I'll get the papers, but yes. Tell Lindsey to get me a new laptop too if that one is broken. Have Sam get the car. I'm calling it a day." My eyes went to Aurora sitting on the couch taking a sip of her drink.

"Of course, sir." Jake turned and went out of the door while I grabbed all the important papers Lindsey had given me yesterday.

I tried to put them back in order because she was going to be pissed if they weren't organized. Sometimes she was a little over the top with the organization. After stacking them back on my desk in my outbox, I came over to Aurora and held out my hand. She took it and left her drink on the table.

The cleaning staff would get that sorted along with the mess from my desk. Aurora and I left the room, and Lindsey was already looking at new laptops. She was going to make sure she was ready in case I had fucked up the other one .

"Lindsey. once you get finished with this, you can take the rest of the day off. I'll be back in tomorrow."

"Of course, sir. Thank you."

We walked past her and the other secretaries and headed to the elevator Jake pressed the down button for us before we reached the doors. All three of us entered it, and it took us down to the garage, where Sam had the car waiting for us.

Jake opened the door, and I allowed Aurora to get in first before sliding into the back seat with her. The door shut, and Jake got into the front with Sam. We pulled away from the elevator and made our way back to the penthouse.

Aurora moved closer to me, and my hand went to her leg. I loved the feel of her legs. Sam and Jake kept their gazes on the front of the vehicle. My hand slid up her leg, and the dress went with it. I made sure to graze her slit with a finger. Aurora whimpered, and she grabbed hold of my wrist. I leaned into her ear and grabbed hold of the lobe. "Oh, temptress, you better let go of my arm or you won't come at all when we get home."

Plunging my fingers deeper inside her, I continued to whisper to her. She let go of my wrist and placed it on my thigh. Tightening her grip. "Tell me how good my fingers feel inside you. But don't let them know."

Aurora's mouth opened slightly as her head tilted back against the seat. I nipped her neck and used the pad of my thumb to run across her clit. Her whimper vibrated against my lips as I moved them down her throat. She widened her legs letting me deeper inside of her.

"You're so wet, temptress. Are you almost there?"

"Yes," Her chest rapidly rose and fell as she kept quiet. Aurora's hand tightened on my thigh as her cunt constricted my fingers. She was doing excellently when the car entered the garage.

The car stopped, and I pulled out of her. Aurora whimpered and gaped at me as Jake opened the car door. I exited the vehicle and held out my hand for her to take. Aurora took it, and I led her to the elevator.

"Sam, Jake, you have the rest of the day off."

"Yes, sir." Jake waited until the doors closed to the elevator before attempting to get back in the car.

Pressing her against the back wall of the elevator, I pulled her arms above her head with one hand and grabbed hold of her throat. Slightly putting pressure around her beautiful neck, she ran her tongue over her lips.

I was already hard from the office and the car. Wanting her right now wasn't really a want, it was a need, and I didn't think that I would be like this when I was the one edging her. Aurora was taking this so much better than I was.

"Temptress. I have so much I want to show you tonight. I want to know if you've ever experienced anal."

"What?" Aurora's eyes widened as she searched my face.

"Has anyone ever had that ass of yours, temptress?" She opened and closed her mouth, and the doors opened just as she was about to answer me. I grabbed her up by her ass and walked her into the penthouse.

"Mr. and Mrs. Churchhill, will I need to prepare lunch?" Gwen came around the corner from the kitchen.

"No. Gwen, we will be busy, so you can take the rest of the day off. Make sure to let the other two know as well."

"Of course, sir. My daughter is in town. I will see you both tomorrow." Gwen grinned and then turned around as I made my way to our room.

Entering the room, I placed Aurora on her feet and started to strip out of my suit. I wasn't going to wait any longer than I had to. I used the heel of my foot to close the bedroom door. Aurora backed up, and her eyes roamed my body. I dropped my jacket and shirt to the floor and Aurora started to take off her dress.

"No, you don't get to take that off. Right now, you are going to watch." I held her gaze and unbuttoned my slacks and slid them down my legs with my boxer briefs.

Aurora's eyes stayed on my cock as I walked up to her. My hand stroked my length, and I noticed her squirming.

"So, I asked you a question, temptress. Are you going to answer it?" I cocked my head to the side as she backed into the post of the bed.

"Um, no. I haven't."

"Then let's get you cleaned up." I grabbed her and slung her over my shoulder. Her dress pooled around her lower back, and the scent of her wet cunt near my face had my cock throbbing.

I stuck my middle two fingers in my mouth and plunged them deep into her pussy. Aurora moaned, her nails dug into my lower back, and her pussy clenched around my fingers. "You feel so good around my fingers. I can't wait to have my cock wrapped up in this ass of yours."

Opening up the shower, I turned on the water and then pulled my fingers from her pussy and sat her on the counter. "Open."

Aurora opened her mouth, and I stuck my fingers coated in her arousal in her mouth. I watched her suck them clean. "Do you taste good, temptress?"

She nodded, and I groaned as I removed her dress, her tits bouncing free. Aurora slid out of the dress, and I unhooked the straps to her heels. Fuck she wasn't wearing anything under that dress. She was wanting to be fucked in my office, there was no question about that. I picked her back up and entered the shower, pressing her against the tiled wall. Aurora hissed as her back connected with the cold wall.

I thrust into her all the way to the hilt, and her legs wrapped around my waist. My hands gripped her hips tightly as I used them to move her up and down my cock. If I didn't pull out of her now, I wasn't going to make it to show her how much pleasure I could give her.

"I'm going to wash you, and then we are going to bed, where I'm going to show you how much pleasure I can give you."

Aurora nodded, and I pulled out of her and placing her on the floor. The thought of being back inside her was too tempting to spend any more time in the shower. As quickly as I washed her off, I did the same to myself. Aurora stepped back out of the spray, and I rinsed off and then stopped the shower.

I stepped out and pulled her out with me. Grabbing a towel, I handed it over to her, and dried myself off with the other one in my arm. I tossed my towel to the floor and grabbed Aurora up as she tried to dry her damp hair. The squeal that came from her brought a smirk to my lips.

"TC! We have all day and night!"

Throwing her on the bed, she grinned at me when she scooted to the middle of the bed. She opened her legs wide and started to play with herself. Aurora's nipples were peaked, making her tits look even more beautiful. I turned to her side table, and her eyes followed me. They widened when I took out her favorite blue toy—the one I had caught her pleasuring herself with.

Aurora was going to need the other stimulation this toy would provide. Her eyes went wide as she continued to watch me, and my hand went to my hardening cock. Fuck, she was already wet as she stuck her two fingers in and out of her cunt.

"On your hands and knees, temptress." Commanding her, I turned on the toy, and she pulled her fingers out of her pussy and then sat up.

She pressed her wet two fingers to my lips and spread her arousal all over my mouth until I opened and allowed myself a taste. Aurora popped her finger out of my mouth and grinned. "Turn."

Fuck, I needed her now more than ever, she turned over on her stomach with her ass up in the air. She eyed me from the side, her hair fanning out on the other side. I used my fingers to find her clit and then placed the vibrating toy on it.

Aurora moaned when I rubbed it against her little nub. Getting her in the mood. I leaned over her and grabbed the lube from the bedside table. Squirting a generous amount on my fingers and then her tight asshole. "TC … Is this going to hurt?"

Her face was scrunched up as her mouth opened slightly.

"Just trust me, temptress, and relax. Just concentrate on the toy. But if it does hurt let me know, and I'll stop." Aurora nodded and closed her eyes. I ran my fingers over her tight hole and pressed in a little. She tightened, and I stopped, allowing her to relax again.

Just as she relaxed, I slipped further in and leaned over her to insert my fingers from my other hand in her cunt. Releasing the toy underneath her. Aurora whimpered while I slowly fucked both of her holes with my fingers.

"Are you ready? I'm going to take my fingers out and fill you with my cock." I pulled my fingers from her ass and grabbed the lube again. Pouring the waterlike substance all over the head of my cock and over her tight hole.

"Take the toy, Aurora," I whispered in her ear. Taking the buzzing toy from beneath her, she held it to her clit as I leaned up and began to slowly fuck her ass.

"TC." Her breath hitched, and I stilled, waiting for her to continue her sentence. "Fuck, why are you stopping?"

I chuckled and started again. She was so tight that I wasn't going to last long, but I didn't want to get to mine before she got hers. Pulling her flush to my body, she continued to use her toy, and I plunged another finger inside her while fucking her ass.

Her whimpers and moans became faster and in bursts as she contracted around my fingers. Damn, this woman. I could feel my balls tighten, and I unloaded inside her. Aurora was coming down from her high, and her head leaned back resting on my shoulder.

"You're such a good girl, temptress. We're going to need another shower." Aurora giggled, and I pressed my lips to hers.

The phone call from the boss' underboss came the following morning, informing me the boss was expecting me to meet him at a superbike racetrack. I dropped Aurora off with Drake and his parents. My parents, along with Emi, were going to be there in a few minutes. Sam and Jake were in the front seat as I made sure I had both my Glocks under my jacket.

Even though we were meeting in a public place, I didn't know whether he actually owned this place or not. The Mercedes SUV passed under the archway into the parking lot, and we headed around the back. I was early because I didn't want to be late when my life could be on the line.

I had a promise to keep to Aurora, and I wasn't going to ruin any chance I had by pissing him off at the beginning. Jake and Sam checked their weapons as well. The under-boss didn't tell me I couldn't bring people with me. Nor that I couldn't bring my weapons.

A limo pulled up beside us, and a guy exited and went to the back door. He opened the door, and an older man stepped out. He had to be in his seventies. His age starting to show on him. Sam and Jake glanced back at me, and I nodded. Jake stepped out and opened my door.

Stepping out of the SUV, the older man glanced at me. His hard brown eyes looked me up and down before he stepped forward and held out his hand. I took his hand with a firm grip, something that my father always told me to do when I met with someone for the first time. The boss' grip was what I was expecting from someone his age.

"Sir, my name is Tom Churchhill."

"I know who you are, Tom. Why don't we take a walk around this place?" He motioned for his guards to hang back a little, and I silently signaled Sam and Jake to do the same.

We entered the pit area and settled into a comfortable walk. I didn't want to outwalk this man. My eyes went to a guy pulling up his leathers and mounting a bike that looked like it needed to be in a junkyard. He gunned the bike and sped off onto the track.

"That man is Riker Kidwell. If someone gave him a chance, he might actually make it in this world." The boss' voice brought me back to why I was here.

"Sir, not to be forward, but I'm sure you didn't bring me here to talk about this racer." I stopped to watch the man race past. He was good, and if I could get my name into this world, I could bring more business to the logistics company.

"No, it's not. I wanted to talk to you about Marcus."

There it was. I knew this was the reason, but I wasn't going to worry about it. I had done right by my woman. He couldn't fault me for that. It was the code. If Marcus wanted to treat me like I was still in the gang, I was going to go by it. He wasn't supposed to touch my wife.

"I will not apologize about what happened to him, sir. He went against the code." I turned to him as the man went past us again. His face was stoic, part of me was trying to place him; other than being the boss he reminded me of someone.

"I wouldn't expect you to. He deserved what he got and more. Along with his captain." The man took a deep breath and turned to walk further down into the pit. I followed him, this was too calm. It had me on guard.

The racer came into the pit and looked up at the timer above the announcer's box. And by his body language, I could tell he was pleased with himself. It looked as if he had beaten a few other times on the board.

"I had you come to meet me because I have a proposition for you."

"Okay?" I was a little confused about this, but I stood there waiting for him to speak again.

"Tom, I want you to run my empire because you are my son."

Three years later

I helped Aurora into our box at the Superbike track. She had been upset when she found out I had sponsored the biggest and tallest racer there was. I knew that look in his eyes when he was searching for a sponsor three years ago. Even though he had beaten most of the smaller rider's time by a lot, he had more potential.

Getting her comfortable, I went and grabbed some whiskey. With everything that had happened since we first got married somehow, we were now going to have our second kid. It was crazy all this was happening. Especially after being confronted by one of the biggest bosses in LA after the whole Marcus diabolical.

"TC, which is our rider?" Aurora's voice brought me out of my head. Her grey eyes were a storm of the hormones that come with being pregnant.

"He's the one in the red and black leathers, along with being the biggest guy out there. You might also notice that none of the reporters will go up to him." I came over to her and sat with my whiskey in hand.

Riker had been winning all his races for these past few years, and I was happy that I had made an investment in him. A lot of the other sponsors had come to me to try to buy in on the sponsorship, but I didn't allow that. If they really would have thought he would be worth something, they would have sponsored him when I did.

"You mean the big man up front on the grid?" Aurora pointed to Riker already sitting on his bike. She had never set foot on the racetrack with me. It was the one secret investment that she didn't know about, which was stupid of me since I was the boss of the crime syndicate that Marcus was stupidly fucking over.

"Yes, and he is one of the best on that track." I smirked as she stared at me.

I knew what she was thinking, but if she knew how much money he had made us, she wouldn't be questioning me right now.

"Just watch and see what he can do with that bike."

The green flag dropped, and the racers were on their way. Riker made it out ahead of the pack—just like he always did in his races. Another racer had broken away from the others and was gunning for Riker before he pushed the bike forward.

On the jumbotron Riker and another racer were battling for first place. Rounding the curve number sixty-four was riding close to Riker's back tire battling for first place. Riker went lower into the curve when the other racer clipped his tire flinging him into the air before crashing into the pavement and smashed into the red and white barrier. Riker didn't move as the other rider continued and the pack rounded the curve.

A red flag was shown and an ambulance with other emergency vehicles raced onto the track. They surrounded him and Aurora gasped beside me while we sat there waiting for news. The mangled bike smoked in the grass forgotten while the entire track waited with bated breath.

<u>Paranormal Romance</u>
The Second Alpha Heir
The Fallen Alpha
Silver Moon Kiss
Silver Moon Kiss: Becoming Alpha

<u>Contemporary Romance</u>
Raising the Stakes: A Dark CEO Romance
Craving the Taboo: A Dark Forbiddin Romance

C. L. Ledford was born in the city of Chattanooga, TN. Where she was raised by her grandparents, to be a strong and independent person. She became an avid reader at the age of eleven, when her fifth grade teacher gifted her the book, The Black Stallion. With this book her love of books gr ew.

In middle school she began to write what would be one of many books swirling around in her head. Silver Moon Kiss came to life with two chapters and multiple scenes before it was packed away and not thought of until after she had become an adult. C. L. Ledford writes in Paranormal Romance and Contemporary Romance. Her first published book The Second Alpha Heir released on June 14, 2022. By this time she had moved to a little town called Ringgold, GA and married her husband where they raise their three children and five German Shorthair dogs. Along with her love of writing and reading, she also enjoys hunting behind her dogs.